T0008186

Advance Praise for .

"Nina is brilliant and drunk. She's also a mother, whose children celebrate her gifts and struggle to survive her parenting. Sabrina Reeves's first novel is as gorgeous, ruthless, and unforgettable as its protagonist."

—Peter Behrens, author of the Governor General's Literary Award–winning *The Law of Dreams*

"A portrait of childhood and motherhood that turns these concepts on their heads, shining a light over all their gaps and insufficiencies. Sabrina Reeves's love of her characters is reckless and palpable, propelling the reader forward across every heartrending page."

—Sean Michaels, Scotiabank Giller Prize winner and author of *Do You Remember Being Born?*

"There are never enough accounts of mothers and daughters; the bedside lamentations, the diversions, the lengths women must go to reach—and care—for each other, and very often, finally, just to let go. In *Little Crosses* Sabrina Reeves wades into the maelstrom with her heart on the outside, and it's that vulnerability that sets the pace here, that makes this book so hard to set down. Cassie's is a compelling journey, one that many of us will recognize intimately, and painfully, as true."

—Sina Queyras, author of *Autobiography of Childhood*

"Nina Wolfe is a force of nature, a free spirit, the life of the party, but as her children know, she can also swallow people whole. Her story sucked me in and left me with a deep respect for writer Sabrina Reeves, who clearly understands the push and pull of dealing with a larger-than-life parent in crisis. *Little Crosses* heralds the arrival of a big talent."

—Neil Smith, author of *Jones*

"A magnetic read. In *Little Crosses*, when a mother requires critical intervention, her daughter balances the brilliant, neurotic exuberance of her mom's life with her own, and with the entrenched aggravations of their complex time together. Sabrina Reeves creates a hypnotic character who invigorates a jubilant, intimate, painful, loving, and astonishing novel."

—Trevor Ferguson, Hugh MacLennan Prize winner and author of *The River Burns*

# Little Crosses

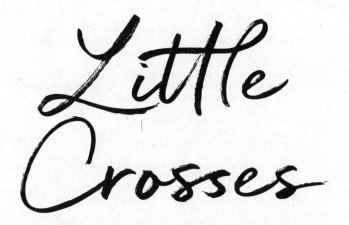

# Little Crosses

## A NOVEL

## SABRINA REEVES

ANANSI

Copyright © 2024 Sabrina Reeves

Published in Canada in 2024 and the USA in 2024 by House of Anansi Press Inc.
houseofanansi.com

All rights reserved. No part of this publication may be reproduced or transmitted in
any form or by any means, electronic or mechanical, including photocopying, recording,
or any information storage and retrieval system, without permission in writing from
the publisher.

House of Anansi Press is committed to protecting our natural environment.
This book is made of material from well-managed FSC®-certified forests,
recycled materials, and other controlled sources.

House of Anansi Press is a Global Certified Accessible™ (GCA by Benetech) publisher.
The ebook version of this book meets stringent accessibility standards and is available to
readers with print disabilities.

28  27  26  25  24     1  2  3  4  5

Library and Archives Canada Cataloguing in Publication

Title: Little crosses : a novel / Sabrina Reeves.
Names: Reeves, Sabrina, author.
Identifiers: Canadiana (print) 20230547575 | Canadiana (ebook) 20230547583 |
ISBN 9781487011840 (softcover) | ISBN 9781487011857 (EPUB)
Subjects: LCGFT: Novels.
Classification: LCC PS8635.E383 L57 2024 | DDC C813/.6—dc23

Cover design: Greg Tabor
Cover image: Nini Reeves, untitled, from *The Horizon Series* (c. 2014).
Book design and typesetting: Lucia Kim

Quotes from *Navaho Religion: A Study of Symbolism* by Gladys A. Reichard (1990) are used
with permission of Princeton University Press; permission conveyed through Copyright
Clearance Center, Inc.

*House of Anansi Press is grateful for the privilege to work on and create from the Traditional
Territory of many Nations, including the Anishinabeg, the Wendat, and the Haudenosaunee,
as well as the Treaty Lands of the Mississaugas of the Credit.*

Canada Council    Conseil des Arts
for the Arts      du Canada

ONTARIO ARTS COUNCIL
CONSEIL DES ARTS DE L'ONTARIO
an Ontario government agency
un organisme du gouvernement de l'Ontario

With the participation of the Government of Canada
Avec la participation du gouvernement du Canada |  Canadä

*We acknowledge for their financial support of our publishing program the Canada Council for
the Arts, the Ontario Arts Council, and the Government of Canada.*

Printed and bound in Canada

MIX
Paper from
responsible sources
FSC® C103567
FSC
www.fsc.org

*For my mother*

*She is beautiful, phosphorescent, pale with bits of black the length of her spine, her bright eyes yellowish-green in the moonlight. Her breath against the cool air creates a plume of steam. Hanging from her mouth is a doll in a torn blue dress; her long canine teeth shine against the dirty fabric. She and I are walking together, moving at the same rhythm, the same speed. I look down at my feet and see that I am a coyote. She begins to run and I try to call out to her that she can trust me, that I'm not really a coyote, but all that comes out is a high-pitched howl.*

# JANUARY 15, 2018

*one*

SUNRISE IN NORTHERN New Mexico is a sliver of cool in a scorching desert, a glimpse of God in a godless land. Wherever you are, there's the sky. When on the I-25, the only north-south highway across this territory, it's easy to gaze across the vast plains and imagine the days of horse travel, of no set roads and ever-shifting borders. They call this southwestern part of the United States the Borderlands, in reference to the border with Mexico, but visually speaking that's a misnomer; everything is continuous, blended in careful gradations like a Georgia O'Keefe painting. There are no sharp edges; it's hypnotic. The mountains roll into plains, which run under-foot for hundreds of miles in every direction; homes are made of earth as if they sprang from the land of their own accord. The only visible line is the ever-present horizon, and at dusk even that line disappears.

The control panel on the dash reads 9:05 a.m. The sun is already glaring as I pull off the St. Francis exit toward the Whole Foods on Cerillos Road. I have two stops to make before my estimated ten o'clock arrival at Meadowbrook. I feel around the console for my cell phone. *Meadowbrook*—meant to roll off the tongue and evoke images of comfort, where the elderly can release their cares with ease—calls up instead an image of that restaurant in New York where Mom and I had had a horrible meal and even worse service but had laughed about it the whole walk home. She'd said, "The Friendly Thai, where they are neither friendly nor Thai." Wordplay was always her favourite kind of humour.

I walk down the wine aisle, where I stand, keys dangling from my hand, and stare up at the Chardonnay stacked on display. On sale for $6.99. These days, $6.99 would seem outrageous to my mother. These days, my mother doesn't spend more than three dollars on a bottle of wine. The refrigerators hum dully. At the other end of the aisle, a man with a thin silver braid and deeply creased skin sits hunched on a milk crate, unloading a box of wine onto the bottom shelf. I decide on a twenty-six-dollar Sancerre. After all, if things go as planned, this will be her Last Supper.

In the parking lot, my phone buzzes with a text from my brother.

JACK:

Boarding now … wish I was there

CASSIE:

It's OK. Better this way

JACK:

Might have slept 2 hrs if that

CASSIE:

Yeah, me too. Try to sleep on the plane

JACK:

K. good luck. Be there soon

I load the paper bag of wine into the trunk.

The lawyer's office is in a long adobe building that also houses an art gallery and a jewellery store.

"Your mother is lucky to have you," he says, holding the door open for me. He's a big man with wavy salt-and-pepper hair and soft jowls. He has reviewed and confirmed the strength of our power of attorney—which is not a few documents in a folder, as I had originally thought when we started tossing the acronym POA around regularly, but rather a large box of documents. He sits behind his desk while I remain standing. I won't be here long. He tells me that he's worked with a lot of siblings, and they don't always get along as well as my brothers and I do. "Nina would be proud of you, Cassie," he says, giving me a distinctly paternal look. "If she were able to see things clearly, that is. You know that, right?"

5

He has intuited, correctly, that parental approval is the one thing we've been missing.

"Yes, of course," I say, knowing the exact opposite to be true. Having her power taken away would make my mother neither happy nor proud.

"I mean that," he says, lowering his head and looking at me earnestly, determined to connect. "It's for the best."

I feel a faint softening, a desire to thank him and give him an actual hug, tell him we would be lost without him. Instead, I say, "Thanks for everything," my voice cracking on the word *everything*. In the silence that follows, I look off to the side and clear my throat. Hoisting the box of documents onto my hip, I adjust my purse and resolve to interact with kind people as little as possible today.

I pull in along the far edge of the Meadowbrook parking lot.

I take the key out of the ignition and sit. In the dog run that borders the lot, a wiry black dog sniffs the perimeter. Adjacent to the dog park is a small shingled house with a covered front porch and a yard filled with cars in varying states of collapse. A plastic bag blows past a wheelbarrow of adobe blocks, tipped sideways in the dried grass. My stomach does a flip at the thought of going inside. I rest my head on the steering wheel.

I don't have to look far to find her. There, just past the central lobby, standing at the entrance to the dining room—ninety pounds at most, blond hair straggly and unwashed, broken purse hanging open, phone in one hand and glass of wine in the other—stands Mom. She is trying to find somewhere she can set her wine so she can operate her phone.

"Hold this, will you?"

Of all the things I miss losing my mother to alcoholism, her being happy to see me is one that I miss a lot. For her, us being together a month ago becomes contiguous with us being together today. The month in between erased. When it first started, I would point it out to her, like you might help someone who was searching for a name you happened to remember. "Mom, aren't you going to say you're happy to see me? I only just got here." But the ensuing look of confusion and frustration that would cross her face made me realize I was being selfish. She hadn't forgotten a name or lost a set of car keys; it was time and space that were disappearing.

"Are you trying to text someone? Maybe I can help."

"I'm trying to text Jack."

"I can help you with that. Why don't we head up to your apartment; he'll be happy to hear from you."

"Okay ... I have some wine in the fridge if you want."

"Sure, yeah. Let's do it."

About halfway to the end of the long corridor that leads to the elevator, she says, "Ow! My knee—it's killing me." And we stop while she reaches down to clutch her leg.

"We should get that looked at, Mom," I say, realizing all at once that she is handing me a critical piece of the puzzle my brothers and I have been assembling for the last week.

Meadowbrook Senior Living is in Santa Fe, one hour north of the Albuquerque Presbyterian Hospital, where we have arranged for her to be detoxed from alcohol and prescription drugs. In the *day-of* portion of our planning, the first challenge was how to get her there. She only ever went to Albuquerque for the airport. When it turned out that Jack had an afternoon flight from Oakland, it provided us with the excuse we needed to get her in the car for that one-hour drive. The problem then became: How do we get her from the airport to the hospital? In her compromised state, we could take her wherever we wanted, really, without offering any explanation. Still, we have learned, not only over these past months but over the course of our lives: things are generally easier when Mom's on board.

We had tossed around ideas—all unsatisfactory—for how we might convince her that a trip to the hospital was necessary. There were any number of creative lies we could produce to explain why we were going, but in the end, it was wasted energy to come up with an elaborate story for someone with no memory. So, much like every other decision we'd made these past two years, Jack and I had decided we were just going to wing it.

"You know what, Mom? I'm going to call today and see if we can't get you in to see a specialist."

After an elevator ride and another impossibly long hallway, we enter her unit. The door is unlocked and I push it open, allowing the rank smell trapped inside to rush out. When I was little, I always thought the wine on her breath smelled like bruised apples and rust. Now all I smell is decay.

Before I can stop myself, my hand is up covering my nose. She pushes past me into the darkened apartment and beelines it for the fridge. The curtains are drawn, and a single lamp at the end of the couch creates a dim circle of light illuminating nothing.

"It's a one-hour drive to Albuquerque; why don't you use the bathroom now, Mom, so we don't have to stop along the way?" I need her out of the room.

"I don't have to go to the bathroom."

"It's a good idea to try anyway. The need to pee can sneak up on you suddenly."

This seems to resonate with her, and she walks out of the room. I quickly pull the two wine bottles from the Whole Foods bag, set them on the counter, and race into the bedroom with the empty paper bag. I rummage through the contents of her dresser, shoving a pair of socks and the pyjamas I sent a few weeks back—tags still on them—into the paper bag, along with the contents of her toiletry bag: Valium, Ativan, Zoloft, and about four other pill bottles. I also manage to get a pair of black pants and two shirts before I hear the toilet flush and quickly close the dresser drawer, taking the bag back into the kitchen. I roll the top closed, open one of the bottles, and begin pouring the wine into two travel mugs. I will save the second bottle as a just-in-case bottle. She comes into the kitchen as I'm filling the mugs.

"What are you doing?"

"I'm pouring some wine for our trip."

"Trip? Where are we going?"

"We're going to the airport to pick up Jack."

"Why is Jack coming?"

"To see you."

"But you're here."

"He's coming too."

"Oh."

She's confused.

"Come on. Let's go."

"One second. I'm going to get a scritch of wine."

"I have some here, Mom."

"I don't like drinking from those mugs."

My mother has been happily drinking wine in the car from mugs like these for two years, driving in unimaginable states of inebriation.

"Sure, Mom. Let's fill up your glass instead."

She needs that glass to get from this second-floor apartment to the car in the parking lot. That distance is too far to go without her glass. Any distance is too far to go without her glass.

She's emptied the first travel mug by the time we hit San Felipe Pueblo, ten minutes into our drive. We pull off the road, so I can get the second mug from the back, which she finishes well before the airport, and we stop again to refill the mugs. We arrive two hours early, both bottles empty, one travel mug half-full. We'll have to find wine in the airport.

. . .

There is one restaurant in the Albuquerque airport this side of security, so we go there. I order a burrito, and she orders a glass of wine and some chips. When drinking in the morning had become a regular thing, it was the chips that had given her away. Whenever we visited, she was sneaky about going to the kitchen to make coffee and then emerging into the living room with two mugs. She would hand me a coffee while keeping her own mug close to her chest. When my brothers and I would visit, we all thought it was coffee—until she started having chips with her coffee at seven a.m. Had it not been for the chips, we never would have thought to peek into her mug. Sneaking, on both her part and ours, had become the norm.

Our food arrives. I take one bite of my burrito and push it aside, not sure why I ordered it in the first place, my stomach is in knots. I decide to initiate the knee-doctor cover story.

Jack is on the plane, so I text our older brother, Oliver, who's at home in Massachusetts.

CASSIE:

Could you call me and when I answer, hang up? I need to have a pretend conversation with a pretend doctor

OLIVER:

OK sure. When?

CASSIE:

Now is good

My phone rings.

"Hello?"

Oliver says, "Good luck. Call me later and let me know how it's going," and hangs up.

I proceed with my fake phone call: "Oh hello, Dr. Valdez ... Yes, I did call you about her knee. It's really bothering her."

She looks over. She's listening. It's working.

"Today would be great. Thank you ... Oh, he's in Albuquerque? Actually, that works out perfectly because we're in Albuquerque right now ... Oh, okay. As soon as my brother arrives, we'll head over to the hospital and have her knee looked at. Thank you so much. Bye."

"What was that about?"

"It looks like there's a knee specialist who can see you today about your knee. He's at the Albuquerque Presbyterian Hospital."

"But I don't want to go to the hospital. I want to go back to the compound."

"I know, but it'll be quick, and then your knee will feel better."

"My knee feels fine," she says. And with that, she gets up and starts walking toward the exit.

I gesture to the waitress that we need our bill, while simultaneously chasing after my mother, trying to block her from leaving the restaurant. It's exactly like when my daughters were little and I'd let them toddle around, all the while keeping an eye on their every move. The only difference here being I can't scoop my mother up under her arms if she goes for an emergency exit or tries to wander outside. Her movement is propelled by a palpable anxiety, somewhere between flight and pursuit; she's unable to be still for more than a minute. I quickly circle around in front of her to distract her without actually touching her. I check the time, forty-five minutes to kill before Jack's flight lands. We watch the monitors showing arrival times, buy gum at the magazine store, use the bathroom, sit down, get up, drink from the water fountain, and when necessary, I pull out the last travel mug. Wandering is apparently normal at this stage. We pass a full hour this way until Jack arrives.

He's wearing his signature black-and-white baseball hat and T-shirt with logo. Today's says Prizefighter. His stock-straight firefighter posture and oversized muscles are usually softened by his good humour and charm. Right now, however, they are contributing to the impression that he's holding his breath. He hugs her, looking at me over her shoulder. I wouldn't have thought it possible, but my little brother looks worse than I do. I bring him up to speed on the knee-doctor cover story. "So, Jack," I say brightly, emphasizing the plot points, "there's a doctor who'll be able to help Mom with her knee, it's really bothering her. Would you mind if we stopped by the hospital on our way to Santa Fe?"

"No, I don't mind," he says, putting his arm around Mom's tiny waist and leading her toward the escalator. I follow behind and we take it all the way down.

*two*

"WHY ARE WE HERE?" Mom asks again as I circle the car past the emergency room for a third time. I look down at the text from my brother. He's inside the hospital speaking to the triage nurse. His words interrupt the rhythm of my thoughts, like fragments of a clear voice through radio static, each word distinct, isolated, loud.

JACK:
We're hitting roadblocks

The emergency room entrance is in the corner of a small parking lot, and as I turn up the first row of cars, I start to count the words out of her mouth, as one might count sheep to fall asleep. She's getting agitated, and I need to be calm.

As we pass the one available spot, between the white

Toyota pickup truck with the rusted fender and the light green Subaru, she says, "There's a spot right there."

I ignore the perfectly good spot, turn left, and then left again down the next row. When we pass the red Dodge Caravan sticking out too far, she says, "Why are we at the hospital anyway?" Further down the row, passing the silver SUV with the Make America Great Again bumper sticker, she says, "Can't we go back to the compound and have a glass of wine?" And starting back up the first row, past the cop car at the entrance, I hand her the travel mug with the remaining wine and the alcohol hits a reset button. Fourth loop.

Toyota pickup with the rusted fender: "There's a spot right there."

Red Dodge Caravan: "Why are we at the hospital anyway?"

MAGA bumper sticker: "Can't we go back to the compound and have a glass of wine?"

Cop car: drink wine and settle down.

With several failed detox attempts behind us and having contacted seven other hospitals before finding a doctor and a program here at Albuquerque Presbyterian, one would think we'd have a plan in place for roadblocks, but we don't. We are worn to the quick and not prepared for any further challenges. What we are prepared for is to hear someone say, "What wonderful children you are. Is this your mother? Let us help you. You look so tired. Why don't you rest here we'll take her, fix her up, and have her back to you in a jiffy."

No. We are not prepared for roadblocks.

I run through all the possible doctors I can call for help.

There's Dr. Katz, the psychiatrist to whom we were referred a few weeks back for a diagnosis that would allow us to take custody of our mother. Dr. Katz had said she'd be willing to give us that diagnosis but couldn't do it until the substances were out of her body: "She has to be clean. You have to detox her." I'd smiled. Maybe I'd even laughed; I can't remember. The casual suggestion that we should detox Mom as if it were the easiest thing on the planet, as if we hadn't already tried, as if the system in this country allowed one person to do that to another without their consent. "You will have to show that she is: a) a danger to herself and others; b) suicidal; or c) wandering."

"She did hit her caregiver across the back with a piece of firewood last week."

"Good. That's good."

We could call Dr. Rasheed, the doctor at this very hospital, whom I had called after the other hospitals had turned us away, all saying variations of the same thing: unless we were her guardians, we couldn't bring her in against her will. Dr. Rasheed had said, "Bring her in." Again, the urge to laugh. Had we struggled through these last two years for nothing? Could these people have helped us before? Or is it only when the brain is fully gone that something can be done? He had assured me we wouldn't run into any problems if we mentioned his name. "Tell them at the triage desk that we're taking her into Geriatric Psychiatry once she's detoxed. We are claiming responsibility; that's the important part to remember." I wanted to tell that Dr. Rasheed that his name didn't carry as much weight as he thought it did.

We could call Dr. Matthews at the UNM Hospital's psychiatric unit, where Mom will go after being detoxed, for a week of observation, if all goes to plan. Dr. Matthews works with Dr. Rasheed. It seems to be a standard route—detox then psych ward. Dr. Matthews had even described the step after those two places. "After the week of observation, your mother will most likely be transferred to a secured memory unit." I flash to all the words one previously associated with prison or the old-school mental institutions, but which have since been repurposed for palatability in the medical context: *locked up* becomes *secured*, *spoon-fed* becomes *assisted*, *freaking out* becomes *agitated*.

"And then?" I had asked.

"There is no 'and then' in this scenario, unfortunately. A secured memory unit is where she will most likely live out the rest of her life."

It wasn't that he lacked compassion, exactly. At least, that hadn't been my take. It was more that he seemed to have run out of reassuring words. In this case, it was the simplicity of his tone that was meant to calm, as if he were saying, "She'll need to take an aspirin and stay off that leg." As if, by virtue of it being an inescapable fact, it would relieve me of thinking of nuances and shades of hope. But it hadn't relieved me; I'd had a flash of Mom sitting in a circle led by Nurse Ratched from *One Flew over the Cuckoo's Nest*.

Throughout this process, there have been things I've shielded Jack from, realities I think Oliver and I are better able to handle than he is. Jack's raison d'être has something to do with strength and helping people in need. To be unable to help his own mother is a torment of a different nature for him. There are details he doesn't need to know. But I wasn't going to be able to shield him from this secured memory unit business. If the doctor said Mom would need to go into a lockdown situation, even if we weren't there yet, there was a high likelihood that's where we were headed. So I'd told him.

"Can't we go back to the compound and have a glass of wine?" She pulls at her seatbelt, trying to figure it out.

I hand her the travel mug, circle back up the first row of cars, and return to my thoughts.

Jack hadn't said anything at first, but in a conversation later that day, he'd said, "This doctor may be very good, but we're not committing her. Hopefully, she's going to be a little better after detox, even if it's only a little—this doctor doesn't know anything about her or her history, what she's already survived. She's not going to be living in one of those places where people are strapped to their beds or propped in wheelchairs with drool spilling from their mouths. No. Sorry. Not happening."

To be fair, Jack's "we will save her" stance is not *exactly* denial. It's more complicated than that. He's a firefighter and a paramedic. Those guys—rescue guys, first responder guys—have accepted a job description something along the lines of: "Believe you can do the impossible." It's an absolute necessity to imagine a positive outcome. They need that kind of thinking—that and about a gallon of adrenalin.

In my body, however, adrenalin functions more like leaky battery acid in a car engine. To say that my brother

last week, she's a single mother. She follows protocols because saving lives requires strict boundaries, and that is how the whole system works. Jack has explained it enough times.

And this lovely triage nurse, in telling me why my mother needed to come in voluntarily, would believe she was protecting my mother's rights. She might even suspect that we are overprotective, meddling children, taking unnecessary control. She might give us that slightly distrustful look we've become familiar with in our attempts to get custody of our sinking ship of a mother—no doubt after her non-existent millions. Any potential for seeing the triage nurse as human or of behaving in a reasonable way would be obscured by the cloud created when the adrenalin shot through my body.

Slipping into fighting stance, my words would remain calm—at first, but I know this drill by heart. I can predict, almost to the second, the point at which I would lose it. I might begin by telling the nurse my mother is slowly killing herself, that she doesn't have the mental capacity to make decisions, that we have a psychiatrist who will testify to that fact. The triage nurse would then tell me that we, the children, must be Nina's official guardians to admit her against her will. My voice would begin to rise as I tell the nurse that we can't become her legal guardians until there's an official diagnosis post-detox, that we've been told she must be cleared of alcohol for an accurate diagnosis to be possible, that we are trying to keep our mother alive, and the longer we are stuck in this Catch-22, the closer she gets to dying. The attractive, but not overly so, triage nurse might, at this point, express compassion for our situation, say that she understands how difficult it can be to want to help someone you love when they don't want that help. I might then take this as an opening to begin crying and begging the nurse, "Please test her liver—do that much—or let a doctor assess her. If you get her to step one, you'll see; I promise—you'll see." The nurse would probably refuse, as turning us away is what she's supposed to do. I might then mention the word *lawyer*, all the while knowing how utterly absurd it is to do so. It would be a powerful feeling to invoke a lawyer. But once I'd mentioned the lawyer, it would be over; the triage nurse would become a high stone wall beyond which we would not pass.

This is why Jack is doing the talking and I'm circling the parking lot with Mom.

"Why are we here again?"

"We're getting your knee looked at. Have some wine, we'll go in in a second." And the answer comes to me all at once. "I have to call someone, Mom."

# *three*

I SLOW THE CAR to a stop and hold my phone to text:

CASSIE:
Should I call Leslie?

JACK:
Yes!

I call Leslie.

"Hi, Leslie … Yes … We're actually *at* the hospital right now … No, um, we're hitting roadblocks."

"I don't see a roadblock."

"Never mind, Mom. It's just a metaphor."

"A what?"

"Okay … Yes, if you're nearby. That would be great … Thanks, Leslie."

Leslie tells me to "hang in there," that we're "doing the

right thing." She says she's ten minutes away and will get here as quickly as possible.

"Who's Leslie?"

"A friend. Remember? She brought you money and wine last week."

"No, I don't remember. Why would somebody bring me money?"

"Because you went into the bank and closed all your accounts."

I wish I could meditate myself out of barking things at her. I used to be good at handling her. I was always the one chosen to talk her out of her black moods. "You go, Cassie. She'll listen to you," my brothers would say. Maybe that's what I've been doing lately: operating in reverse, trying to *bring on* a mood. If I take up yelling, reminding her that she should be angry about her life, maybe there will be a spark, maybe she'll lift her head and look right at me, and behind those flat, dim eyes will be the regular her, the old her, back on the planet and ready to rage.

Or, I have to admit, maybe I'm being selfish, attacking a woman who's unable to defend herself, and this is my pathetic attempt to make her see what a disaster she's made of her life, and consequently ours.

I text Jack:

CASSIE:
Leslie said to invoke 5150 and make it
clear that you refuse to leave

JACK:
Oh man

CASSIE:
Do you know what that is?

JACK:
Yeah. Shit. OK

CASSIE:
Are you going to do it?

JACK:
I guess so, but what about that doctor?
Can't we call him?

CASSIE:
Can you call him? It's a little hard to talk
about Mom while I'm with Mom

JACK:
OK

Section 5150, also known as the seventy-two-hour law, dictates that when a person is a danger to themselves or others, or is suicidal, or wandering, the hospital *must* keep them for a seventy-two-hour period.

LESLIE:
OK. I'm here. where are you?

CASSIE:
I'm in the car with Mom but Jack's inside
at the triage desk. Could you go in and
see if there's anything you can do?

We first met Leslie nine months ago, when we reluctantly accepted that our then seventy-two-year-old mother did not have Alzheimer's—as friends and neighbours had suggested in their numerous phone calls—but alcoholism. Jack and I had flown out to New Mexico to get a sense of how serious things were. Google had led us eventually to Leslie: senior care advocate. Leslie was our brass-tacks saviour. She'd conducted one assessment session with Mom, lasting a little over an hour, after which Jack and I had gone to her office.

"Your mother is an alcoholic in the end stage of the disease. I suggest you conduct an intervention with her as soon as possible, preferably in the morning when she's lucid, with the goal of getting her to commit to detox. If you're successful, we'll take it from there. I'll be honest and tell you it's more likely that you'll be unsuccessful, in which case I'm afraid there's little you can do to turn things around. You will need to accept that your mother is walking a path and all you can do is accompany her. She is an adult with the constitutional right to live her life as she chooses."

She'd laid these facts before us like a street vendor with a limited selection of wares. It had taken all of a minute. The two years it has taken to play out have felt like an eternity.

*four*

I TRY TO HOLD her arm as we walk into the ER, but she brushes me aside: "I'm fine."

Her agitation has become near constant. The travel mug is empty, and it occurs to me that she's going to begin detoxing before she's officially admitted. When we enter the ER, she sees Jack sitting in front of the triage desk.

"What's going on?" she asks, going to him with more speed than I've seen her use all day.

"We're here to see the doctor about your knee," Jack says, eyeing me over her shoulder.

"About her knee?" The triage nurse looks up from behind the desk.

"Come on, Mom, let's go sit down," I say, taking her arm more firmly now, realizing we probably should have stayed in the car a little longer. As I lead her away, allowing Jack to explain our cover story to the triage nurse, a wave of guilt comes over me. It's a particular type of guilty feeling we've become well acquainted with these past two years. With every one of her rights we've taken away or tried to take away, we've been confronted with suspicion. "You want to take over her bank account? ... revoke her driver's licence? ... invoke your power of attorney? ... see her medical records? ... detox her?" Side tilt of the head. "Why?" Narrowing of the eyes. "She seems fine to me." The problem with having a beautiful blond mother who was (once) highly intelligent is that she doesn't fit the image of Serious Alcoholic, and if one doesn't speak to her for more than a few minutes, she can appear as "just fine" and we seem like the bad guys.

"Don't touch me." She wriggles her hand away and starts walking down a hallway toward a door that says Ophthalmology. I catch up and walk alongside her.

"Mom, we have to wait for the specific doctor we came to see."

"I'm not waiting. I'm going to tell them I need to see a doctor now or we're leaving."

"But this is Ophthalmology. They aren't going to be able to help us here." I make the mistake of trying to take her arm.

She yanks it free. "Fuck off." Her look flattens to a nickel.

The realization of how far out of my depth I am is starting to dawn on me.

My mother has always been combative, of the mind that nobody is going to tell her what to do, she controls her universe and nobody else. As the alcohol has gradually increased its hold on her, the expression of this certainty has lost its refinement. "Cassie, please. I'm able to make my own decisions" has become simply, "Fuck off."

She approaches the Ophthalmology desk and launches into a description of the pain in her knee: "I can hardly walk on it. The pain is all the way around the knee and shooting down to my feet. I'm not going to sit and wait, I need to see the doctor now or I'm going home."

Just as the receptionist—who looks like she's trying to unscramble a long anagram in a word game—is about to say something, Leslie appears from behind us. "Nina, the doctor's ready to see you now; it's right this way." She turns Mom around and starts down the hall, looking back over her shoulder to silently gesture an apology to the receptionist.

"Here, have a seat while I find out where they want us to go." Leslie sets Mom into a chair and walks toward the glass-protected reception area.

"Well, this is good," I say, sitting down next to her.

No response.

Leslie returns. "He's getting the room set up. Why don't we go get something to eat?"

After a trip to the vending machine for a chocolate bar, another trip to the triage counter and then to the bathroom, it dawns on me that Leslie has lied. There is no doctor ready to see Mom; Leslie has been buying time. What she knows—as surely she knows how to take someone's blood pressure or listen to their heart—is that, with dementia patients, one must live in the moment, do what is needed in any given instant, and much of the time that involves lying. Because it doesn't matter what you say: the demented person will not remember it even one minute later. So Leslie keeps Mom believing she's about to see a doctor "any second now."

As I watch them ping-pong across the waiting area, I think of a story our grandmother used to tell us when we were kids: "It was a dark and stormy night and the captain and his crew were sitting by the fire and the captain said, Alphonse, tell us a story. So, Alphonse hitched up his bootstraps, poked at the fire, and then he began: 'It was a dark and stormy night and the captain and his crew were sitting by the fire and the captain said, Alphonse, tell us a story ...'" She would go all out building up the drama, usually making it a full three or four rounds before we started shouting at the injustice, "Grammy! Come on, tell us the real story."

Now they are standing in front of the gift shop. Mom has her hand on the arm of an orderly and is smiling up at him. I cringe. Leslie turns to me and rolls her eyes. Mom's trying to flirt. This happens everywhere lately; it's as compulsive as the drinking. If a man is in the room, she'll move to him as if pulled by a magnet; she has no control over it. Ten years ago, when she was subtle and refined, this worked. But now, her once beautiful features are sunken and bloodshot and it's awful to watch. The orderly has managed to pull himself away, and Leslie is leading Mom back into the waiting area. The uneasy part of my relationship with Leslie is around these shared *can-you-even-believe-it?* moments. For two years—or ten or forty—I've been wearing my "everything's fine" face. To have someone to talk to—someone who really understands what's going on—has been a saving grace. But in certain moments, like when Leslie says something off-the-cuff like, "Wow. She really has no boundaries whatsoever," I feel like the worst kind of traitor. *How dare you talk about my mother like that.* I shut down.

"Nina Wolfe?"

"Okay, Nina. It's time." Leslie's hand is gentle on Mom's back.

I turn to Jack. "Do you mind going with them? I need to make a few calls. I won't be more than ten minutes."

"Okay," he says reluctantly, following Mom and Leslie through the double doors.

*five*

I LOOK DOWN at the text from my daughter:

LUCY:
How's Grammy? Did you say hi from me?

Yesterday, I was in Montreal. Yesterday, I was in my own bedroom looking through the sliding glass door at fat snowflakes falling on our roof deck. I was with my own family, watching from the safety of my home as snow fell and the world lost its shape. In the summer, the lights I'd strung up on the deck cast an amber glow on festive nights, but yesterday they were encased in ice that dripped from the roundest part of the bulb in long icicles, the six-foot evergreens drooping with the weight of snow, like old men destined to face the ground in penance.

I was packing my metallic blue suitcase for the seventh time in as many months when Lucy appeared at the top of the stairs, a vision in faded red tank top and long, unbrushed hair. "Mama, where are you going?"

"Hi, sweetie. I'm going to see Grammy." I touched my daughter's cheek as I set my purple folder of New Mexico documents in the suitcase. "Is your show over already?"

Lucy ignored my blatant attempt at changing the subject. "But you just got back from Grammy's. Why are you going again?"

She was only eight but desperately wanted to be a teenager like her sister. She didn't want to need her mother still and was mad at me for underlining that need by leaving so often.

"Grammy's buying a house" was the story I'd come up with for my last trip, so I stuck with it. "I have to go out and help her with the details. That's all."

Lucy sat on the step, in front of the long sliding glass doors that led from our bedroom onto the roof deck. Her red top and wild hair silhouetted against the falling snow gave her the air of a queen.

As a newborn, she'd had an inch of thick black hair and alert eyes that followed your every movement. She was like a small woodland creature, with finely tuned responses. The nurses had all come in, wanting to see the "baby with all the hair." As she grew, I tried to imagine what she would be like as an adult. At every stage, there was something otherworldly about her, regal from the get-go. Looking at her then—such beauty in her fury—I could see clearly that the tree had always been visible, even in the acorn; the imprint of what she would become had been there from birth.

"Why? Why does she need your help?"

She wanted a real answer, and she wasn't leaving until she got one. She wasn't falling for this "buying a house" nonsense. Kids have such a keen radar for lies. I decided on the old trick of saying something that was true, but not the whole truth. "Well, sweetie, Grammy's been having memory problems, like Yaiya. So she needs a little bit more help these days."

"I know that. You already told me that. So why doesn't she move into a place like Yaiya's if she has Alzheimer's?" She added the word *Alzheimer's* to make it clear that she wasn't a child and didn't appreciate being spoken to like one. I didn't correct her. It was easiest to let Lucy think it was Alzheimer's. I told myself I would explain later. After.

"I'm presenting my project this week," she said, looking at the floor.

I sat down on the foot of the bed and faced her. "Is your project this week? I thought it was next week." Lucy shook her head, not looking up. "I'm sorry, sweetie. You're going to be great, and Daddy will be there. I know I've been gone a lot lately, but this trip is an important one." I took both her hands in mine. "There's a hospital that will be able to help Grammy, and hopefully after this trip, other people—professional people—will be able to take over what Mama's been doing and I won't need to go out as much."

"What's wrong with her?"

"We're going to find out exactly that on this trip, and I promise that when I know everything, I'll tell you."

She looked at the floor.

"Would you like to visit Grammy sometime?"

"Yes! Can I come with you?" She jumped up.

"Not this trip—because you have your project and I have to get Grammy settled, but maybe next time."

I text Lucy:

> CASSIE:
> Grammy says to say hi to you too! She was asking how your project went

LUCY:
It was fine

> CASSIE:
> I'm so proud of you, sweetie

LUCY:
Will you come next time I'm presenting?

> CASSIE:
> Yes I promise

LUCY:
I luv u mama

> CASSIE:
> I love you too

I call my advisor and, after exchanging pleasantries, apologize for missing our appointment. She tells me not to worry and asks again if I'd like to defer my thesis. I tell her no, I'll be fine. Having already pushed it once, I don't want to put it off any further. She suggests we wait until after my final workshop for our next meeting.

My phone buzzes with another text.

ISABEL:
Hi mom, how's Grammy? Tell her I say hi.
Also, do you know where my passport is?

CASSIE:
Hi sweetie. Second drawer down in my desk - Ziploc bag.
When I'm back we'll get you a toiletry bag, promise.
Back soon X

Isabel has been accepted into an exchange program and leaves for Seville in a week. Her intellect is a river that runs like a sword, a streak of heroism in lapis blue. Top grades in every class; "an elegant thinker," her Modern Religions teacher had commented. For the application, she wrote an essay in French on her desire to learn about other cultures, which she wove into describing her love of Montreal and how much it would mean to her, not only to go to Spain but also to welcome a Sevillana student into her home. It was eloquent and personal. And now she's flying to Seville and I'm not there to help her prepare for this epic adventure.

Finally, I make the call I've been putting off for weeks, hoping my situation would change.

"Hello?"

"Hi, Jude. It's me."

"Hi, Cassie. How are you? ... How's your mother?"

"I'm good. We're at the hospital. She was just taken in. It shouldn't be too long now. It's the waiting that's hard."

"Ingrid and I are thinking about you."

"I appreciate that. So, listen. Go ahead and teach my part to Sia. I'd really love to do this tour, but I just can't commit right now."

"I feel like shit about pushing you, Cassie, it's the time crunch. We need to move forward."

"No, no—don't feel bad. It's not your fault. The timeline pressure is real. Who knows, maybe after this European tour, there will be an American tour and I can come back on board then. Really, I'm fine with it. In fact, I'm relieved you guys can stop thinking about it and focus on the work."

"Thanks. That means a lot. Take care of yourself. Let us know how things go."

"I will."

I get a Reese's Peanut Butter Cup from the vending machine, and it melts all over my hands when I open it. Licking my fingers, I use my teeth to scrape the melted chocolate from the wrapper. As I am pulling the wrapper through my teeth, my gaze is drawn to the opposite side of the room where a tiny woman with thin gunmetal hair is wearing a full-length black mourning dress and furiously working a strand of rosary beads. Her glaucous eyes lift to meet mine, her body rocking back and forth. She's out of place in this modern fluorescent waiting room, like an unlucky tarot card. I look down at my fingers, muddy with chocolate, and decide to forego the second cup. I task the tiny brown wrapper with cleaning my fingers before dumping the whole melting mass into the garbage.

I am not fine with somebody taking my part in a show I've spent years creating, right as the work is done. No, I'm not fine with somebody touring Europe in my place. I'm not fine with missing Lucy's presentation. I'm not fine with leaving Isabel to prepare for the first big trip of her life all on her own. I'm not fine with dropping my entire life to come help my mother pull hers from the dumpster where she left it. No. I'm not fine with any of it.

I text Jack:

CASSIE:

I'm ready to switch with you

JACK:

K

CASSIE:

How is she?

JACK:

She's pissed off and it's hard to keep her
in this room

CASSIE:

I'm coming

JACK:

It's room 9

I buzz at the glass-protected entry to the ER. When the muscle-bound attendant who works the locked door leans forward, I tell him through the intercom that I'm Nina Wolfe's daughter. He buzzes me through.

Jack and Mom are mid-argument. "It's okay, Mom. There's plenty of time. It's only five o'clock."

"It is not five o'clock. It's seven o'clock." They're facing a large clock in the corner of the room and Mom's gesturing at it angrily.

"Okay, fine, Mom. It's seven o'clock." Jack takes his phone from his pocket. "I'll be back, I need to call Iona."

"What is Iona?" Mom yells at him.

"Iona is my wife." He gives me a tight grin and walks out.

"I'm here, Mom. It's okay, it shouldn't be long now."

I sink into one of the two plastic chairs against the wall and watch her pace. Every so often, she rests on the bed and closes her eyes, but never for more than a minute or two. She complains about the lack of pillows and the hardness of the bed. She picks up the travel mug and tries to take a sip, though it's been empty for hours. She repeats this every few minutes. It was hard enough to watch when the mug was full; it's worse now that it's empty and she tips it all the way upside down with her head bent backward, like a dying person in a desert.

# six

SHE STANDS IN THE corner staring blankly into space, as if she were about to say something but can't remember what. Her eyes are lakes emptied of water.

"I've asked for a pillow, Mom. Why don't you try closing your eyes for a minute?"

Growing up, whenever we stumbled in on her napping, we'd stop dead in our tracks. "Oops! Sorry," we'd say to the muffled rumple on the bed, and as we tiptoed backward through the half-opened door, we'd hear, "It's okay, I'm not sleeping. I'm just closing my eyes for a minute."

According to my mother, she didn't sleep, she just closed her eyes for a minute.

She won't lie down or close her eyes. There's a small drop of blood on her arm where she's pulled out the IV port the nurse had inserted. I give up on trying to get her to rest and try the same effort on myself. I cross my arms and settle into the plastic bucket chair. My eyelids fall to half-mast. I search for deep breaths in the outline of a kidney-shaped pan. My mother's blurry silhouette flutters indistinctly as she opens cupboards, searches her purse, pokes her head out the door, sighs, complains, and finally, *finally* lies down.

As my brothers and I inch ever closer to passing her into the hands of professionals, my grip on the endless necessary details attenuates. Facts and numbers and doctors' names stop circling; something akin to relief is in the air. I cross my arms and slide deeper into the sloped plastic, my head coming to rest against the wall. Mom's constant motion transforms the room into flickering shades of light and dark, a moth in the half-light. My eyes close all the way and a thin veil of the past hangs threadbare like an old woman's shawl; yesterday's laughter wafts through the air lifting the shawl like a breeze, circles of light through lace.

*I'm in a faded polyester nightgown, with mud boots and tangled hair, leading our horse back through the wet grass. I turn to look back over my shoulder and you wave. You're in your green terry-cloth robe, leaning into the paint-stripped door frame of the farmhouse you renovated, coffee cup in hand, steam spiralling into your contented face.*

*You're doing dishes at the kitchen sink and your little goldfinch comes to sit on your shoulder, and you talk to him quietly as you do the dishes. You don't see me, and I listen as you tell the little bird your plans.*

The room is quiet. I open my eyes. She's gone. I leap from the chair and peer out into the brightly lit hall. I see her down to the left standing next to a nurse who's taking the blood pressure of a man bleeding from his head. The man's emaciated body is perched on the edge of a gurney like a blade of needlegrass unable to right itself after a storm. He's connected via stethoscope to the nurse before him. Her gaze is pinned to the dial she has pressed into his outstretched arm. Hunched there, counting heartbeats, she seems to be praying, as if standing in front of a fading Jesus, asking benediction. So devoted is she, that even Mom's insistent rapping on her left shoulder won't pull her from this task.

"Mom!" I sprint down the hall to take her arm with one hand. I am gentle. Steering her requires finesse; it has to be done without her realizing it. I try the Leslie variety of lying. "I talked to our nurse, and he's getting a pillow for you. We should get back to the room."

"I don't want to lie down. I want to go home."

"But the doctor is on his way right now, so we won't have to wait anymore." This second lie works, and I'm able to lead her back to the room.

Her feet barely lift from the floor when she walks. She's as thin as the man on the gurney and almost as dirty. As we make our slow way back to the room, I turn to look over my shoulder at the nurse and the man. They are a silent sculpture of grace, given a flash of backlight when a door beyond them opens. *Give me your tired, your poor, your huddled masses yearning to breathe free.*

I am helping Mom into the bed when Jack, gone in search of a blanket, returns. We help her to lie down; she allows us to take off her shoes and we drape the blanket across her, and at last, she closes her eyes.

Jack and I sit side by side in the plastic bucket chairs and I whisper that we're going to need a sedative soon. Jack whispers back, "Yeah. We should get one for Mom too." We chuckle and he gets up from his chair. "I'll go talk to our nurse."

The lights are low. Jack goes out and closes the door behind him. I follow an impulse to pull my chair closer to the bed and hold her hand.

"I ruined your vacation," she says, sadly, opening her eyes.

I don't know if it's the holding of my hand, or the fatigue of the hours, or the alcohol draining from her body, but she's actually looking at me, talking to me.

"I didn't come here for vacation." I just say it. "Jack and I came here to help you."

"With my knee?" She rolls onto her side to face me. She takes my hand in both of hers. Her eyes close for a moment and then open again. She seems profoundly tired, like a fighter returning to his corner after a brutal round. Maybe she's tired of fighting us, of fighting whatever chemical reaction is happening in her body, of fighting life for years on end.

"No, Mom, we're not here for your knee. We're here to help you get the alcohol out of your body. It's killing you."

Jack slips back into the room and stands at the foot of the bed. She doesn't look up and I continue. "Jack and I planned this trip, we booked our flights and arranged the hospital and the doctor, and you're not here for your knee and we're not here for vacation. We came for one thing, and one thing only, and that is to detox you from alcohol."

There's a long pause before she looks at me with clear understanding, and then over to Jack, who says, "We love you, Mom. We want to help you," and wanting to hold her in some way, squeezes her feet through the thin hospital cover. She looks back at me. It's the old her. The old her is seeing us. We are talking to *her*.

After a long pause, she says, "Wow. That's impressive."

## seven

THE NURSE COMES IN with a small tray, on which sits a Dixie cup and a single pill. *Male nurses give me hope for the world*, I think as he explains what Ativan is. Neither Jack nor I interrupt him to say we are well acquainted with Ativan. Mom doesn't want to take the pill. She even says, "I don't take pills." Jack leans in to gently touch her cheek, he tells her it will help her sleep and she takes the pill. I realize I've been imagining it as more dramatic than this, that detox would involve tubes and wires. But seeing my mother still for the first time all day, I realize the drama happens *inside* the body.

A few moments later, the doctor comes in. He's a tall man with shiny unkempt hair and huge globe eyes, holding a folder against his chest like a schoolboy would hold his books. He swivels a rolling stool out from under the counter to sit alongside Mom. He is kind; he asks her about her knee and listens attentively while she pulls a few loose words through the fog of her fatigue to describe pain. The doctor explains that drinking alcohol has caused damage to her liver and that he would like to keep her for a few days to help her get better. Then he is saying things like "hepatic liver" and "peripheral neuropathy," and her eyes become inkblots. When they close all the way, the doctor turns to Jack and me. He tells us she'll mostly be sleeping now but they'll be monitoring her closely; the bloodwork reveals damage to the liver, but he won't know the extent until he has the ultrasound results. After he leaves, two men in scrubs wheel Mom, now sleeping, out of the emergency area. Jack and I stare down the hall as she disappears around a corner.

It's a little after eleven when we step through the glass doors of the emergency room and out into the cool January night. Everyone has been telling us we're *doing the right thing*. But there is no accompanying feeling of rightness. We drive back to the hotel in silence.

Jack pulls into the parking lot and shuts off the car. We are facing the road that leads to the airport, but it's late and there are no cars. Neither of us makes a move to get out. Jack looks down at the keys in his hand. "Can I ask you something? It might be kind of a stupid question considering these past few years."

"Yeah?"

"Do you think, when we were growing up, that she was an alcoholic?"

We're parked directly under a streetlamp. It reflects off the hood of the car, washing our faces in a flat yellow light.

"I guess we always knew something wasn't right, but I see the drinking as more of a result. Something was wrong that she couldn't overcome, so she drank. I guess something like that. Leslie says—"

"Yeah, I know what Leslie thinks. I have to be honest; I hate that shit. It's reductive. I don't accept that a label can negate everything she's done and made and given to the world."

The night is blue and quiet. Jack's being defensive; I recognize the posture. I wear it often. But at the same time, I agree with my brother. Our mother was a woman of awesome power. Leslie was trying to be helpful, giving me the pamphlet "Recovering from Life with a Narcissist," but it rubbed me the wrong way. To my thinking, the bullet point list in the little guide read like a how-to manual for women breaking through glass ceilings. Be out of touch with reality, be grandiose in your need for recognition, rage at devaluation, don't trust those around you ... Like they say, you're not paranoid if they really *are* out to get you.

Jack interrupts my thoughts. "If we had only seen it coming earlier ..." He's doing that impossible equation where you line up the facts of your history and shuffle them this way and that hoping to come up with a different ending. "I remember her drinking wine with dinner and at parties."

"Yeah, and who doesn't drink wine with dinner? Technically speaking, if we go by the strict definition, most of my friends are alcoholics."

"I don't remember her being out of control or drinking so regularly or so much that I thought, 'Whoa, Mom's got a problem.'"

"I understand some things better now that I've passed through the toddler phase with my kids. When Isabel and Lucy were little, I felt like I was never going to have a life again, like it would be dirty diapers and playdates and tripping over toys for the rest of my life."

"I think Iona's feeling that way right about now. And—my God, think about *us* as kids. We must have been hell—writing on the walls of the den with that blue marker, and the time I smeared diaper ointment all over my bed and my dresser—"

"And your body and your hair. Oh yeah, I remember ... And Oliver with the apples."

"What was that story ... when I was a baby and Mom asked Oliver to watch me, and he set me on the dining room table and went out to play with his friends." Jack laughs.

"Oh man, Ollie ..." I shake my head.

"Do you remember that snowstorm? You guys took me sledding at the Jones Road dead end—I think I was six?"

"You were five. And Mom said we could only do a couple of runs and then straight home because they were calling for a blizzard. The snow was two feet deep by the time she got there—it was up past her knees. She appeared from out of nowhere—that bright blue down coat and the plaid hat with the leather earflaps, the snow swirling up behind her."

"And she pulled us all home on that rickety toboggan with the yellow cord."

"Well—she pulled me and you on it while Oliver and Stan Press trudged ahead, clearing a path."

"Stan Press. Shit, that's right. How could I forget about him?"

"The best was you yelling—"

"Mush! Mush!"

"And Mom howling like a wolf at the moon every time you did it. You guys did that the whole way home."

"Yeah. I remember …"

Mom had made us blueberry pancakes for dinner that night, and the snow had continued to fall, and school was cancelled for the whole week, and Stan Press stayed over for three nights.

All at once, Jack gasps for air. His shoulders heave, and his face twists up as he lets out a sound somewhere between a sob and a moan. He brings his hands up to his face, trying to hold in the sounds, but they escape through his fingers. After some number of minutes, he wipes his eyes with the back of his arm and says, "Jesus fuck."

"What time is your flight?" I'm sitting on the edge of the bed and look up from programming the alarm on my phone.

"Six thirty-five."

"Okay. Mine's at six fifteen, so I'll set the alarm for four thirty. Sound about right?"

"Sounds good to me."

I set my phone on the bedside table and open my purple

New Mexico folder. The doctors who will see Mom after detox are people who've never met her and know nothing about her. Dr. Katz thinks it will help them if they have a history to work with. She's instructed me to write Mom's history as a narrative. She thinks it'll be easiest this way. "Put what you think are the relevant names and events into a story. Have fun with it."

I open my laptop.

I open a Word document.

I click the Save button and name the document "Mom relevant facts."

I look at the tiny vertical line flashing at the top of the page.

I trace the edge of the keypad with my forefinger.

I lift my head and look at my brother's back. He's hunched over the small hotel desk talking quietly into the phone. "... Because I have my chief's interview on Wednesday, and I couldn't change it ... Do you mind if we talk about this when I get home? I'm so tired."

I try again to think of how much I knew as a child. How could we have grown up thinking we'd had a normal childhood? And even as the thought is entering my mind, I can hear her over my shoulder with her life's mandate. "Normal? Please. Who wants to be normal when you can be extraordinary!"

*I wouldn't mind a dose of normal.*

According to Google there's nothing extraordinary about becoming an alcoholic. It's about as average as things get. Mom appreciated irony, but not when it applied to her directly.

1977-1987

# eight

LIGHT STREAMING THROUGH tall trees turns the car gold and green, Mom sings over the wind and I check my seatbelt. She has one hand on the steering wheel and the other resting in the open window, and the warm air lifts her long blond hair like wings. We pass manicured lawns the size of football fields and houses tucked behind little groves of trees, and then a bump in the road, and we are airborne. Jack reaches for my hand and Mom hoots and Oliver sticks his face out into the bright blue morning.

A woman watering a small patch of garden with a long green hose shakes her pink gloved fist in the air and yells something at Mom as we fly by. I turn around to watch through the back window as she disappears in the distance. And then it's dark and we're in a cool, wet tunnel. I turn around to see that dense forest has replaced suburbia. The only remnant of civilization: two crumbling stone walls keeping pace with our blue Plymouth station wagon on either side. I lean across Jack and take hold of the window ledge. The stone walls are low and small and definitely losing the battle; vines climb the utility poles and encircle the phone lines, honeysuckle and baby maple tumble over the walls, and the canopy of towering trees allows only speckles of light to break through. Mom drives a little faster and I slide back into my seat, and we sit awed silence at the strangling, crushing beauty.

Then a flash of brilliant daylight and we are out, flanked once again by front lawns and swimming pools and white post-and-rail fences and Mom turns up the volume on her Beatles cassette.

"Nina, slow down!"

But Mom is singing "Eleanor Rigby."

I wait for the instrumental break to tap her on the shoulder, "What about goats?"

She looks at me in the rear-view mirror with that glint in her eye like we're bank robbers on a great heist. "At least five or six."

"What about a llama?" Jack starts kicking his car seat excitedly.

"I want a snake," Oliver says out the window. Then, turning to me, "Look!"

We fly by an old-timey sign spanning the front of a white clapboard building: Ye Olde Towne Market. "Good grief," Oliver says as we watch the little house recede into the distance. "We're really in the country now!"

"This is that waterfall, remember?" Frank is trying to hold the map, but all the windows are open and the wind is bending the thin paper in every direction. He gives up and lets it drop into his lap.

"Dad!" Jack starts kicking his car seat. "Dad! Dad!"

"I'm right here, Jack. I can hear you."

"I want my lollipop."

"Magic word."

"Please."

Frank hands Jack the remains of his yellow lollipop. Mom and Frank have been married for three years. Jack calls him Dad but Oliver and I already have a dad, so we call him Frank. Mom says we will be using Frank's last name from now on, instead of our old one, Albrecht. So now our last name is Wolfe, like the animal but with an *e*.

Mom slows down. Banking our left side is a wall of very tall perfectly spaced evergreen hedges ... or ... "Are those trees or bushes?"

"Arborvitae. They're trees," Mom says. "And they're ours."

She flicks on the blinker and turns in to a barely visible opening between the trees. Frank shuts off the music. Nobody says anything, tires rolling over loose stones the only sound as we creep up the long, narrow drive.

Wild flowering bushes of purple and yellow drag across the windshield, what's left of the concrete drive is decorated with cracks, and every bent and broken line is a burst of green. A chaos of wings erupts beside us and a hundred tiny sparrows dart from the yellow bush, becoming one as they hit the sky.

"Look!" Oliver's entire torso is out the window and I follow his pointing finger to a large bird with a bright red head, puffed chest and long, straight tailfeather. It strolls across a patch of grass and then picks up speed to trot in front of the car. "That's a pheasant," Frank says. Then Mom says to herself, in a voice barely above a whisper, "There it is." And the house comes into view on our left. It's a tall, skinny thing that gives the impression of looking down and judging—which is ironic, considering its condition; it seems to have once been white, but flaking paint gives it the ashy look of an old man. Nests poke out from the eaves, and tall climbing vines obscure the first-floor windows. We follow the driveway past the house to where it ends in front of the garage. "The realtor called this the carriage house." Oliver and I exchange a look; it's a garage—or, correction, it was once a garage. Beyond it are two more structures, one tiny and one huge. The tiny one looks like an old playhouse. "That would have been the caretaker's house," Frank says. It has one window, of which every pane is broken, and there's an old wooden door hanging askew from a single rusty hinge. And finally, the barn Mom's been telling us about: a massive, wood-shingled, woolly mammoth of a building that is—if such a thing were possible—in worse condition than the house. My heart sinks at the sight of this dilapidated stretch of wreckage. Oliver's mouth hangs open. As if reading our minds and wanting to keep our spirits up, Mom says, "Isn't this exciting?"

That's not the word we were thinking.

She shuts off the car, I release Jack from his car seat, and we follow her up the front walk to the house. With a bit of effort, she pushes open the thick wooden door, and one by one we step inside. There is flowered wallpaper, stained and yellowing, and a dark wood floor that looks about a hundred years old. In the wall opposite us is a large hole revealing thin strips of lath covered in bits of plaster. A shaft of light slices a diagonal through the dusty air, illuminating a patch of floor in front of us, across which saunters a large rat. He's so casual there, basking in the light, so unruffled by the presence of five humans standing in his house that any scream or sudden movement on our part would seem disproportionate and even a little rude. Jack, taking his lollipop from his mouth, says quietly, "Mousie." Frank says, "Let's check into the motor lodge and come back in the morning, fresh." Mom nods absently and Frank says, "Who wants milkshakes?" And we happily take the cue to run down the walk and pile back into the car. All except for Mom, who stands in the doorway for a few extra seconds. With her dark blue sleeveless T-shirt and bangs pushed to the side, she looks like a grown-up, woman version of Oliver. It's clear she would have started working right then and there if she didn't have us with her. She's probably picturing all those things she's been talking about nonstop: a kitchen with herbs hanging from exposed beams, wide plank floors, and a large table where we will all eat together, drinking milk provided by our own goats, eating eggs from our own chickens, and vegetables and herbs and "we'll be completely self-sufficient." She's going to turn these rundown old buildings into a home. Her vision for what she's going to give us just a long list of all she never had.

# nine

IN THE STILL DARK of early morning, Mom drags us up and
out of the motor lodge. She starts the tiny coffeemaker
and shakes our feet one by one. "Come on, everybody up."
Oliver cocoons himself further into his covers, moaning. Jack
flips his head from one side to the other, his gentle snore
not missing a beat. Mom stands over me. "Hey. Sweetie, I
need your help. We need to get them moving." The bathroom
floor is cold as I brush my teeth. Frank rolls up the drawings
from where they're spread on the table, snapping an elas-
tic around each end as I stuff my books into a bag. Oliver,
hugging his pillow to his chest, shuffles to the car and Frank
buckles a still-sleeping Jack into his car seat and we drive
to the Friendly's on Speen Street in Natick. Our new town.
We wake in silence over pancakes and eggs as businessmen
order coffees to go and bacon sizzles in the kitchen and the
silver-haired waitress chats her way from table to table with

a steaming pot of coffee. The first hint of morning is just turning the edges of the sky transparent when Frank takes the bill up to the counter to pay and we pile back into the car.

The road is wet, and beyond the waterfall the sky is an upside-down rocket popsicle, reddish pink at the bottom fading into white and then blue and getting lighter by the minute. By the time we pass through the arborvitae the sun is fully awake, sitting unabashed on the horizon, yawning a lazy greeting, stretching long fingers of light through the soft, wet grass, turning the whole scene white gold. There is the smell of dew and grass and a warm breeze, and magnolia blossoms twirl to the ground and even Oliver smiles. Every morning here is the first morning in all of time, the world born before us, open-armed and welcoming, and I love Mom for moving us here. With the sun pouring through the windows of the house, even the dingiest room is golden with fairy dust, and Mom takes a sip from her coffee and throws an arm over my shoulder and surveys her kingdom.

Frank sets the drawings on the makeshift table and comes to stand next to Mom. Frank is from the tough East Boston neighbourhood of Chelsea and has a moustache, sharp cheekbones, and overwide eyes, like he's ready for a fight, like nothing is going to catch him off guard—except, everything does. "When you grow up with nothing, you're always expecting someone to come along and take everything away." He makes things out of leather—bags and belts and hats—and sometimes he makes pillows out of bits of old rugs and sells those too.

Oliver comes in and sits on the stairs. He's still holding his pillow, and he closes his eyes and leans against the wall.

Jack and Oliver both have blond hair like Mom. Oliver's hair is ash blond, and his eyes are deep blue like winter. His hair is too long and he's always flipping his bangs to the side, and he's got about a million freckles and his teeth are too big. Jack's hair is yellow like sunshine, and he's round and wobbly and run-walks to keep up with everyone. When he was brought home from the hospital, I decided then and there that he was going to be mine. Mom was way too busy to take care of him, and Oliver didn't have the first idea how to take care of a baby, so it would be up to me. I don't look like Jack, though, or Oliver for that matter. I have light brown hair that hangs in braids to my waist and turns reddish in the summer. My knees are too big, and I have a space between my two front teeth that I want to get closed up. The dentist said he could do it with a special wire and super-strong glue, but Mom said, "Absolutely not. We're not changing anything that makes you you."

"Ollie, do you want to keep going on the basement?"

"Want to?" Oliver says, opening one eye, but not lifting his head from the wall.

"Let me rephrase. Oliver: basement."

"And Murphy, you and Irene can finish stripping the wallpaper in your bedroom." Mom has called me Murphy for as long as I can remember, I don't know why or where it came from, it's just her name for me—which is so like her, to give me a long fancy name like Cassandra and then never use it.

Like that guest bathroom in the old house; she spent two months renovating it and nobody ever went in.

Irene is pulling up the driveway in her yellow Volvo.

"Hellooo? Sorry I'm late," she calls through the open window of her car. Irene is Mom's best friend. Her high-pitched voice has always seemed to me an attempt to lessen the strength in her height. She would never dream of taking up too much space—which is challenging at six foot one.

Irene and I scrape old wallpaper in what will be my bedroom while Mom pulls up mildewing carpet in the hall outside the door and tells us stories that Irene greets with bright explosions of laughter, and every so often she and Mom slip into British accents like from Monty Python.

By the end of two days, the big blue dumpster is full and we need another. Things that don't get thrown out include: the hundreds of old canning jars Oliver finds in the basement; the antique toys from the attic that Frank will clean up and sell in his shop; a pair of baby booties, so dirty with cobwebs and dust and mouse droppings it's impossible to say what colour they might have been; and the treasure Irene finds, a love letter from a soldier named William, dated June 8, 1917, to his "Sweet Claudette."

Despite his complaints, all this dusty old junk is heaven for Oliver, who was well known for trash collecting back in our old town of Newton Center. In that well-to-do suburb of Boston, Mom had neighbours complaining on more than one occasion, "Your son is in my front yard going through my trash."

She would ignore the implication that Oliver's behaviour was out of the ordinary. "Hey, you threw it out—that's your tough luck. Finders keepers." And she would hang up the phone and wink at Oliver, who loved her for it. She'll defend any one of us to anyone and she never apologizes for anything. Ever.

Sometimes she'll defend us even when we we're not under attack. Like when Oliver's teacher commented that he was "special," telling Mom that, on the one hand, he remembers everything he's ever read or seen or learned, in its exact detail, can write at a level far in advance of the other students, and is perfectly ambidextrous. "He's quite astonishing, really. But on the other hand," she continued gently, "he has difficulty concentrating in one-on-one conversations, and I really think he might benefit from working with a specialist."

To which Mom replied, "Are you a specialist? I didn't think so. Thank you very much for your opinion, but my son is fine." Even Irene tried to convince Mom to go the specialist route, but she wouldn't budge. She said Oliver was his own person and that was that; she wasn't about to change anything that made him unique.

Oh, he's unique, all right. There was the time he wanted to know how many peas would fit up his nose and if they would start going down his throat once they reached the top. Mom had to take him to the emergency room to get them all out. And when he was five, he climbed out John Finkle's window, onto the roof of his porch, and then onto the roof roof and wedged himself down the chimney. Said he wanted to see if it was even possible for a fat man in a red suit to fit down with a bag of presents. The fire department had to come that time.

"Cassie! Come on," Oliver calls up to the open window. I lean my head out but he's already walking off toward the barn with Jack toddling along behind. I look to Mom.

"Go ahead, Murph, and keep an eye on Jack. Lunch is in an hour."

I drop my scraper and run down the creaky stairs out the front door to the barn, where Oliver is pruning a large stick with his Swiss Army knife. "Find a walking stick," he says, and I do, and after some breaking and whittling, the three of us set off through the long blowing grass, pilgrims in a new land. The woods are a million shades of green, and we run over a tapestry of roots and ferns and old logs sprouting with new life at every edge. There is a brook carving its way through the woods, and Oliver and I help Jack to cross the wet stones. We use our sticks and I hold his hand, and we continue deeper into the woods. About ten minutes in, we find ourselves standing before a derelict stone wall, beyond which stretches a massive apple orchard—rows and rows of perfectly kept trees running as far as the eye can see. The apples are tiny and green and nowhere near ready, but we scramble over the wall and start climbing the trees anyway.

Heading back home our chests are puffed out in pride, our pockets overflowing with the tiny green apples. We know Mom bought this house to "do it on her own" and we've just contributed apple pie and apple crumble and cider and ...

"It has to be up to code." We hear Frank yelling before we see him. "We need an engineer and that's all there is to it."

We slow down as we approach the house, the mood spilling from the doorless threshold.

Mom is speaking in that low, even voice that circles the room like a snake. "I'm not paying for something we don't need. It's obvious which are the supporting walls, the beams are a foot square." We are frozen on the front walk, all thoughts of apples gone. She hasn't had a mood in a while, and we are unprepared. Irene is way down the driveway, steering clear of the situation. She sees us and waves, but her smile is forced.

Mom has apparently decided she wants to knock out all the walls on the first floor. Frank is saying we need to get an engineer in if we're going to start knocking out walls.

She takes the sledgehammer from the sawhorse.

"It has to be signed off on." Frank's voice has a *don't-you-dare* edge to it.

Mom notices us standing there on the walk and waves us in. This is the very last thing we want to do, but our feet know we have no choice and start walking. She directs her lesson at Jack. "Demolition is how all construction begins. You can't build anything new until you destroy what came before." And with that she brings her arm back like a baseball player and swings the sledgehammer straight into the wall between the dining room and the kitchen, creating a crater the size of a stop sign.

Jack, four years old and not yet adept at reading the room, yells, "Demolize it!"

Mom laughs. "What was that, Jack?"

"Demolize it!" He jumps up and down as she swings the hammer again, sending another huge cloud of dust into the air.

"Nina!" Frank yells.

Jack starts chanting, "De-mo-lize it! De-mo-lize it!"

After three more swings of the hammer, Frank stops shaking his head and yells over the noise, "Fine."

Mom smiles triumphantly, Jack stops yelling, and Frank says, "At least put a mask on."

Irene appears behind us in the open front door and sets her hand on my shoulder. "So, no walls?"

Mom swings the sledgehammer up onto her shoulder like a railway worker and puts an arm around Oliver, "*They drink their cakes and eat their tea ...*"

She and Ollie made up this rhyme and we kids all join in to finish it:

*They climb the river and swim the tree,*
*You say, "Wait! That's the wrong way 'round!"*
*But maybe it's you who's upside down.*

# *ten*

THE LILACS AND ROBINS of spring and summer are replaced with the crunching of boots on crisp frosted grass, fall coats, and plumes of warm breath in the icy air. And as we kids settle into our new school, the house gradually becomes livable—or what Mom considers livable—so she and Frank start on the barn. They work overtime to build horse stalls, a goat pen, and a chicken coop. But as the weather gets colder, so does the air between Mom and Frank. The bickering becomes near constant; they're unable to agree on anything, and the work on the barn turns into one long series of cut corners. They tack up a sheet of plywood to close in the goat pen rather than building a proper wall, they rig a tarp over the hay in the loft rather than patching the holes in the roof, and when Mom tells Frank the door to the chicken coop will need to be redone eventually, Frank retorts that it will have to get in line behind the fifty other things that need to happen for the humans to have a livable home, and he storms off into the house for the hook-and-eye latch. Mom, unfazed, calls out after him that it's on the kitchen counter next to the hot plate.

They work overtime to replace the floorboards in the main entry and ready the barn to house actual animals—which Frank says is "absurdly ambitious," but Mom is undeterred.

With all the sawing and hammering, Jack, Oliver, and I are more than happy to get on the school bus each morning at seven thirty. Jack's preschool is attached to our elementary school, and we walk him all the way in before going to our own classrooms. And most days, when the bus drops us back home at three thirty, we are greeted by the sound of the circular saw and raised voices. We drop our bags, grab a snack, and head straight back outside.

With each season we pass in South Natick, our suburban family learns a little more about life in the country and we manage to settle into something like a routine. I now know the buzzing in late summer is from cicadas, the wind is strongest in October and November, and one needs a tractor to shovel a driveway fifty yards long. I love the smell of freshly dried hay and the organization of the tack room. I learn to ride a pony and filter milk and clean a milking stand. Jack often trails along behind when I do my barn chores, but not Oliver. Ollie's interest in the barn fades with the warm weather. He is the first to make a friend in the neighbourhood, and so, the first to realize farming is *not* considered cool and that chores can use up an entire after-noon. His best friend, Stan Press, lives down the street. How Oliver managed to find someone as weird as himself I have no idea, but they're peas in a pod.

Oliver trots down the stairs and through the dining room with his blue skateboard in hand. I get up from the dining room table, where I'm doing my homework, and follow him through the kitchen. "Are you going to Stan's?" Any attempt to hang out with Oliver and Stan is futile, but I *really* don't want to be here for the cider party.

"Dream on, dork," Oliver says, walking out the back door, dropping his skateboard onto the driveway and gliding away.

I sigh; not only will I be here, but I'll have to watch Jack. Oliver gets out of everything by disappearing, and I'm stuck doing everything because Mom depends on me. I'm dependable.

"His name is George," Irene is explaining to Mom as I come back through the kitchen. "And he teaches at the Boston Architectural College. I spoke to him last week and mentioned the cider party and told him you were someone he simply *had* to meet."

It's late morning, and the two of them are chopping toma-toes for bruschetta. The smell of basil fills the kitchen. There are platters on every counter: little sausages on sticks and mini quiches and doughnuts. Frank has come in from setting up the cider press and is washing his hands.

"Oh, Irene, you're the best." Mom hugs her.

Irene laughs her big *who, me?* laugh. "Don't thank me yet. The truth is, he's a bit daft—but he is a good person to talk to if you want to study architecture at the BAC; their continuing education program is excellent."

Frank's drying his hands. "I don't know when you think you're going to fit in architecture classes, between the new job at the furniture store and this place."

"Oh! Did you get the job at Design Research?" Irene asks, taking no note of Frank's tone.

"I did. It's only part-time. I start this coming week, nine to one, while the kids are at school, and"—Nina leans in and whispers conspiratorially to Irene—"I get a twenty percent discount on everything."

Frank is pouring a glass of whiskey and says, without turning around, "Jesus, Nina. Maybe we should figure out how to pay the mortgage before you start paying Newbury Street prices for housewares." He storms out before Mom has a chance to respond.

She shakes tomato from her hands like she's hitting someone. "Sometimes I wonder how I married someone so utterly lacking in imagination."

"Money stress does things to people," Irene offers awkwardly.

Jack and I are sprawled out under the lilac bush putting the roof on an elaborate Lincoln Log house, slightly sick from the obscene number of doughnuts we've eaten, when Mom,

Irene, and George walk over to the food table on the other side of the bush. George is handsome in a TV show sort of way, with straight white teeth, perfect posture, and too much hair gel. Irene is in the middle of apologizing for some inside joke he didn't get. He does seem slightly put out.

"You'll have to excuse us; Nina and I get carried away sometimes." Irene touches his arm. "But George, what do you think of the house?"

"Oh yes, the house. Thank you for giving me the full tour. I think Nina has a real knack for interior design. It's quite lovely, very ... rustic."

Irene flashes a look at Mom, whose smile has disappeared. Irene speaks before George has a chance to continue. Interior design is not architecture, and Irene wants to steer him in the right direction. "Nobody has Nina's design sense, that's true enough. But also, the structural work she's done is remarkable. You may not be able to tell by how well she's integrated the new materials with the original structure, but Nina took out four walls on the first floor—and added that room off the dining room, as well as the greenhouse. The first floor is heated entirely through solar and wood-burning stoves. She exposed the beams and the subfloor and has plans to transform the upstairs of the barn into a painting studio."

Jack and I are frozen in place. Though Mom is obscured from our view, we can feel her mood darkening, as sure as a drop in temperature.

"I think what Irene is getting at"—it's Mom speaking now—"is that I'm interested in studying architecture.

I understand you run the continuing education program at the BAC. How does one apply?"

"Oh! Well ..." George looks completely caught off guard, his gaze darting back and forth between the two women before turning down to his drink. "The BAC—well, if I may say, it's a rigorous program of study. I can't see how a woman—with three kids, no less—living forty-five minutes outside the city is going to be able to keep up with the demands of the coursework."

I pull down the branch in front of us, giving me and Jack an unobstructed view of Mom, standing rigid in front of George, her face impassive. Irene, in contrast, shifts from one foot to the other, smiling awkwardly and fluttering her hands. "Surely, you aren't suggesting that Nina drop the idea altogether?"

"Well, of course she's welcome to do whatever she wants, but I wouldn't want her to harbour illusions that because she can decorate a farmhouse, this qualifies her for a program as rigorous as the BAC."

At that moment, someone hollers across the party, "George, come. You must tell Judith about the overpass—she doesn't believe me."

"Excuse me." George nods curtly and walks away.

Irene, stunned, looks at Mom, who isn't moving, doesn't seem to be breathing; the air has shifted. Mom sets her drink on the table beside a platter of wilting cold cuts and walks off in the direction of the barn. The noise of the party fades into the background and Jack and I look down at our Lincoln Log construction unsure of what to do.

About an hour later, as the party is winding down, she re-emerges. She seems ... sort of ... fine? She thanks people for coming, walks them to their cars, accepts compliments on the house and barn, and waves as the last of the guests drive away. Over the next few days, we watch her closely. Study her. From all outward appearances, she is our mother. She is the woman who feeds the animals and sweeps the kitchen and talks to us at dinner, but there is something else, something inscrutable ... not a mood, exactly ... It isn't until the third day that we will learn that "something else" has been the tending of an inner fire, the stirring of a fierce and unrelenting determination: Nina has a plan.

Three days after the cider party, three days after she is told in no uncertain terms *not* to apply to the Boston Architectural College, she drives to Boston and fills out her application.

With a handwritten letter of recommendation—from a dear family friend and well-known architect in the Boston area—as well as photos of the house, she walks straight into the main office. Though she has missed the application deadline, the letter and photos are impressive enough that she is accepted on the spot. She will begin night classes the following Monday. She rearranges her days at the furniture store to line up with the nights she has class. On those days, she leaves the house at seven a.m. for her eight-hour shift and then goes straight to the BAC for her night classes, not getting home until eleven. On those days, Jack and I and a reluctant Oliver do all the barn chores, and Frank makes dinner.

Throughout this period, Mom is brimming with things to tell us. "Architecture is *life*. By transforming space, you transform everything—society, people, relationships—even families are defined by their shape and construction," she says, gesturing grandly as if the ultimate family model were on display at this very table. Oliver laughs out loud, almost choking on his food. And then Jack and I laugh at Oliver. But it's okay. It doesn't really matter what words come out of her mouth. We all feel it. When Mom is happy, everyone's happy.

# eleven

AT LONG LAST THE day has arrived; it has been four years since
we moved in, and Oliver and I are finally going to California
to see our father. Mom says we have to stick together at all
times. "Do you hear me? At *all* times." The high-heeled flight
attendant in the dark blue suit with the shiny silver buttons
clips along in front of Oliver and me, wheeling her tiny suitcase and swivelling her polished head to look back and smile
and wink. She smells of too much perfume and we don't
smile back. She is walking fast, and we scurry along behind
her past magazine stores and restaurants and carts selling
jewellery and popcorn. Palm trees and sunshine brighten the
tall windows, and Oliver has a big, genuine happy smile plastered on his face. All at once we are standing before a crowd
of people holding signs and waving, at the front of which is
a man in blue jeans and a short-sleeved grey button-down
shirt holding a sign that says Oliver and Cassie.

Even though I've had four years to prepare for this moment, I'm not ready. My heart is racing.

"You're the father?"

"That's me."

"Joe Albrecht?"

"Yes."

"I'll need to see your ID." The flight attendant pulls a clipboard from her bag. There is some signing and exchanging of papers, and then she turns and disappears into the crowd. Oliver and I, each wearing a backpack and holding a small suitcase, turn to face our father. He opens his arms so we can run to him, like in *Kramer vs. Kramer*—which I find strange, since we don't really know him. Like, maybe we should exchange a few words first or shake hands or—Oliver drops his suitcase and dives into his arms. I try to rouse the same courage but settle for hugging Oliver's back and part of my father's arm. This is okay. This is a good amount for now. He steps back to get a better look at us. "How did you get so big?" I'm thirteen and Oliver is fifteen and he hasn't seen us in four years, so I want to make some joke about kids growing like weeds, but his eyes are all wet, so I don't say anything. It makes me uncomfortable when adults cry.

When our bags are loaded into our father's big green van, and we are buckled side by side into the seats that are as wide as beds, he says, "I hope you like camping." And we set off on our journey north, driving beside the ocean with the windows down and the music playing. We have a dinner of hot dogs and ice cream at a small oceanside food shack and arrive at Grizzly Creek State Park as the sun is sinking below the hills. The giant redwoods and sequoias make it feel like we've stumbled into a fairy tale; this place exists but not in the real world. This is a magical alternate universe where trees are the size of houses, and the king of the land is our *yes-he-really-exists* father. Oliver and I help him build a fire and we roast marshmallows, and he pulls out a guitar and we sing along while he plays. Oliver looks at him like he's a rock star. And when he goes over to the van and pulls out a second smaller guitar, Oliver's smile threatens to extend beyond the borders of his face. "Thanks, Dad." I try it too. "Yeah, thanks, Dad." It feels forced but also good. He must find the whole thing as awkward as I do because he laughs, not at me but like he's going to cry again. Dad shows Oliver a few chords, and the next day while I swim, Oliver and Dad sit along the bank of the river and play guitar and sing. He and Mom had met in college when Mom was studying art and he was in the music program majoring in piano performance. He plays the piano, the guitar, the saxophone, and the harmonica. "Try this combo: G D Em C. You remember the E minor, right? Same as the E but lift your second finger off the string ... that's it, you got it. Now you can do 'Take Me Home, Country Roads.'"

A deep orange sun has long since sunk beyond the hills when we pull out our sleeping bags. Eucalyptus leaves rattle in the wind and Dad leans close and says, "I love you, Cassie." I pull my sleeping bag up to my chin. Nobody says that at home. We watch him walk off toward the van with a guitar in each hand, and Oliver crosses his arms behind his head and looks up at the stars and says, "Can you imagine Mom sitting by a campfire with us, roasting marshmallows and singing?" He barks out a laugh. I recognize his "mad at Mom" tone and I don't like it. It makes me nervous. Sometimes he can get *really* mad. If Mom were here, the tone would mean they were about to get in a fight. I want to defuse whatever he's building up to. "Sure, yeah, I can imagine it."

"Come on, be real. You can imagine her sitting out under the stars, doing nothing for hours, hanging out with us—all night?"

"Well, maybe not all night."

"Not even an hour, I bet."

"She's busy."

"She's always busy."

"What are you getting at?"

"She never stops working and doing things. She's always doing something."

"Well, maybe Dad's able to hang out with us because he doesn't *have* to do anything, like in the category of actually taking care of us." Ollie is making me mad; I don't want to be upset at my father, who I only get to be with for two weeks. "I don't understand what you're getting at."

"I'm saying if she really cared about us, she would spend time with us sometimes. And not because she has to."

"How can you say that?" I realize I'm whispering. I'm not sure where Dad is, and I don't want him to hear us talking about Mom. I lean on my side so I'm facing Oliver. "She moved us to a farm so we could have more places to play and things to do and a better life. All the things she's doing, she's doing for us."

"Really? Come on. She moved us to a farm so she could stick it to Grammy and Pappy."

I don't say anything. It's kind of true. I know Grammy and Pappy paid for our old house and that's why she wanted to move out of it. Oliver and I were together when we overheard her saying that exact thing to Frank. "Why are you so down on Mom right now?"

"Why do you have on rose-coloured glasses about her?"

"Why do you have on rose-coloured glasses about Dad?" He doesn't say anything for a few minutes. "Okay, listen. I don't mean to be down on her but let me ask you this: Why do you think she got so mad about us coming out here?"

"You mean when I lost my ticket and Dad had to send a new one?"

"Oh man, you're so naive ... do you really think you 'lost' your ticket? You never even *had* the tickets; *she* had them."

"What are you saying?"

Right then, Dad calls from the van. "Ollie?"

"Yeah, Dad?"

"Come here. I want to show you something."

Oliver gets out of his sleeping bag and is about to walk away but turns to face me. "It's for your own good that I'm saying all this. You know that, right? You need to wake up, Cassie."

. . .

Mom is waiting at the entry to Logan Airport when the flight attendant brings us out and she signs the paper on the clipboard. This time, it's me who dives into the summoning arms and Oliver who stands back. And how was the flight? Are you tired? Did you get to see a movie on the plane? It was good, we got to go into the cockpit, and the pilot gave us these little wings, see? And no, we're not hungry; we had food and nuts and Ollie kept asking for more nuts, and more. You're such a tattletale. And we saw *Murder on the Orient Express*—twice!

We gather our suitcases from the baggage carousel and Mom is turning to leave when Oliver stops her. "Wait. We have to go over to special handling for my guitar."

She turns. "Your guitar?"

"Yeah. Dad gave me a guitar." Oliver glances at me then as if to say, "Pay attention." I look to Mom. *Please prove him wrong.* I want to be the one to say, "I told you so." But instead, I watch it happen. And though I've seen it a million times, it's the first time I really allow myself to stand back and take it in. Her green eyes darken like a mood ring. I don't look away. I don't feel any need to pretend it's not happening or make it better. Two weeks of distance has put a little space between us and it's like I'm seeing someone on a TV screen; I can't change anything, I can only observe. Oliver is standing quietly, holding his ground. After all, it's only a present from his father. She is stock-still for a mini-eternity. Then she exhales in a slow, deliberate stream. Summoning calm. She lifts her head to the array of signs, lands on Special Handling, and takes a ridiculously dramatic inhale. I hear a funeral dirge soundtrack in the background. I want to laugh. *Who directed this?* The level of drama is wildly out of proportion with the action. I follow an impulse I would normally ignore. I tug at her sleeve and as she turns, I reach into my backpack. "Look. Dad gave me something too." I pull out the model horse with the bright red bow still on it and hold it up to her face.

She takes the horse by a single stiff leg, with an expression of sheer malice. I can see the inner battle raging beneath her green eyes and for the briefest of moments I think she might win. *Please, Mom, try.* But she thrusts the horse back at me. "No. Sorry. A plastic horse does not qualify him as a father. Do you think he's paid even one cent of child support? He sits on the beach in California, does whatever he wants, and I'm the bad guy?" She stops herself and shakes her head. "Never mind." She puts up her hand to indicate the Herculean level of self-control that is being exercised, for which we are to be thankful. We should feel simultaneously guilty and thankful that she will say no more about our derelict father.

Her silence is a black hole. It has its own force field: pulling our insides to the surface, turning the air dark, making it hard to breathe, like all the oxygen has been sucked from the room. I want to say, *Can't you let us have this one thing? Can't our father be something that's about us instead of you?* Oliver is right. It's always been there. I've seen it, but I didn't *want* it to be there, so I put my energy into pretending everything is totally normal and fine. *Great, in fact. Everything's great.* Keeping that ruse going is my job in this family. I want to cry, but I can't breathe.

At last, the guitar is ferried through the little black flaps, gliding toward us behind a pair of skis, and something in the appearance of the guitar snaps her out of it. "Oh! I can't believe I haven't told you yet. We're almost finished with my painting studio." She takes hold of the guitar handle and continues talking excitedly as if nothing has happened, leading us toward the exit. "Irene helped me bring up my easels—and you know that couch we saw in the *Want Ad?* We bought it. And we've installed sixteen feet of windows—you can see all the way beyond the woods to the orchard ..." At the car, she tosses the guitar into the trunk as if it were just another one of the suitcases.

For the whole ride home, she rattles on about her painting studio and the crane that had to be brought in to install the massive windows and how now you can see for miles and miles. Oliver, who gets to sit in the front seat, looks back at me only once. She will paint over our trip as if it never happened. We will not be allowed to talk about it. There will be no more said about the guitar or camping or our father. He exists least of all. I have the whole back seat to myself, but I feel cramped. I can only get tiny bits of air in the narrow spaces between her sentences. We've gone from the great wide open into a straitjacket. I want to scream—*I have a father who lives on the other side of the country, and he showed us redwood trees; and we swam in a river and slept under the stars.*

*He took me to see the Lipizzaner stallions and bought me this horse and he plays music and says, "I love you."*

When we get home, I set my horse in the middle of my dresser on display. This is my act of defiance; these fifteen inches of jet-black plastic the measure of my daring.

But Oliver is braver than me—or maybe angrier. He plays that guitar every day for hours, his concentration never wavering. In his single-focused attention is the conviction that the guitar holds the power to change everything about his life he doesn't like. It is a show of will that, ironically, proves him to be every inch his mother's son. But he turns out to be partly right; there is something in the power of music that changes not only him, but all of us. What starts as an act of defiance reveals itself to be a natural facility. Mom's grudging admiration transforms into pride. She wants Oliver to be the best he can possibly be. Within a matter of weeks, she has signed him up for Saturday classes at the Berklee School of Music. She is flaunting his skill on the guitar to whoever will listen, as if she were the source of his newfound talent.

# twelve

"SO, WHAT'S THE DEAL with your brother?"

"My brother?"

"Yeah. Oliver."

"What do you mean, what's the deal?"

"Well, like he's ambidextrous—that's *so* cool—and he has a frickin' iguana living in the rafters of his bedroom, and on the guitar, he can play, like, anything. What, is he a boy genius or something?"

"Hardly." Delilah Toobin and I have been friends since she moved in three months ago, and she's *my* friend. Why does she have to find Oliver cool? It's *very* easy to find him uncool.

"Yeah, he was supposed to see some specialist because he has like a learning disability or something ... ADD, I think it's called."

"A learning disability? What is he, too smart?" Delilah is an only child, she's lean and wiry and has red hair that can't seem to decide whether to be straight or curly, like hundreds of tiny arms waving at a rock concert. And she's cool. Like, she's *from-New-York-City* cool. She sits on her shag carpet and starts flipping through records.

"Mom wouldn't let him see the doctor, though, so we don't really know what's wrong with him," I say, trying to lean into the *wrong with him* part.

"Ha!" She laughs and drops the needle down on Led Zeppelin's *Physical Graffiti*.

"What?"

"Your mother sounds like my parents. 'If it ain't broke, don't fix it—but if it *is* broke, hide it in the closet.'" She takes a pair of mirrored shades from her dresser and puts them on.

The Toobins bought the old Varick Farm on the other side of Sellers Orchard and are renovating it. Mom and the Toobins have become fast friends. As transplanted city folks renovating an old farm, the Toobins have a lot in common with Mom and Frank; they also drink like fish and swear like truck drivers and—probably what Mom likes best—speak perfect French. Mom minored in French in college and loves having the opportunity to dust it off. Whenever they come over, she's all "Bonjour, comment ça va?" Happy hours and dinner parties at our house have become a regular thing; they seem to be Mom and Frank's solution to the relentless fighting. The arguing hasn't exactly stopped, it's more like discovering nettles and thorns can be used to decorate. Now the barbed comments and raised voices are bathed in laughter and alcohol.

Delilah stops air-guitaring and slides her sunglasses down her nose. "Want to go down to the bustling centre of Hicksville and get some snacks for tonight?"

"Sure. I have to be back by five, though, so I can do my chores before everyone gets there."

"Ugh. Fucking barn chores, I hate them. Give me the grime of the city any day."

"I don't usually mind that much. It's just, sometimes it's a lot."

"What do you mean you don't mind?"

"I mean ..."

"Are you saying you like to shovel horseshit?"

"Oh no—I didn't mean that ... I mean I like being around the animals is all."

"Yeah, I like animals too, it doesn't mean I want to shovel their shit."

"I guess I don't *love* it."

"Don't love it?"

"Well, one thing I really hate is the chicken coop. It's disgusting."

"Now we're talking. Go on." Delilah sits at the head of her bed and crosses her arms behind her head like a director awaiting a performance from her star actor.

"And we have this huge pit where we dump the manure. I gag every time I go near it."

"And?"

"It's fucking vile."

"Fucking right, it's vile. We have one too."

"And the fly tapes hanging everywhere. What the fuck? They're fucking disgusting."

"All right! Much better." She hops off the bed and goes to shut off the record player. "Don't worry. I lie to myself too."

"What?"

"You know, try to convince myself I like things when I don't. It makes it easier. But be careful what you trick yourself into, or you'll start to forget what you *actually* like."

I look around her room. It's a sea of rock posters and hanging beads, knick-knacks and records and books, and on her dresser is a lava lamp from Spencer's. I know it's from Spencer's because I saw it there a couple months ago and asked Mom if I could get one and she said, "You don't want something so tacky in your room, Cassie. Come on." Delilah's Shaun Cassidy poster: also from Spencer's. "We don't want to ruin your nice wallpaper by tacking up posters, do we?" Mom always says *we* when expressing an opinion, as in, "We don't like her makeup. We love that show." I don't think she does it with Jack or Oliver. I think about my room, with the wallpaper of tiny pink rosebuds—the wallpaper she chose. I wanted the wallpaper with the green climbing vines and blue stripes, but she talked me out of it. I have a four-poster bed which is a "valuable antique" and a dresser that was my grandmother's, and an antique doll I got for Christmas—with eyes that never close, guaranteed to creep the fuck out of anyone who comes in my room. I suddenly want to trade it all in for shag carpet and beads and rainbows of colour.

Later that night, all of us kids are piled into Jack's room

watching *When a Stranger Calls*. We eat potato chips and drink Orange Crush and hold on to each other as the young female protagonist fumbles with a series of locks when she realizes the danger is inside the house. When it's over, we crowd around the window behind Delilah, who's already moved on to the next show: watching the adults down in the yard. The floodlight over the back door creates the effect of a spotlight in a circus. Frank is standing on a tree stump dancing with a napkin on his head as the Toobins egg him on. "Incroyable!" "Encore!" Mom spins Irene in an overenthusiastic waltz that sends her flying headlong into the lilac bushes, and the party erupts in laughter and screaming.

"What a bunch of jackasses," Delilah says, shaking her head.

"Hey!" Jack pokes Delilah, pretending to be mad. "Don't say jackasses."

"Sorry, Jack. You're right. They don't deserve your name. What a bunch of assholes."

Jack copies her in a whisper, stretching his mouth around the word, testing it out. "Assholes."

I stifle a smile. What must it feel like to be Delilah? To say exactly what she feels—about anything? To be able to look at something and say truthfully, "No, I don't like that wallpaper, I like the one with the green vines and the blue stripes. No, I don't want you to write a letter to my music teacher telling her she knows nothing about teaching music. No, I don't want you to call the school and insist I'm moved into honours English. No, I won't lie to Aunt Aggie that we're missing the reunion because I have a rehearsal."

In our house, Mom curates how our family is presented; what's said to this or that person, what story is told after the fact to explain why we didn't do what we said we were going to do. And arguing with her or telling her you don't want to go along with her story is something you do only once; the depth and darkness of her anger ensures that—like those test mice that get a shock when they press a certain button, you will never press that button again.

I want to be like Delilah. Delilah is a superpowered Eveready flashlight shining in every corner, naming things and moving on. I gaze at her there, looking out the window, her red hair glowing in the moonlight and wonder if she's even of this world. As if reading my thoughts, she turns to face us all. "Who wants to raise the dead?" Stan's huge brown eyes beam at her from under his afro and I realize I'm not the only one who has a crush on Delilah.

It's two a.m. when we finish with the Ouija board, and the party winds down and everyone goes home, and it's four a.m. when I go down to the kitchen for a glass of water—and find Frank lying on the floor in front of the sink. He's on his back with his arm thrown across his eyes and his cheeks wet with tears. I tiptoe back upstairs.

I sleep late the next morning and when I come down, Frank is standing at the kitchen counter looking out the window, coffee cup in hand. He is quiet but otherwise normal. He doesn't say anything to indicate he saw me. But later that night, his chair at the dinner table is empty. Same thing the next few nights. Mom explains that he has some meetings, and none of us question her. After about two weeks of this, on a Saturday morning, Mom calls us downstairs.

"All of us?" I holler down.

"Yes, all of you."

Getting called downstairs usually meant getting in trouble, and getting in trouble didn't usually include me. "Frank would like to speak to you."

Once we're seated at the table, where Frank sits waiting for us, Mom walks out the back door. There is an awkward silence and Frank shifts in his seat. We steal glances at each other until he clears his throat.

"I'm an alcoholic. I've always been one, and I always will be one because it's a disease. But I've quit drinking and joined a group called Alcoholics Anonymous. That is where I've been going in the evenings and will keep going, so I don't start drinking again." He says some more stuff about "hitting rock bottom" and having a "moment of clarity," and the three of us stare at the middle of the empty table as if something vital resides there. There is a pause in which he seems to be deciding whether to continue. He settles on: "Things are going to get better, you'll see."

When he finishes, he tells us we can ask him questions if we want. I steal a glance at Oliver, who's looking back at me from under his bangs. We're in high school. There's a keg party every weekend and we're usually at it. We drink. We've been drunk. We drive drunk. Are we in trouble? But then we realize if we were in trouble, it would be Mom doing the talking. And Frank seems not to care about any of that. He seems to genuinely want us to understand something. It's the word *alcoholic* that confuses me. That word applies to people on street corners drinking from bottles wrapped in paper bags. Frank and Mom both drink, sure. But so do all our parents' friends—and all our friends' parents. Pretty much every adult we know drinks—and every teenager. Are we all alcoholics?

Jack breaks the silence. "Why does everyone drink if it's so bad for you?"

"At first, alcohol doesn't seem bad at all. At first, it seems like the best thing ever, like getting a nice, warm blanket after being outside in the cold. But somehow it goes from being something soft and comforting to being a hammer that smashes everything to bits."

None of us say anything. I don't understand how something can go from being a blanket to a hammer. And I'm pretty sure, from the looks on my brothers' faces, they don't understand either.

"Things are going to get better. You'll see."

# thirteen

IN THE WEEKS and months that follow, however, it becomes clear that things aren't getting better, as Frank had promised, they're getting worse. Much worse. Not all at once, and not for each of us equally, but more like the speed of a cruise ship turning, the tension mounting as our family heads for an iceberg. Mom seems stunned, like someone who's been abandoned at a party—or maybe he's at the party, and she refuses to come in. Either way, they're in two different spaces and can't seem to come together. At the dinner table, one of them will say something to the other, and Frank will storm out the door and peel off down the driveway. Mom will say evenly, "Don't worry, he's just going to a *meeting*." But there's something in the way she says *meeting*; she goes to the kitchen and mixes herself a rusty nail—which is, according to her, a real doozy. I'm pretty sure she fights with Frank so he'll leave and she can drink.

But it isn't only Mom who clashes with the newly sober Frank. No longer a happy-hour kind of guy, Frank takes to napping at four o'clock every afternoon. Religiously. He protects that time like it's all he has left. Every day after school, the three of us are told to go outside or to a friend's house, or if we're going to be in the house, to be quiet. Jack and I do what we always do, which is to not make waves. But Oliver is a magnet for getting in trouble. And it's not totally his fault, he has ADD. It's a real thing. But instead of getting medicine or treatment, he gets yelled at and punished until he realizes he's never going to get any help; he's on his own. So he gets angry. Instead of being apologetic about having a messy room or playing guitar while Frank is napping, it all becomes part and parcel of one great big "fuck you."

I keep waiting for the announcement that Mom and Frank are getting divorced, or that Oliver is getting medication, or that Frank is going to therapy, or that Mom is quitting drinking—or something, anything. But instead, the house turns into a battlefield. I drop the happy-making song and dance, Jack develops a stutter, Oliver practically moves into Stan's, and the rusty nail replaces Sauvignon Blanc as Mom's nightly beverage of choice.

One afternoon, after a pretty bad fight between Oliver and Frank, I go to Oliver's room and stand in the doorway. Oliver is lying on his bed and doesn't look up from *The Age of Innocence*. "What?"

"Nothing." I go over to a stack of books perched precariously on the edge of his desk and pretend to be looking for a particular one. "I was thinking that if you played without the amp in the afternoon, maybe Frank would get off your back."

He doesn't respond. He keeps reading. I don't say anything else. When I'm almost out the door, he says to my back, "It must be tiring being so perfect all the time."

I walk down the hall to my room and slam the door. I throw myself on the bed and punch my pillow. *Fuck you, Oliver.* I take the pillow in my arms and flip over onto my back and stare at the ceiling. *You have no idea the things I don't say, just to keep this house from falling apart.* I press my face into the pillow and scream. I hate the adjectives that are always applied to me: reliable, independent, easy. I've heard Mom describe me as *easy* to Irene more times than I can count. As in, "Thank God Cassie's such an easy child. I don't think I could have handled it otherwise." "She's so independent" is the latest incarnation of this. To hear Mom tell it, it's as if I was born in flight. "Your birth took a grand total of thirty minutes. My water broke in the bathroom—there wasn't even time to call the doctor. You've always done things on your own." *No need for help. I'm here.* By age five, I was allowed to babysit Jack, and by six I walked to first grade on my own. I have, according to Mom, always been independent and strong. But, as life would have it, even the easy kids eventually need *something.* The problem is that by the time I needed help, it was too late to ask for it—a precedent had been set.

So when Oliver and I were playing hide and seek with the O'Reilly boys back on Beckham Road, and Jimmy O'Reilly cornered me in the basement, lifting me onto the washing machine, pulling my pants down, and putting his hand in my underwear, I didn't tell anyone. I froze until he started fumbling with his belt, and then kicked him the chest and ran up the basement stairs out of the house. I was seven. And at age nine, riding my bike to Jack's Little League game, when a car pulled up beside me asking for directions, and it turned out to be a man with his dick in his hand, I didn't bother Mom with it. Not the first time it happened, and not the second or third time either. And last week, when I had sex with my boyfriend for the first time and it hurt so badly I bled, I didn't call for a ride but walked home the three miles at midnight on my own.

Sure, fine; it's probably better to be the "easy" child than the "difficult" one, but one thing it isn't, is easy.

"Murph? Can you come downstairs please?"

I throw my pillow against the wall and go downstairs. "What?"

"Frank and I are having dinner at the Toobins tomorrow night. I need you to babysit Jack."

"Oh, sorry, I can't. Tomorrow is the Donahues' big spring bash. I'm going with Delilah."

"Well, you need to change those plans because I need you to babysit Jack. I won't be able to find a sitter last minute."

"What? No. I can't. Wait, last minute? Are you saying you *just* made these plans?" She's emptying the dishwasher and not even listening. "We've been talking about this party for weeks. Stan and Oliver are playing. There's a stage being set up for them—it's the biggest party of the year. You can't tell me I have to babysit without asking me first. That's not fair!"

"Actually, I can. You're babysitting. End of story."

"Well ... I'm not doing it."

She turns to face me with a mug in each hand and starts waving one of the mugs at me. "Do not speak to me in that tone, Cassie. There's a party every weekend. I'm sure you'll survive if you miss one."

"Are you listening to me *at all*? This is the biggest party of the year. Oliver and I have been talking about it for the last month. His band is playing, and Delilah and I are helping them. We've told you about it at least ten times. You should try listening sometimes!"

"One more word out of you, and you're grounded for a month."

"I can't believe this. This is *so* unfair." I storm up to my room and slam the door as hard as I can. I shove my Pat Benatar cassette into the boombox and crank it to ten. Jack pokes his head in my door.

"I'm sorry," he says, slipping in and leaning against the back of the door.

"It's not your fault. Fuck." I throw myself down on the bed.

And then, looking at him standing there in his *Star Wars* T-shirt and tousled blond hair, I suddenly have an idea.

"Can you keep a secret, Jack?"

# fourteen

A MAGNOLIA BRANCH reaches for my open window, its small furry hands holding shoots of pink in offering. The warm, wet smell of spring spreads through my lungs and I want to dissolve into it, to disappear from this house and never come back.

If it weren't for Frank's sobriety, everything would have gone off without a hitch. But I guess it's not fun to be at a dinner party when everyone is drunk and you're stone cold sober. Frank left early, arriving at home a full hour before me and Jack.

We took Delilah's Chevette to the party and Jack, with his first-ever very own red SOLO cup of beer in hand, followed all our instructions. And Oliver and Stan brought the house down. By nine the sprawling backyard was a mass of teenagers, all dancing, drinking, or making out. By midnight, I was untangling Jack from a gaggle of sophomore girls. "We have to go. Mom and Frank will be home soon," I yelled, as if volume would make my slurred speech more comprehensible. Jack came right away, and Delilah dropped us off. But we were too late. Frank was already home sitting at the dining room table waiting for us.

It wasn't the getting yelled at or being grounded or any of that that bothered me, that part was normal. It was her. The way she reacted to the whole thing was messed up. Like I had betrayed her in some deep, unforgivable way. Like she couldn't get that I just wanted to go to the party. No, it was more like she'd been left out, like she was hurt in a personal way. She didn't speak to me for three days.

I grab my windbreaker and wade through the long, wet grass of the back field and into the woods, through the ferns and up to the edge of the brook now overflowing its banks. I sit on a large stone and look down into the rushing water, at least two feet higher than usual. I lift a tiny branch from the ground beside me and break it like a wishbone, dropping the pieces, one after the other, into the water. I watch them slip and bob, and then there is the soft brushing of ferns and she appears beside me.

She sits down on the rock next to mine and reaches out to rest a hand on my knee. I try not to flinch. I'm not mad anymore, but I don't want to give her anything either. She makes me feel suffocated. I want to be free of her, and that's not something she can help me with.

We sit in silence.

"The brook is so high this spring," she says.

When the brook is low, you can see the moss-covered rocks and loose pebbles that make up its bed, an intricate system of rising and falling for the water to tumble and fall and then climb and burst forward in sprays of foam, its movement a melody of birdsong through velvet, rain on a tin roof.

But not now. Now it is pure rushing force.

"Are you and Frank going to get a divorce?"

She pulls her knees in against herself and wraps her arms around them. If she's surprised by my question, she gives no indication. "No."

I feel small pieces of myself seep through the moss into the rushing current and disappear.

She picks a stem of bloodroot from the water's edge and rests her chin on her knees to study the flower. She looks like a teenager, picking at the tiny petals. "Did you know your grandmother was Phi Beta Kappa from Smith College? She was accepted at fifteen and graduated at eighteen. She translated Greek and Latin and spoke five languages fluently. There's nothing you can ask her that she doesn't have the answer to."

I turn to look at Mom for the first time since she sat down. I conjure an image of my quiet grandmother, in her beige pants, her dark blue button-front shirts, her grey-brown hair cut short, no makeup. Everything about her an attempt to blend in, to not be seen.

"I can't get a divorce."

"Why? I mean ... what does Grammy have to do with it."

"Everything. She has everything to do with it. I've already

been divorced once, which is completely unthinkable to someone from Grammy's time, from her class. She won't hear of me doing it again."

She lays the remains of the tiny flower gently across the toe of her boot. I am dazed, trying to absorb the fact that there exists in this world a person who can simply say the word and Mom will do as she's told.

I think of my grandmother, of the times my grandparents have come to visit. How Pappy sets himself up on the couch by the wood stove, with his books and notebooks spread across the low table before him. How Grammy always brings him black coffee, and how, if he's engrossed in something important and doesn't want to come to the table, Grammy will bring him his food on a tray.

My grandparents own 130 acres of land in a small town in western Massachusetts called Otis. According to Mom, they were always moving when she was growing up. She lived in half a dozen different houses over the years, moving to wherever Eliot was teaching. Eliot N. Wentworth, my grandfather, is a tall, hulking man with small brown eyes and a head as bald as a cue ball. He wears wide-wale corduroy jackets with elbow patches and expects perfection from everyone; he has the air of someone who really wants to like people but is, instead, perpetually disappointed. My grandmother, Florence Jane Heed, is even smarter than my grandfather. But she became a mother rather than a professor—one position she was eminently qualified for and the other she knew nothing about and had no natural instincts for.

Mom told me, "Before Pappy taught at Harvard, he taught at the University of Chicago, but lost his job during the McCarthy era. That's when the moving started. Every few years we would pick up and move to wherever the next teaching job was. Each house bigger than the last, until the houses got so big when I was sixteen and we lived in St. Louis, the house had an actual ballroom—and half of the house never even got furnished."

I think of how important education is to both of my grandparents. And all at once, there it is in neon lettering: Mom married Frank as an act of rebellion. Marrying someone without a college education was the worst thing she could do to her father. Of course she loved Frank once, and of course their marriage wasn't only that, but ... My mind is racing to keep up with itself, thinking of everything she has built on an act of defiance, not only her marriage, but our family, buying this house, the farm. I suddenly feel the inevitability of its fall—of our fall. We are origami birds on a wire, rice paper in the wind; one strong gust and we're gone. I look at her there, gazing down into the water, how much she has fought to get where she is. "I love you, Mom." She doesn't say anything but takes my hand and presses it to her cheek, wet with tears. Her cheek is wet. We walk back to the house as dusk ebbs into night, not knowing the first bird will blow away within the hour.


It happens at the dinner table. Oliver is dishing himself spaghetti, lifting the serving fork high in the air, and carefully circling long strands of pasta onto his plate in a perfect nest. As he stirs the bolognese, he says casually, "I'm moving to California to live with Dad." He lifts the spoon over his plate, pouring the thick sauce onto his spaghetti, and returning the spoon to the pot. He reaches for the grated cheese. "I've talked to him, and it's all planned out. I'll have my own room, and there's a high school around the corner where I'll do my senior year."

Frank's fork hovers in mid-air. Jack and I are frozen in our seats.

She isn't moving. Only Oliver has begun eating. Calmly. Happily. The silence is eternal.

She reaches for the bottle of wine and fills her glass to the rim. "Fine."

Oliver smiles down into his plate. She sets the bottle back on the table and we eat the rest of the meal in silence.

Later that night, Oliver goes to the attic and takes down the small leather suitcase he used when we moved into the house. He flies out to California after the school's end-of-year picnic.

*Fine* becomes Mom's favourite word that summer.

"Mom, I'm going to Delilah's to study."

"Fine."

"Mom, can I loan Stan the wrench set? He needs to fix his bike."

"Fine."

As soon as I realize she'll say "fine" to almost anything, I push it a little further, sometimes on Jack's behalf.

"Mom, can Jack and I ride down to White Street and watch the Little League game?"

"Fine."

That's the summer she takes to sitting down at the piano to play Beethoven's *Emperor Concerto* whenever a mood overcomes her. It's a clear signal Jack and I appreciate. If we come up the driveway and hear the piano, we know to steer clear of the house. Sometimes, though, we sit on the steps to the screened porch and listen. In those moments, I imagine we are thinking the same thing: *How does something so beautiful come from someone feeling so bad?*

With everything turning upside down, Jack and I manage to fly under the radar. Even in your average summer, Mom is an active non-subscriber to suggested norms. So things like summer camps, or sports clubs, or SAT prep classes—any of those things our friends are doing—we are definitely not going to be doing. "I'm not raising my children to be sheep."

Then, on the Saturday of Labor Day weekend, Oliver comes home.

Not a word is said or asked about his trip. Everyone acts as if he never left. Even Frank seems to feel sorry for him. Back in June, when Oliver was preparing to leave, I'd kept him company while he packed his suitcase, helped him organize his things. He'd told me then, with excitement, that he was going to go to school in Oakland, and Dad was going to get him a new skateboard, and they were going to jam together, and that when I visited next summer, he would be able to show me around, because surely by then he'd know his new town.

A few nights after he comes home, I go into his room with a deck of cards and sit on the floor playing solitaire. He's lying in his bed reading. For a long time, we don't say anything, and then he says, "Dad has a new girlfriend." He lays his book across his chest and tells me the whole story. When he finishes, I swear to myself that I will never speak to our father again. I had always fantasized—ignoring ample evidence to the contrary—that he was going to be the man to stand up to Mom, take the raising of his children firmly in hand, do the right thing, grow a pair. But no, his new works-in-finances girlfriend had found Oliver "challenging," said it was too much to have him around. He didn't put up a single argument in defence of his son. Did he know that we'd been faithful to him despite the years and the miles? That he'd remained our father in our hearts, despite the minuscule amount of effort he put in and in the face of Mom's campaign to eliminate him from our thoughts? We'd stoked that fire ourselves, we'd held out hope. If we could do it, why couldn't he? I realize he'd been a mirage all along.

Our family is like a teacup that has broken and been glued back together; tiny pieces are missing, the cracks are distracting, and it no longer holds tea. But for some reason, we've put it back on the shelf just the same.

# *fifteen*

"WHAT ARE YOU doing here? Mom was supposed to pick me up."

"Well, you got me," Oliver replies through the half-cracked window of the car. I stumble and fall as I walk around to the passenger-side door. Ever since I dented the front fender of Frank's Prelude driving drunk, I'm not allowed to go anywhere unless I have proof of a ride home.

"Maybe you should be happy it's me instead of Mom, or you'd be grounded again. How much did you drink?"

"I might have had a few." I close the door on my coat, open the door, pull my coat in, and close it again. We leave.

It's October 30, 1984, the night of the cast party for *Oklahoma!* Oliver picks me up just after midnight, and for the whole ride home, I babble on about the party. It's not until we get to the end of the driveway that he interrupts me. "Grammy died."

"What?" I turn to look at him, but he doesn't say anything else, just pulls up the driveway and parks.

Mom is sitting on the brown velvet couch in front of the wood stove. She has a tissue in her hand and Grammy's tartan plaid blanket wrapped across her legs. The door to the wood stove is ajar, and the crackling flames bathe the room in soft amber.

I sit down beside her and rest my head on her shoulder.

Her hand fumbles with the edge of the soft wool blanket. "This was Grammy's," she says. "She was told to pack a suitcase when she went to the hospital, that she was going to be there for an indefinite period. And the only things she put in the suitcase were five pairs of underwear and this blanket." Mom smiles. "It was her mother's before her."

Grammy had never been much of a housekeeper, or a cook for that matter, and Mom, Uncle Larry, Aunt Doro, and Aunt Aggie were mostly left to their own devices. There were weeks when they wouldn't see her for days at a time. On these occasions, Eliot would say, "Your mother has taken her medicine. She needs to rest now." Mom was younger than her three siblings by almost a decade—she was five when her brother and two sisters were teenagers and they would run off with their friends, leaving her completely alone in those hours when her mother "disappeared."

Eliot purchased the home in Otis, the one they came to call the Farm, in the hopes that it would keep Florence from lying in bed day after day with the door closed and the curtains drawn. Maybe animals would keep her company, make her happy, maybe she would grow a vegetable garden. But Florence never got beyond a German shepherd, a hay rake, and a .44. Mom said it was probably a good thing that the Farm had never become an actual farm because that would require constant tending, and Florence was not a constant sort of person.

The realization that she was a grandmother seemed to hit her from time to time and she would do something out of character with her normal reclusive behaviour. Once she took me, Oliver, and Jack to TJ Maxx and set us loose in the store, told us to choose whatever we wanted and she would buy it for us. We began tentatively. "Is this okay?" I asked, holding up a shirt.

"Throw it in the cart," Florence nearly hollered, gesturing grandly, with the same fervour as when we were raking hay. As if to say, "We're getting it done. Let's do this thing!" Oliver asked if he could get a pair of pants. "Toss 'em in." Jack wanted a water pistol. "Good choice." The more we threw in, the more involved she got, like we were out at sea in a great storm. "Hoist the sail. Pull the line. All hands on deck!" We filled the cart and left with four exploding bags of clothes and toys. After the clothing store, she took us for ice creams and insisted we all get double scoops.

For her funeral, Florence has left instructions. She is to be cremated and buried on the hill beyond the pond. Set up at the top of the hill are little white chairs in perfect rows and a table holding flowers and an urn; there's also a podium and a minister. There are about thirty people and Mom sits with us several rows behind my aunts and uncle, who sit beside my grandfather in the front row. As far as I can see, Mom hasn't said a word to her father since we arrived. I saw her hug Uncle Larry and Aunt Doro when we came in and she nodded tersely to Aunt Aggie when we were walking to our seat, but that was it.

The minister is talking about my grandmother's courage in fighting the cancer ... but I am looking at the back of my grandfather's bald head, his black suit jacket, the slope of his shoulders. The shape and placement of bodies in space doesn't lie: who sits with whom, who stands, who walks away, who doesn't even come. You can have confidence in what you see; it's words that are unreliable. Secrets and wisps of half-truth stretched into stories and told so many times we believe them to be true. But what is truth? What are facts? My grandmother died of lung cancer: solid, medical, veri-fiable. Facts are stones that can be placed on the wall that circles the property of you, so one day you can bring your children and say, here is where I fell off my bike in first grade and lost my front tooth, and here is where my grandmother died of lung cancer. Neat. Solid. But there will be no stone to say my grandmother stopped breathing the day she got married, the gold ring on her finger was a form of black magic that shrunk her into bringer of husband's coffee, cleaner of husband's shirts, translator of husband's notes, and when the magic wore off and the anger threatened to strangle, taker of pills and drinker of wine. It is early November, and the clumps of grass rise and fall in waves of silver and the pond is

# sixteen

THE GUST THAT will lift the mother bird from the wire, and in so doing send the family airborne, is appropriately named Perfect Storm and arrives one dreary day at the end of February. It is late afternoon, and I am reading in an armchair by the wood stove when Mom appears at the back door, trudges through the kitchen in her barn boots, and summons for me to follow. "I want to show you something."

There's a thin layer of snow on the ground, and we crunch along in silence. She takes one of the heavy barn doors and I the other and we slide them open, allowing sunlight to pour through the dark interior and illuminate, there in the centre stall, one of the most magnificent creatures ever to walk this earth.

"Meet Perfect Storm." Mom walks slowly to the stall door as the beautiful black horse stamps and sidesteps and whinnies. "Easy, girl."

Perfect Storm is the shiny black of crude oil, with not a speck of white on her sleek, sinewy body, standing at least two hands taller than Phantom, our small white gelding, who hovers meekly in the far corner of the adjacent stall. The goats, normally outside at this time of day, are also here, not wanting to miss the action. Perfect Storm is several classes above the animals that surround her, this much is clear in the first instant of seeing her. Her presence transforms the entire space.

She allows Mom to lead her from the stall and clip her in the entry to the barn. I imagine this majestic animal is accustomed to being groomed regularly. Mom picks at her hooves and brushes her coat to a high sheen. The horse shivers occasionally, holding her head high, throwing it up and back when I try to approach.

"Easy now," Mom says. She brings her cheek in to lean against the regal mare and closes her eyes. "Beautiful girl." After a moment, she pulls her head away and looks at me. "So? What do you think?"

"I think she's incredible."

"Yes. She is that, isn't she?" Mom smiles then, for what seems like the first time in months.

She starts taking horseback riding seriously. The tack room behind the chicken coop now has an additional saddle and two new bridles. Frank helps her set up arrowhead jumps in the field beyond the garden, and she rides twice a day. Every day. And on Tuesdays and Fridays, Maureen Whelan comes to give her lessons. We've known Maureen for years; we've been getting our hay and grain from the Whelans since we first moved in. The Whelans have the biggest barn this corner of Massachusetts. And Maureen is well known as top of the top for all things equestrian.

By the end of March, Mom has decided she wants to enter Storm in the spring show and, at Maureen's suggestions, takes her to the Whelans' to begin training. Their field is already set up as the show course and Maureen says they will be better able to prepare Storm over there. So Storm is moved to the Whelans' horse barn and Mom now leaves the house every day at noon and doesn't return until after four. We see her in riding pants more than anything else that spring. She is aglow with her love of that horse and of riding. Even her fighting with Frank lets up; she is chatty at meals, asking us kids what we're up to, and laughing at our stories.

Two weeks before the show, she asks me if I will take notes at her upcoming training sessions: times, comments from Maureen, things she needs to work on. It doesn't sound very thrilling, and I am trying to think of how to get out of it when she says the magic words, "You'll have to miss a little school."

Four days before the show, Mom realizes she has a dentist appointment she can't miss and so moves the training to late afternoon. It's four o'clock by the time we get to the Whelans'. The rain has been heavy for the last three days, and we are sinking in thick mud as we trudge to the barn. Storm—used to being ridden every afternoon at one—is all but kicking down the walls of her stall. I look at Mom. I don't think getting on this animal is such a good idea. Mom is out of sorts from having her tooth drilled and not fully up to dealing with a finicky horse. She looks at me and then at Maureen, who is coming from the tack room with the saddle. "Maureen, maybe we should pick this up tomorrow." But Maureen shakes her head. "We need to stick to the routine, as much for her as for you. I'll be out in the field."

It takes three tries for Mom to get the saddle across Storm's back; she is tossing her head and pulling the leads, each time lifting her front legs from the ground in little hops. "Easy, girl," Mom says, tightening the girth. Storm blows out and stomps her front foot.

Straight out of the barn, she is stepping sideward in a staccato dance of defiance. Mom pulls hard on the right rein, digs her heels in, and rides her mare out to the training field.

"Bring her once around the course to warm her up, and then we'll work her combinations," Maureen hollers from across the field.

Mom pulls on the reins, and Storm rears again. "Come on, girl. Let's go. Same as every day."

Maureen cups her hands to either side of her mouth. "Nina, you show her who's in charge now. The other horses are being fed back at the barn; she's not going to let up. You're the boss and it's time to work."

Mom nods and adjusts her helmet. "Come on, girl." She pulls Storm around the turn to take the first jump. It's a simple chevron, and they've done this course easily a hundred times.

She digs her heels into the horse's ribs and drops her voice lower, pushing through the pain in her back tooth. "Let's go, Storm. Come on."

They set out at a canter, Mom sitting tall against the blackening sky like she's entering the Acropolis. They round the starting turn and head for the first chevron, but even here in the field the mud is thick, and halfway to the first jump, Storm skids and Mom slides left in the saddle. I climb onto the bottom rail of the fence for a better view. Mom adjusts, and they regain an even canter. But just shy of the first chevron, Storm pulls to a near halt as if spooked; her front legs rise high into the sky, her body is a twisting mass of muscle, her mane flying back. Mom hangs in the air like a rider in a rodeo ad. But the image doesn't last. Storm's back legs slide from under her, and she crashes onto Mom.

From where I stand, frozen in place on the bottom of the post-and-rail fence, I see Storm get up easily, fluidly, giving a light shiver before trotting off. Mom lies still and broken in the muddy grass. I can only stare. Maureen is screaming to the barn, "Call an ambulance!" Now she is running to Mom. I step down from the fence, but it's as if I'm in somebody else's body and don't know how it works. I walk until I am standing beside her. She is pressed into the mud like she's making a snow angel. Except she has one boot on and one boot off and I think she's dead. Maureen is hunched over her, her ear almost touching Mom's face. It is quiet except for a cool wind. All at once, Maureen sits up. "She's breathing."

. . .

In the days and weeks that follow, Mom will describe it vividly; the sky passing in slow motion is Grammy's black stone bowl filled with tufts of dusty cotton. She describes cuts in time like splices to a film reel: seeing the storm clouds, cut to ... Maureen standing over her, cut to ... all sound disappearing ... cut to a flash of silver scissors and paramedics placing an oxygen mask over her face ... then the inside of the ambulance ... then the hospital and the return of sound at full volume ... "Code blue! Code blue!" ... water dripping from a bag hanging above her, Maureen crying ... Frank by the side of the bed ... a bright light coming from the end of a tunnel ... floating over the entire scene ... seeing herself lying in the bed, doctors rushing, prodding ... three children standing stock-still at the door ... Jack, the elected holder of a few torn lilac branches stepping forward ... the smell of lilacs filling the room ... cut to ... descending back into her body and continuing on ... not giving up ... staying. She will tell us, years later, it was the smell of lilacs that brought her back down into her body and that she can't smell lilacs without thinking of her three children standing in the doorway that day in the hospital.

She remains in intensive care for eight days and then in the hospital for another five weeks. The list on her chart includes nine broken ribs, pelvic bone fractured in four places, broken collarbone, punctured lung, cardiac arrest, and concussion with possible further head trauma. Her memory slips in and out, but the doctor assures Frank this can happen with a concussion. "We're keeping an eye on her. Nothing to worry about yet." They keep her at the hospital on monitors of every kind, only releasing her into our care in early June.

The day before she is to come home, I'm doing my homework out on the screened porch when I hear Frank in the kitchen making an appointment for her with a psychiatrist.

"Hello? Yes. My wife was referred to Dr. McKinnon ... My name is Frank Wolfe ... Oh, he did? Great ... Yes, that's right ... for Nina Wolfe. Yes, she's being released tomorrow ... Not that I know of, no ... I believe only Valium ... After the birth of her second child ... postpartum depression ... Yes ... severe. She was institutionalized ... Five weeks, I believe, I could check on that for you ... Yes, she did ... electroconvulsive therapy ... It did, but there was some memory loss during that period. I believe she got all of that back, though ... You'd have to ask her about that ... Walden Hills ... Mondays are good, yes. I should also let you know that she and I were on the verge of separating when the accident happened. I'm not sure what the psychiatrist, um ... Dr. McKinnon would advise, but obviously, I'll do whatever you suggest ... So, Monday at four p.m. with Dr. Hugh McKinnon ... okay. Thank you."

My geometry homework rests in my lap ... *a pivot point marks the intersection of two lines* ... After her second child ... *the angle of the pivot point will define the shape of the object* ... electroconvulsive therapy ... *pivot points are also key in physics and architecture* ... five weeks ... I look through the screened porch at the wind blowing the last petals from the magnolia.

When we bring her home, she is a broken doll in need of great tenderness. The rancour and sharp edges of months past are smoothed, and we all pitch in to care for her. In addition to her weekly psychotherapy, she begins intensive biweekly physiotherapy. She still has too many bones healing to do stairs, so we set up a convalescent suite on the screened porch. She and I will sleep on the two couches, with a long bench serving as our joint bedside table.

It is late at night, and Jack, Oliver, and Frank have all gone to bed. The only light still on is the reading light we share.

"What's electroconvulsive therapy?" I venture.

Mom lifts her head from her book, takes off her drugstore reading glasses, and faces me. "Where did you hear that term?"

"I heard Frank on the phone making an appointment for you."

"I see." She closes the book in her lap. "Have you heard of ECT before?"

"Like when they shock you?"

She turns and looks out into the night. "Yes, like when they shock you." She is silent for a few minutes.

I hold my breath.

She faces me. "Your father and I got married when I was twenty-one, did you know that? You're almost eighteen now. Try to imagine that three years from now you are married and pregnant. All your plans of being an actress are over and suddenly you're a mother. And with every sleepless night, every fever, every load of laundry, you're watching your dreams recede a little further. Into an unreachable distance."

I feel like I've been caught eavesdropping on a private conversation. I want to slide from the room but she looks right at me then. "Your father was studying music, studying to be a concert pianist, and I was an art major, painting every day ... I got pregnant with Ollie almost immediately after we were married, and the realization was slow in coming, but when it came, it hit hard."

"What realization?"

"That I was never going to make art again."

"Oh."

"Everything seemed so dark. With every step I took, it was like the ground itself was threatening to swallow me whole. After you were born, I guess I gave up trying to stay above it all and let myself sink. I—I don't know if I should be telling you this," she says, as if realizing just this minute that I am one of the characters in her story. But I can see it in her eyes; the thought of stopping is still faint, and I can override it if I act fast.

"It's okay. I want to know. Really, you can say it."

"Well, after you were born, it was ... I was suffocating. And finally, your father asked Pappy for help." She laughs, but not the kind of laugh that means something is funny, more like a sad laugh. "Pappy, as you know, when he sets his mind to something he does his research. And his research led him to a place called Walden Hills and a treatment called electroconvulsive therapy. When I got out of the institution, I would see people on the street or at the market, and they would come up to say hello as if they were my oldest friends in the world, and I would have no idea who they were. I gradually got my memory back, but it took a while."

"Who took care of us while you were away?"

"Your father. You were little—I guess about eighteen months old?"

"How long were you in that place?"

"Six weeks—is it okay that I tell you all of this?"

"Yeah. Of course," I say. "Totally fine." But I can't get a full breath. I have that homesick feeling I sometimes get but can't put a name to.

And then she says, "Frank and I are getting a divorce."

## seventeen

WE HAD MOVED into the beautiful old farmhouse together, and we would leave it in much the same fashion, not all at once and not in the same direction but within a year, we would all be gone, like seeds scattered in the wind.

Frank finishes hitching the trailer to his car and comes to stand beside me on the sunbaked driveway. Our family has always functioned best in units of two: me and Frank, Ollie and Mom, Jack and Frank, me and Jack—but never Frank and Oliver or Mom and Frank, not anymore. Maybe never.

"I hope I don't just become 'that guy Mom was married to,'" Frank says. He means for it to come out as a joke, he even tries to smile, but his eyes well up. I hug him. He taught the three of us to play baseball and built us a treehouse and taught me to drive a standard. He looks past me to the house. I turn. The house was well built, just not the family inside.

Jack is next to go. One month after Frank leaves, he returns for Jack. I try to register the fact that he's only visiting, that he's not pulling up the driveway with groceries, about to make dinner. He and Jack are headed off on a father-son camping trip to Nova Scotia. I watch him park and walk up the cobblestone path to the back door. From my window, I can see everything except his arrival at the door. Does he knock? He installed that door. I helped him hold the level and draw the pencil line to mark where the hinges would go. I listen to him downstairs talking to Mom. For years—for more than a decade—the two of them downstairs talking was the soundtrack to my life. This is different. It's not background noise; each word is charged, carefully chosen, overly polite. They have learned the hard way the power of words to ignite and scorch.

Jack passes my open door with his sleeping bag and backpack, sets them on the floor at the end of the hall and sits on the top stair. I come out of my room and sit beside him. We listen to Mom and Frank, talking about "the Jack situation." Oliver emerges from his room and leans against the railing beside us.

Despite all my lessons on surviving high school, Jack has managed to get himself into trouble—which is to say he did what all kids do, but he got caught. Three times. We hear Frank say in a friendly tone that the all-boys boarding school is only nine miles from his new home in Great Barrington and that Jack will be able to stay with him on weekends. We hear Mom comment on the grounds and the beauty of the architecture. We listen to the two of them amicably reaching a decision about their son's life, a decision they are making without so much as a nod to Jack. I feel the spirit seep out of him as the verdict is reached. All three of us saw the brochure sitting on the table yesterday: every page plastered with the smiling faces of the kind of prep school kids we hate.

"Jack?" Mom calls up. "Come on. Time to go."

Jack stands silently, takes his pack and sleeping bag, and heads down the stairs.

"And then there were two." Oliver sits down beside me on the top stair.

"Not true. What about when you go to UMass?" I ask. "Then there will only be one."

"You've got me for another four months. Enjoy it while you can."

Oliver has already taken a ditch year, which he probably would have turned into two or three if Mom hadn't insisted he fill out some college applications. But by the time he got around to it, it was too late for September, so he applied for January entry. After Christmas, he'll be on his way to UMass.

"You're only going an hour away. You'll probably be home every weekend," I tease him.

"It's two hours away, not one. And don't worry, I don't plan on coming back."

"We'll see about that. Me, I'm going all the way to the other side of Pennsylvania. I won't be able to come home even if I want to."

"Awfully sure of yourself, aren't you? You haven't even auditioned yet."

. . .

It's 1:55 p.m. when I'm called from the large auditorium to sit in the "on-deck" chair, waiting to be called in for my audition to Carnegie-Mellon University. I close my eyes and try to breathe evenly.

"Cassandra Wolfe?" The young student with the clipboard motions for me to go in.

Sitting in the back of the audition room is a short man with a burst of grey hair that most likely began the day smooth and flat but was now expressing as much exasperation as the face it sat above. He doesn't say "Welcome" or "Please begin" or anything at all for that matter; just looks at me over wire-rimmed glasses with an expression of utmost boredom.

"Hello. My name is Cassie Wolfe. My contemporary monologue is from *Playing for Time* and my classical is from *Antigone*."

By the time I finish both monologues, he has perked up and is looking at me intently. He says, "Tell me, Cassandra, how do you deal with your father's alcoholism?"

My mind races. *How does he know Frank's an alcoholic? Could he have found out somehow? Is there something on the application?* And then it hits me: he wants me to improvise.

I launch right in.

"It's very hard for me to talk about," I say, turning slightly to the side and folding in on myself. "He locks us in the closet when he goes out..." I continue until he interrupts me with, "How did your boyfriend react when you told him you were pregnant?"

I become indignant, throwing my hands in the air. "Typical. So typical."

"How did it feel to win the Tony for best actress?"

"Words can't even describe ..."

He asks me six questions in all and when he stops, I am forlorn. I could do this all day; I'm soaring. Like putting someone who's been deprived of oxygen in a barometric chamber. It's never been okay to show all my emotions. I never felt like I owned something, like there was something out there I could do that was wholly mine; but this? I *owned* this. In this moment, I know exactly what I want to do with my life. If he doesn't take me, I'll go somewhere else.

But he does take me; he follows me out of the room and tells Mom the school will give us whatever we need.

We go out to dinner that night and get huge margaritas with our meal, and back at the hotel, we order dessert from room service and call Oliver and Jack to tell them the news. And for the whole twelve-hour drive back to Massachusetts, we blast our favourite songs and sing at the top of our lungs.

## eighteen

MOM IS STANDING at the edge of the kitchen, twisting a dishtowel in her hands. "I'm inviting a friend for dinner." It's the day after our return from Pittsburgh. I'm at the dining room table doing homework and Oliver is on the couch playing guitar.

"Okay." Neither of us pays much attention.

"I really want you to meet this friend," she says, taking a few steps into the dining room.

Her caginess makes clear to both of us that "friend" means "boyfriend."

"Yeah, okay. Sure."

We exchange a look and go on with what we're doing. Mom spends a good part of the afternoon preparing dinner, followed by another hour upstairs getting ready. When she comes down, she's wearing a dress. And makeup. I close my book. I didn't know Mom even owned a dress. Oliver puts away his guitar. Mom is beautiful, but not in a makeup-wearing, high-heeled-shoes kind of way. She wears jeans and plain crewneck shirts or sweaters, and if it's a special occasion, a button-down shirt. I once asked her why she didn't get manicures, and she replied that her hands were her tools and getting a manicure would be like painting her paintbrush. This is going to be good.

At six o'clock precisely, a powder-blue Mercedes rolls up the driveway. Mom checks her reflection in the kitchen window and goes out the back door to greet her "friend." Oliver and I watch from the dining room window as a tall, gangly man with silver hair emerges from the car. His hands face backward when he walks, giving the impression that he's paddling.

"He has to be at least twenty years older than her," I whisper to Oliver as we watch Mom and the silver-haired man walk up the pathway to the back door.

We stand politely as Mom introduces us to Hugh. His blue eyes are pale and bright at the same time, like the side of a glacier. He's wearing a beige suit without a tie. While I help Mom get dinner on the table, Hugh chats with Oliver, who is holding a glass of red wine; it's like a real adult dinner party—the civilized kind, that is. Hugh is funny and a little shy and very interesting, and Oliver and I are on our best behaviour. Strangely, it isn't until about forty-five minutes into the dinner that Oliver asks, "And what do you do?" It sounds funny coming out of his mouth. Like he's heard adults asking this question and is trying on being an adult.

Hugh gives Mom a quick glance, and in the split second of it happening, I register it as important.

"I'm a psychiatrist," he says slowly, knowing he's dropping the bomb this night was designed to absorb. I flash back to hearing Frank making appointments for Mom after the accident ... "Dr. Hugh McKinnon."

The picture comes together like laying the last piece in a thousand-piece jigsaw puzzle. Oliver looks at me, fork in hand, mouth half-open; we are finishing the same puzzle. Oliver swallows, sets his fork on the table, and wipes his mouth with his napkin. He turns to look at Hugh. "And how did you meet our mother?"

Hugh takes his time. He's probably nervous; he must know he's broken a cardinal rule in the medical code of ethics, and we may react badly to this information. But he doesn't show any of this. He seems altogether in control.

"I met your mother as my patient, which, I would like to clarify, she no longer is."

Oliver and I look at each other. Perhaps we should react, object, accuse him of taking advantage of Mom, of crossing a line. Maybe we should be angry. But we aren't. What this man doesn't know—or maybe he does, since he's spent hours listening to her talk—is that we don't really have lines in our family; that this is the most relaxed we've *ever* felt at the dinner table; that this level of calm is something we could get used to. And later, when Oliver and I debrief we will both confess to being quite okay with having a mental health professional in the family. But most of all, there is something about this man that is implicitly trustworthy. And so, in an unspoken agreement made in a moment, we decide that a potential abundance of benefits outweighs his lapse in judgment and that he can be trusted to handle Mom. *Here you go.*

Oliver says, "Okay."

And I say, "Right, then."

And no more is said about it.

He comes to dinner again next week, and the week after that, and as weeks turn into months and fall turns to winter Hugh is coming to dinner every night and staying over on the weekends. He asks Oliver about his music, what classes he's signed up for at UMass, and what he wants to do with his life. Oliver mentions a literature course he's looking forward to and tells Hugh he loves the classics. On his next visit, Hugh brings Oliver a book on William Blake. It's nothing spectacular; a simple and unremarkable gesture, really. Nonetheless, I try and fail to remember the last time an adult male asked Oliver what he wanted to do or what he thought about his life. When Hugh asks me similar questions, I tell him I want to be an actor and that I write stories, and somewhere in there I mention keeping track of my dreams.

Sure enough, on the next visit Hugh brings me a journal and a book on dreams by someone named James Hillman. "If you're interested in mythology and dreams, I think you'll find Hillman fascinating."

Everything has become so civilized, seemingly overnight. And Mom is changed too. The accident has slowed her down. She's calmer, happier. Nothing sets her off.

The day of her accident when the ambulance drove away, I remember Storm grazing at the edge of the field with her saddle still on as if nothing had happened. I remember wishing that horse had never come into our life, thinking that she had destroyed everything. But now I see it differently, like somehow Mom knew only a deus ex machina could get her out of her stagnating marriage; like she didn't know what Storm would bring, but she knew it would be radical, and she's never been afraid of radical.

It is with this new easy tone established that Mom informs us Hugh has quit his job with Harvard Community Health Network and accepted a job with Indian Health Service on the Navajo reservation in Fort Defiance, Arizona.

"We're moving west," she says and goes on to tell us all about the move and how she and Hugh will live in housing provided by the government, but that she intends to find a place where they can live more permanently, where they can have animals and a home of their own. And within a week, there is a For Sale sign hanging at the end of the driveway.

1994–2002

## nineteen

THE CHEAP CHRISTMAS LIGHTS strung along Second Avenue blink with mesmerizing monotony. In the window of the vintage clothing store Love Will Save the Day, a hastily dressed mannequin in a teal dress and Santa hat inclines to the left. Yellow taxis and delivery trucks honk at nothing, swerve, pass, and fly through just-turned-red lights. Groups of people bundled against the snow, carrying bags and packages, cross between cars, not waiting for the Walk sign but filling any pause in the rushing stream. I let go of the curtain and crawl back into bed. My mother bought me these sheer curtains when I moved in two years ago, in anticipation of the sun-drenched life I was sure to lead in this East Village apartment—rather than the drug-addled, velvet-curtained life I am leading. I pull the blanket up to my chin, feeling as thin as a leaf. I wish she was here, in the kitchen making chicken soup, about to poke her head in and ask if I want to watch a movie.

I pull the phone under the covers and dial her number.

"Hello?"

"Hi, Mom."

"Oh, hi, sweetie. Hang on a second. I'm letting the dog out ... Go on, Elvis. Go!"

My head is throbbing. I stretch a leg out to kick my bedroom door closed; in addition to the delivery trucks and sirens piping up from Second Avenue, my roommate is in the living room blasting Missy Elliott.

"You should have seen him yesterday, with the big dogs herding cattle he got right in there. No awareness of his size whatsoever." Water is running and pots clank in the background. "So, did you hear anything?"

"I didn't get it."

"Oh, rats. I'm sorry, sweetie. You must be feeling crummy."

"A bit, I guess."

"Theatre jobs in that city must be so hard to get. Probably the actresses with the big names get those parts."

"Yeah. I did book a commercial, though. And it's a national, so the residuals will be good."

"A commercial? Are you sure commercials aren't ruining your reputation? Maybe you shouldn't be doing those?"

"No, commercials aren't ruining my reputation. Actors have to pay the bills, and that's what the commercials do. Vanita made almost fifty thousand dollars on her Burger King spot."

"Really?"

"Yes, really."

"Hang on a second, Murph." She opens a door and calls the dog in. "What do you think about taking a break and staying in Truchas after Christmas? Maybe even staying through the winter?"

She and Hugh have been living in this small mountain town at the edge of the world for six years now and it's been a kind of mental and spiritual dialysis, flushing all the waste from her cells and bringing her back to full and vibrant life. We talk every day, and every call is packed with stories. "A herd of cattle is crossing the back field ... a screech owl has taken up residence in the dead tree by the acequia ... I'm helping to renovate the old church up the road ... Francisco, the whiskey-drinking wood carver has more talent in his little finger ..."

"I wish I could, Mom, but I can't come for that long ..."

"Why not?"

"Because I have an agent. I can't tell them I'm going to be away for two months for no reason and expect them to stay interested."

"Why not? They're your agent, aren't they supposed to care about your mental health?"

No, that's definitely not part of their job description. "They want actresses who are hungry."

I started out hungry. Arriving in New York fresh out of college, I was going to take the city by storm; my name would be up in lights in no time. Two of the three agents who gave workshops at school the semester before graduation told me, "You, my dear, are going to work. A lot." Straight out of school,

I'd been introduced to a major film director and came within a millimetre of getting a large role. I even flew out to LA for a screen test. But that was two years ago now, and the memory of what was supposed to be my sure and easy success only makes me feel that much worse.

In truth, I'd like nothing more than to go and hang out with my mother in the mountains of New Mexico, but doing that would fall under the category of giving up. And lately, anything that resembles quitting is appealing to me more and more—and that scares me.

"What about your friends from school?"

We had all gone into the drama program at Carnegie-Mellon wanting to be actors and knowing we were survivors, and gradually coming to realize those two things were related. In our classes, we were praised, insulted, picked apart, and pitted against one another. We got rid of our small-town dialects, lost weight, learned to breathe in a corset, to dance and sing, and most of all, to take direction. The drama program was testing the strength of our resolve, pushing us to the edges of our emotions. The universally accepted methodology had—for the most part—no regard for "safe space." From a starting class of fifty, eighteen of us made it through to the end.

In our course on professionalism in the industry, we were taught that our attitude was to be "Yes, I can!" to whatever was asked of us. My agent would call and tell me the date and time of the audition, whether it was for Bounty paper towels, or Shakespeare in the Park, and whether I was to dress as a young mom, or a drug addict, or an ingenue. I went to every audition and to all the open calls listed in *Backstage* magazine. Can you sing? "Yes, I can!" Do a Russian accent? "Yes, I can!" Ride a horse? Play the piano? Dance in toe shoes? Drive an eighteen-wheeler?

Eventually I learned to occasionally say, "No, I can't." But *no* was a word I had never felt comfortable saying. I was discovering, however, it was a word one needed in New York City.

"Oh Murph, I just don't want you to burn out."

"I'm fine, Mom, really. A little tired is all."

I pull myself as far as the living room and, with my hand over the receiver, whisper to my roommate, "I'm coming with you." I sprawl out on our threadbare couch and close my eyes against the throbbing in my head. This morning, I vowed I was going to stop all the drinking, stop doing drugs, see more daylight, get my life headed in some sort of direction— any direction—but as my mother's voice surges through the line I feel my willpower usurped with each question I fail to answer; shame makes way for defeat, and I decide tonight is not the night to make a change. I watch as my roommate taps two lines of coke from a tiny plastic pouch onto the scalloped mirror that has become a permanent centrepiece on our broken coffee table. She hands me a rolled-up dollar bill. "Mom, can you hang on a sec? I'm grabbing a glass of water." I set the phone on the couch and hunch over the mirror, focusing on the lines of white powder rather than my own blurred face staring back from the broken glass. The line of coke is a shot of cold wind to my brain. I sink back against the tattered couch and close my eyes. In a matter of seconds, all soft edges will be replaced with clear sharp lines. My thoughts will be crystalline and absolute.

"Sorry, what were you saying, Mom?"

"I really think you need to get another job."

I work at a fancy hotel bar in Midtown called the Whiskey. When I first applied for the job, I was worried that my lack of experience would be a deterrent in hiring me, but my application consisted of a single Polaroid picture and I was hired that same day. The uniform is a catsuit—which does not have ears and a tail as I first thought when I heard the word, but is, rather, a skin-tight grey bodysuit worn with a black belt. The hours are brutal but the money is good, and my days are left free for auditioning.

"All of these auditions ... it's like you're auditioning for the right to have a life. It's absurd." She makes a *pfft* sound to indicate disgust. "What are you saying, Hugh?" She yells to Hugh.

"Mom, can you hold the phone away if you're going to yell."

"Hugh says I should give you some space."

"You should listen to Hugh." It comes out sounding more annoyed than I'd intended.

"Well, excuse me. I thought I was expressing concern. I'll try to be more psychologically savvy in the future." I can't tell if her sarcasm is directed at me or Hugh.

"It's not that, Mom. It's not you, really. You're right that I'm tired, but that's all."

"Fine."

I try bringing up Christmas to change the mood. "So, I'm going to be out there in a week. I can't wait."

"Mm-hmm."

"I gave you my flight information, right?

"Yes." She's mad now, and nothing's going to change that.

"Okay, well, I'll call you tomorrow."

"Fine."

"Bye, Mom."

"Bye."

# twenty

AT CHRISTMAS, I FLY OUT to New Mexico. Whenever I arrive in that part of the country that extends wide and endless in every direction, the part of me that is floating and spinning and hopeless settles. If I've been getting acting gigs and working regularly, this landing resembles a soft, gentle sinking into welcoming arms; but if I've been drinking and partying more than usual—which is most of the time lately—it's more like being thrown from a moving vehicle.

The sight of Mom there at the end of the hall, beautiful in her turquoise necklace and simple beige sweater, gives me an instant visceral feeling of home. She has a new haircut and seems softer, radiant. She's happy.

"Murphy!" she calls, waving and pushing to the front of the crowd. "Oh, sweetie. You look so tired." She releases me and takes the handle of my suitcase to wheel it along behind us as we walk. "Did you eat anything on the plane? We could stop in Santa Fe before we head up the mountain—unless you're hungry now?"

Truchas is an hour up the mountain past Santa Fe. "I'm okay, I'll be fine."

"Ollie and Jack should be home by the time we get there. Hugh won't be in until around seven. He did a sweat lodge last night and has been on the rez for the last week, so be prepared to hear all about it."

Mom and Hugh moved to Truchas after a year of living in government housing on the reservation. Mom said she felt like a homing pigeon when she saw the For Sale sign on the little adobe house on the side of the road. She let the realtor give her the full tour, though it wasn't necessary, she knew instantly. She bought the house and the twelve acres that came with it that very day. And after two years of living in the house at the edge of the dirt road that snakes through town, she chose the spot where she would build her first, her own rammed earth house. It was way down beyond the front house on the other side of the acequia, by the Gambel oak grove. She finished building that house last year and they sold the front house to Roberta, a stout woman with red cheeks and silver wind-swept hair. Roberta is a painter from California whom life seems to have hit like a strong gust of wind and who consequently faces all interactions with like vigour, not mincing words or suffering fools. Mom tells me she "gossips shamelessly," in a scandalous tone, as if she's never heard of such a thing. She and Roberta have become fast friends. It's Roberta who convinces Mom to get back to her painting.

. . .

"I might crash out early tonight if that's okay ... you know, with the altitude and the time change and all," I say.

"Of course, sweetie. We still have four days until Christmas. If you're feeling up to it, I was thinking we'd do the Farolito Walk again this year."

"Sounds great."

We stop at Kokoman for mezcal, and as we pass the Santuario de Chimayo and start up the last peak to Truchas, the sun slides behind the mountains. The air is thinner by the mile up here where sky and land fuse into a cold blue dusk and my eyes give in and close all the way.

"Murphy?" Her fingertips are cool against my forehead as she brushes the hair from my face. "We're here."

I open my eyes. It's dark and we're parked in front of the house.

Jack and Oliver are both there. I smile. It's good to see them—good to see them together.

During dinner, Jack and Oliver laugh at each other's jokes and we all laugh at Hugh, who loves it. He wants to be part of the banter but exists in another realm: coming at everything from a mythic angle, seeing everything in its larger context, his responses are often in the wrong key. On the surface, he's gentle bordering on bumbling. But the image of benign, warm-hearted septuagenarian is a ruse that disarms—before you know it, you're showing him all your cards while behind his wink and smile, he's holding four aces. I can see so many ways in which he gives Mom permission to be her best self, her large, wild self. I would wager there aren't many mothers who can build a house from the ground up or have pigs for pets or feed their family exclusively from their farm or find their way out of a bad mood by playing Beethoven, who are equally comfortable discussing politics or art as herding cattle. Mine was that mother who evoked envy in all my friends. A lot of kids had parties in high school when their parents were out of town, but the only party my brothers and I hosted was the one Mom dreamed up: our Goodbye, Natick party, the biggest event our high school had seen in years. It was the summer before we all moved out. She helped us build a stage in the back field for Oliver and his band and set up the front field for parking and made a sign for the end of the driveway. We'd told her we were thinking of getting two kegs of beer and she'd said, "Get five." People are probably still talking about that party.

After dinner, we drink margaritas in the living room. I fall asleep with my head in Mom's lap while Oliver plays the guitar, Jack keeps the fire going, and Hugh reads some book on Navajo religion, occasionally reading random sentences out loud. "Listen to this: *Even death has no power over coyote. He keeps his vital principle in the end of his nose and tail; when the rest of him is destroyed, he pulls himself together and comes to life again.* Wonderful. Simply wonderful."

When Oliver moved west, Hugh—at long last—proved to be the father figure he'd needed so desperately. They take walks together, joke, go camping, and Hugh takes Oliver to men's group meetings. Oliver seems different: more mature, less angry. He's happy.

Jack did a brief stint at the University of Arizona before deciding that college wasn't for him. I don't know if his two years at boarding school turned him off the whole "rich kids" aspect of higher education or if he really was called to be in nature. But three years ago, he quit university and started working as a woodland firefighter with the forest service. He's away for weeks at a time and when he's home for a few days, he mostly sleeps.

Hugh drives us down the mountain to the Farolito Walk on Canyon Road. He's more excited about it than any of us. "Of course, the nobility never walked. How much or how little one walks has always been a mark of social status. Kings and queens were carried everywhere, their feet only touching the ground a very small percentage of their lives. Beggars, children, monks, and women walk the most." He looks to Mom, as if expecting a response. When she says only "indeed," he turns around to face the three of us in the back seat. Jack presses his foot against an imaginary brake. The car is going seventy miles an hour down the mountain. Finally, Hugh turns back to face the road, laughing. He takes Mom's hand and holds it up as if in a show of solidarity. "Solvitur ambulando!"

. . .

We light our luminarias and join the river of paper bag lanterns snaking up the hill. There are bonfires here and there along the side of the road and people are singing Christmas carols. Walking away from one of the bonfires, Mom slips her arm through mine and asks the question she's been holding in since I arrived.

"So ... when do I get to hear about the boyfriend?"

"Oh. Well ... he's not a boyfriend, Mom. It's ... there's not much to tell."

"But it's been almost six months, hasn't it?"

I don't answer and hope she takes the hint. When I tell her anything about my life, it immediately becomes something "we" are facing—which can be nice, sometimes. But not with Kai. Kai's not a "we" thing.

"You said he's from Thailand, right?"

"No, he's from Canada. His mother's from Thailand. But the thing is, he's in a band ... it's just, it's complicated."

"Yes, you told me he's a musician. He's the singer, right?"

"Yeah."

"Why does that matter?"

"It matters because he just signed a huge record contract and is about to tour the world."

"Oh."

She puts her arm around me and pulls me close. I rest my head on her shoulder. "There's no way you can try to make it work?"

Hugh and Oliver are walking ahead of us, and Hugh is pointing out something up in the distance.

"Is it okay if we don't talk about this right now?"

I met Kai at the Whiskey, and we got to know each other over the course of the summer and into the fall, while he was "doing the New York circuit." The record label put the band up in an apartment in the city, a home base while they toured the outlying areas. They were signed to EMI earlier this year and are just starting to break. He says it's all about touring right now but that it won't always be like this. He seems to genuinely believe I will sit and wait while he tours the world. Yes, I want him to "live his dream." I had a vision for my life, too; I graduated university and moved to New York City with an image of what the actor's life was, what my life was going to be—and this isn't it.

"Hello? Anybody in there?"

"Sorry, Mom. What did you say?"

"I was asking if you want to go all the way to the top?"

Jack sneaks up behind us. "All the way to the top." Mom lets go of me, laughing, and Jack shakes me by the shoulders. "We're no quitters. Solvitur ambulando!"


The rest of the week we stay at the house. I sleep late in the morning and in the afternoon take long walks on the mountain. At night we drink margaritas with dinner and read by the fire. In the city, tight labyrinthine ways of moving make my thinking and understanding shrink to fit the maze. But out here, my thoughts can breathe; I settle into myself and the horizon expands.

On one of my afternoon walks, as I'm coming down off the mountain, past the black tree that always reminds me of the *Joshua Tree* album cover, I sit on the large, flat boulder on the hill before the acequia. Out of seemingly nowhere, Hugh emerges and asks if I mind him sitting down beside me. I move over to accommodate him. We sit in silence. Silence is not something I'm used to, or comfortable with, coming from New York. There's no such thing as silence in New York City, no matter the time of day; one never walks down a street void of people, it just doesn't happen. It's disarming to sit with someone this comfortable with silence.

"Beautiful, isn't it," he says at last, as we both look to the mountains in the north, between which hovers a tall, about-to-tumble rain cloud.

"Yes, it is."

"It must be nice after the city."

I don't know what it is about this statement, how such a simple comment is able to unlock something so deep. I feel the heat rising to my face my eyes are filling with tears and I squeeze them closed against the building pressure, but they break forth anyway, falling until I'm submerged and sobbing deeply, my stomach and chest caving in. It is a wave of grief that has no name. There are shades of my life now, of Kai, but it is so much deeper, further back in time, mythic: the tone of absent fathers, and the shape of mothers who would—maybe—have been better off without children, and the longing of children who want to be loved for who they are, but who will, more likely, repeat the cycle of their parents. I'm aware of not being embarrassed or self-conscious, aware that I don't feel like I should stop making things awkward. Apart from reaching into his pocket to give me a tissue, Hugh remains completely still, completely quiet. We sit for a long time in silence and a peace descends over me like a change in the weather. The towering clouds forming in the distance turn the mountains purple.

"Do you know of Ariadne? Wife of Dionysus?" Hugh asks, as if it's the most natural thing ever—and somehow it is. "She was a master spinner and half-sister of the minotaur. There are many different versions of her myth and each one has her dying a different death: she died in childbirth, Dionysus had her killed, Artemis killed her, she hung herself. Our modern thinking wants to say, 'Well, which one is it? What's the real story?' The point of therapy is not to simplify or somehow solve your life. The idea is to find a way to live with the paradoxical nature of it all, to get to a point where we can stand at the edge, call out through *all* the stories, and listen for the shape of the echo."

Hugh loves to speak in riddles. I try to think of conversations I've had with Hugh, and ninety percent of the time they're conversations with both him and Mom. Aside from our trip together to see James Hillman speak when I was in college, this is the first time I've been with him alone. I wonder in that moment what it must be like to have a father, to *really* have a father. It makes me momentarily jealous of what he and Oliver have ... but only momentarily: if anyone deserves a Hugh in their life, it's Oliver.

"Is this your way of telling me I need therapy?" I say, trying to lighten the mood.

He doesn't bite, just sits there quietly. Patiently.

And why am I joking? Nothing is funny. My life is passing like some drunken dream. I drink to a blackout point, wake to strange men in my bed, sometimes go whole weeks without seeing daylight; I have a non-relationship and a non-career and no impetus to change anything.

I stop laughing. "That's beautiful, Hugh. But I don't understand why you're saying it."

"In one version of your story with your mother, you're close, you tell each other everything; you lean on each other. But in another version, you're your own person, separate and unique. A therapist would most likely look at your family and see a lack of boundaries, and that would be accurate, but seeing *only* that would be disallowing for another truth, another story."

"I suppose I could go to therapy ..."

He pauses to choose his words carefully, "I'm not telling you what to do, but I am saying you have the right to your own psychic material—as separate from your mother's."

I grin and raise an eyebrow at him. "My own psychic material?"

He smiles slightly to acknowledge my teasing but holds my gaze long enough to make it plain there will be no joking until we reach a clear understanding.

"So, what do you say?"

"I say, yes. Let's get some boundaries around my psychic material."

Finally, he laughs.

That night, we have some of Mom and Hugh's Truchas friends over for dinner: Francisco, Roberta, Philemon, and Margaret. I feel an inner calm I haven't felt in ages. I see my mother in a new light, a little bit less as a mother and a little bit more as a woman. She's designing the house of a big New York jewellery designer and it's turning out to be a game changer for her. It's a massive construction in Chaco Canyon. Magazine articles are being written. I smile proudly as they sing her praises, talk about all she's brought to Truchas, call her brilliant and inspired. I understand why she's different out here. The archetype of the uncompromising genius has typically been male. Typically, men don't like a woman telling them what to do. Back east, she had ruffled more than a few feathers. But out here it's different, she has her own crew who respect her. She's the boss and that's that. The great, lawless West has opened its wide arms to her, and she has given back.

out west, before this grid of steel and cement, this endless cellblock, wears away at me, strips me down to my marrow. I try to hold the pieces of myself I've gathered, like stones from a river, but anything gathered is eventually lost. It's only a matter of time.

I walk up out of the subway as morning comes into being. In the still dark of not-yet day, sidewalks are being shovelled off, corner stores set up, white pails filled with carnations behind sheets of heavy weatherproof plastic, and the days' headline shows through the graffitied doors of magazine stands. I get a coffee and cross Lafayette as the sky lightens. I cross Astor Place and the Bowery, and the sidewalks fill with businesspeople carrying briefcases and mothers pushing strollers and ravers emerging from Save the Robots, and the cold air is now clear with the new day, where the disparate become one, crystallize into a singular multitude, coffees in hand crossing the street; these are New Yorkers with direction and I step in line; I join the horde, step to the rhythm of the many, togetherness that becomes its own heartbeat. We pass the door to my apartment and walk through the Lower East Side past the fish vendors of Chinatown and the towering steel of the Financial District. The faces change, the day is cold and raw and I keep moving, part of the great show that is New York City. I can't stop now. I am impervious to hunger and the heavy sky, to the tiny sun shrouded in thick layers of grey, to the moisture and absence that dissolve my skin and the buzzing that is in my head but is also the silent scream of the city. Bodies replaced and replaced and replaced, bundled against a chill I can no longer feel. I walk until the city and I are one, until there is no more me.

Night has fallen again when I turn the key on my own small square of space in this dead zone. I sleep, wake, watch TV, drink coffee, eat leftover pizza, drink vodka, sleep again.

On the third day, I wake with a feeling of purpose, decide that I'm going to get my life back together, that I'm going to be fine—that I *am* fine. I'll call my agent, set up a lunch or something, refresh his memory that I exist. I take a shower, get dressed, and dial the number. The secretary puts me through. My agent tells me in a cool but cordial tone that my contract has been up for a month and he isn't interested in re-signing. I hang up the phone and study a worn spot on the hardwood floor. The phone rings again. It's Kai. He has called to say he misses me, that he wishes things could be different, that he ... I hang up on him in mid-sentence, slide under the covers, and curl into a ball.

I sleep often and at all hours. My dreams turn into nightmares that stay with me long after I wake, images that float in space with no binding logic ... like me.

Winter turns into spring.

I write: *A dream is a poem. A poem is a polished stone. A stone is solid.*

I roll the stone over in my hands; I look at my notebook of dreams, these scratchy pencil lines nobody will ever see or know, and think perhaps they are my own sacred texts. I go to my dresser and take Hugh's note from the top drawer: *Dr. Brallier, Jungian dream analyst.*

At my first appointment we focus on my recurring snake dream. I tell Dr. Brallier about Mom—I try to describe her magnetism, and Dr. Brallier listens. Later in the session, he connects the image of a magnet pulling shards of metal to that of a snake capturing a mouse. I tell him that Oliver had a snake when we were little, and I go on to describe the grim feeding ritual, how it would take nearly an hour, the frantic mouse always moving, moving until it tired itself out and in that moment the snake would attack. One swift lunge. Then came the squeezing, suffocating, sucking the life out of, the swallowing whole. Dr. Brallier suggests that maybe my fear is not of snakes but of being swallowed whole. He asks if I feel engulfed in her presence. Yes. Yes, I do.

At certain moments, he'll stop me to ask why I rolled my head a certain way or changed the subject or cried. The weeks progress and I come to depend on my sessions. The things we talk about are helpful. He asks me to be more aware of my responses when I'm feeling trapped. He gives me vocabulary to use. I do the work. And he listens. Sometimes I think it's as simple as that: somebody listening. I go every week and it's not so much that I feel better, but rather that I start to feel real. Solid.

I leave Dr. Brallier's office every Thursday afternoon feeling the weight of myself in the space around me, myself as separate from the city. I remember one of my teachers from college, a Peruvian woman who was the stuff of legend in the Carnegie-Mellon drama department. We all loved and feared her in equal measure. Her note to me was always, "Feel your weight, girl." I would smile and nod and thank her for the sage advice and walk away having no idea what she meant. But now as I walk slowly down this street lined with trees whose crimson leaves twirl to the ground before me, the sounds of the city quiet to a distant backdrop, I breathe slowly into myself; I feel my weight, and everything begins to change.

I stop drinking. It isn't one of my usual big resolutions; it just happens that one night the bartender pours me a shot and I don't want it. And then I don't stop at the Lafayette liquor store on the way home. I sign with a new, smaller agent and get back to auditioning regularly. I book a part in a film— not a huge part, but a principal role with two scenes, small but not minuscule. I feel my appetite coming back. I give my notice at the Whiskey the Friday after Thanksgiving and start working at a restaurant called Revolution. It's still a job waiting tables, but it's a neighbourhood spot and it feels good to know I'm done with the catsuit and the late hours. My latest shift is midnight, and I can wear my own clothes.

It's a snowy night one week before Christmas and I'm at work, walking back to the kitchen window for a food order, when the manager taps me on the shoulder and tells me there's somebody at the front to see me. "Very exotic looking," she adds.

I have a plate in each hand, and my heart goes into my throat. I know in that instant that all my hard-won stability is going to be for nothing around Kai. I set the plates on the service window and turn to see him standing by the hostess's podium. He is taller than I remember, his black hair that was long past his shoulders is shorter. He's clutching his hat like a woman might hold a small purse. He lets go and waves tentatively. I smile. He's nervous too.

"Hi."

"Hi."

"I'm sorry to bother you at work. We got in this afternoon ... I called and your roommate told me where you were. I thought I could wait until tomorrow, but ... What time do you get off?"

"Midnight."

We look over at the clock by the bar. Twenty minutes.

"Do you mind if I wait?"

"Sure ... okay."

We sit at the end of the bar together. He tells me I look thinner and asks if I'm okay. I tell him I am, that I'm very okay, that I've signed with a new agent and am working on an independent film and I'm happy not to be working at the Whiskey anymore, and he tells me about the tour. He gives me a CD of songs he's written for me. He takes me home in a cab and walks me to my door. He doesn't kiss me, but instead asks if he might see me again. As if we've just met. As if this is a first date. A first date except that in the morning, over breakfast at Sidewalk Cafe, he asks me to move to Montreal with him.

Tiredness has lodged deep in my bones, and I know it will never fully go away as long as I live in this city. I have no idea what Montreal is like, other than that they speak French and it's cold. But I know I'm going to go; I need a break, not only from waiting tables but from auditioning—from being told I'm "too tall" at five feet, eight inches, or "too old" at twenty-four, "too serious," "too light," have the "wrong colour hair," am "not compatible with the male lead," or of simply being dismissed with the old standby, "We've decided to go another way." Something's happening that's good. I feel, at long last, it's my own two feet I'm standing on. Even if I'm a one-room shack, my architecture is mine and mine alone.

# twenty-two

THE COUNTDOWN ON the orange flashing Don't Walk sign shows four seconds, a sea of yellow cabs is held at the starting line across five lanes of traffic on Sixth Avenue, and Mom steps out into the street, head held high as the sign clicks to show three seconds remaining. It is not a hurried *I-have-three-seconds-to-cross-this-street* walk, but rather her *I-rush-for-no-one* walk, a walk that borders on strolling. I'm watching from across the street, since I sprinted at the nine-second mark (while Mom pulled on her gloves and tightened her scarf like she had all the time in the world). A light snow is falling when she crosses the first lane and steps into the second, and the light turns green. I grit my teeth against the inevitable mayhem, waiting for the honking, the windows rolled down, the arms gesturing obscenities; I wait for the infamous impatience of New York City taxi drivers. But it never comes. Nothing comes. There's no honking or swearing or flipping the bird;

Mom walks her queen's walk across the street, and they wait. As if all of time stopped for those few moments. She arrives at the other side smiling contentedly, and in that moment, I realize how funny she is when you're not the one being reigned over. I can't help but laugh and take her arm and tell her that she broke a New York record. That week, we have the best time we've ever had in New York: we go into chi-chi boutiques and try on clothes we can't afford, get hot chocolate and watch breakdancers in Washington Square Park, order takeout for all meals and sit up talking into the night, and in the morning have toast and coffee in bed. Any thoughts I had that the old Mom, the one we grew up with, has been tamed out of existence by the riding accident or Hugh or the southwest is put to rest. Yes, she is different since moving west, more sure of herself, grounded. But she's still in there, wild and unconstrained.

Curled together on the couch, we watch the ball drop to ring in 1997, and on the first morning of the new year, we haul my boxes and suitcases down the four flights of stairs and pack them into the U-Haul. We say goodbye to my roommate and drive the six hours up and across the border to Montreal, my new home. Kai is waiting at the apartment where he's signed a lease, in a neighbourhood called the Plateau. It's snowing when I introduce the two of them on the sidewalk, and the cold keeps us from lingering. We unload the van with supreme efficiency, and after a quick survey of our empty apartment, devoid of food, heat, or furniture, we decide to get lunch at a café around the corner. We are walking down Prince Arthur Street in a fierce wind when a group of teenagers runs up and crowds around Kai, asking for his autograph. They have no care for the weather; some of them want pictures with him, others are already taking pictures without asking, and Mom and I, elbowed off to the side, stand in the blowing snow while Kai signs and cameras snap. I am smiling, almost laughing—I've never experienced this before, and then I immediately have the worry that this will frustrate Mom. I peek over at her watching the scene, but she is smiling too. She is glowing.

At the café, the waiter is also a fan and hovers relentlessly, asking about upcoming shows and refilling our already full water glasses, and Mom laughs. She gets the picture—and she likes the picture. From one celebrity to another, this is something she understands. As we sit there eating lunch, a small part of me wonders if she would like him this much were he just a regular guy: no fawning, no special treatment. But as the week goes on and they laugh at each other's jokes and get into spirited political debates, it's clear their fondness for each other is genuine. She stays for a week and helps us furnish our apartment and buy food and set up the kitchen, and when we drive her to the airport on Friday, it is with promises to come out and visit her and Hugh in Truchas.

Our little apartment is on a cobblestoned street and features a pot-bellied wood stove on a wobbly brick platform, and we spend our first few weeks alone in total hibernation, leaving the house only for groceries. We make love at all hours of the day and night and sleep long and deep and the snow continues to fall. The weeks pass and I sign up for a semester at McGill, I take French classes and read for hours and learn to cook. And Kai and I take long walks. And we talk. I miss the theatre, but I don't miss the feeling of being raw material in someone else's vision. I want to find a way to make my own work. Kai says he has two friends who recently moved to town. "They do experimental work, and they need an actor for a piece they're performing tomorrow night."

Kai went to school with Jude and Ingrid. This showing is one in an evening of excerpts from works in progress. Ingrid is going to be throwing Jude against the wall and they want me to speak the text in the moments when he's hitting the wall. Jude is nervous as we wait to go on and is talking a mile a minute. "The tyranny of narrative in theatre needs to be subverted, we're creating a visual action that's violent but not misogynistic, as most theatrical violence is, we're creating an action completely unrelated to the text being spoken, in the hopes of forcing the audience to stop obediently placing text at the top of the hierarchy of stimuli ..." Or something like that. I'm running lines in my head and only half-listening. "Don't forget, keep the lines as monotone as possible."

The next night, there's a party at a dancer's loft in Old Montreal and we meet at Jude and Ingrid's place beforehand. We pick up a bottle of cheap wine at a corner depanneur and go up to their loft on Saint-Laurent. I am fascinated listening to Jude and Ingrid talk about their work. They create site-specific interdisciplinary performance; they want to upend the strict categorizations of the arts, to challenge preconceptions, surprise audiences. I am invigorated imagining what it must be like to create shows from the ground up. Jude tells us about their new project based on Nietzsche's *Birth of Tragedy* and we all go to the loft party, and dance, and drink, and in the wee hours of the morning find ourselves back at Jude and Ingrid's where we started. Kai and Jude are mid-argument as Jude fumbles with his key to open the lock.

"But they fucked goats," Kai prods Jude.

"Well, take a look at what they created—maybe we should be asking ourselves why we don't fuck goats. I mean ... come on ... okay, what did they invent? Like ... um ..."

"Mathematics." Ingrid rescues him.

"Philosophy," I add. "And art."

"Civilization, for fuck's sake." Jude is attempting to extricate himself from his coat, his attempt at an emphatic gesture getting stuck in his sleeve. "Goat-fucking might have been essential for creating one of the greatest civilizations in the history of man. We don't know. But that's exactly the point. It's morality that tells us goat-fucking is wrong. And that's Nietzsche's point, don't you see—morality is at odds with our true desires."

"I've got to be honest, I have no desire to fuck a goat."

Jude is undeterred. "The true Dionysian imagined original man as a satyr."

"What?"

"Oh no," Ingrid interjects. "We have to cut him off at the pass." She gets down on her knees in front of me, upstaging them both. "Dear Cassie, will you work with us? Will you do our show?" They've told me how much they loved my performance the night before—all night they've been speaking about the project as if I'm doing it, talking about how I'll make the perfect one-woman Greek chorus; they've done everything short of outright asking me. And now, here it is.

"Yes! Of course, I'll do it."

Ingrid hugs me and Jude hugs me and then Ingrid says, "We have to think of a name."

"A name for the piece?" I ask.

"No, a name for our new company."

## twenty-three

THE SNOW STARTS slow and silent like mist, so faint I'm not sure it's even snowing. I look out over the rooftops of the city. They have a pinkish glow in the half-light and Montreal seems, at that moment, like Narnia. I smile. Somehow, I managed to fall north, out of the battle zone of my life in New York, where I had spun myself around so many times I'd lost all sense of direction, of what had once been important to me. I knew where to get a dime bag of coke on Avenue B but not how to get a library card for the New York Public Library. I knew where shoes were on sale that week but not what artists were on at the MoMA. For a while, my agent had continued to send me on auditions and I had continued to go, but mostly out of routine, maintaining the illusion that I was an actress. Living *as if*, as Hugh calls it. But I'd never walked into an audition room with the belief that I would get a large role that would put me on a path to a career. And now, here in Montreal, I am going to be making work from the ground up. I will have a say in what the show is, I will contribute to the writing and the creation and the staging. Kai asking me to move to Montreal has been a lifeline. And just like that, I pushed my way through the madness of my New York party life into a winter wonderland where people take tea by the fire, read into the night, travel here and there on sleds, and speak multiple languages. Where a covering of snow gives life the literal sense of a blank canvas.

About two hours after I arrive at Jude and Ingrid's loft for our first rehearsal, there is a loud knocking at the door. It's Kai. "Your mother called ... she was crying."

"When? What did she say?"

"She asked that you call her as soon as possible. She didn't say what it was, but it didn't sound good."

"Can I use your phone?" I ask Ingrid.

"I'm sorry, the phone's been out since yesterday because of the storm. Wait, let me double-check." She goes to the little table by their old green couch and lifts the receiver, only to shake her head apologetically.

"Okay, I'm going down to use the pay phone."

I pull on my coat and boots and trudge out to the pay phone on the street.

I pull the phone card from my pocket and dial the impossibly long number.

"Hello?" Her voice is shaky.

"Hi, Mom, it's me." I hop from foot to foot to keep some warmth in my body, my feet crunching snow against metal as I speak.

"Oh, Murphy. Thank goodness."

"What's up?"

She starts crying almost immediately, "It's Hugh." I stop moving. "He has cancer."

My exhale curls slowly into the icy air.

"Murphy?"

The word stops hovering and sinks like a stone.

"I'm here."

This can't be right. Everything is going well, they're happy—Mom is happy. I can't think of any of those useless words that come in handy at moments like this—words that make people think they have some control over the reckless limbs of life and death that are constantly tossing us up in the air and randomly deciding who to catch and who to let fall.

"I'm sorry, Mom."

How can this happen to Hugh—to Hugh! He is ours ... our—*finally*—patriarch. He's the binding of our loose-leaved family.

"He has a tumour in the lacrimal sac," she is explaining.

Lacrimal, lacrimal ... means what? Mozart's "Lacrimosa" starts playing in my head—must be something to do with crying.

"Which is the base of the tear duct," she continues.

"Will they be able to take the tumour out? Has it spread? Is it treatable?"

"They say that it is, but—" She is starting to panic. "What am I going to do up here on the mountain without Hugh?"

I am wondering the same thing, but keep my voice even. My mother has never been out of a relationship, has never been alone—can't be alone.

"Slow down, Mom. They said it's treatable. That's a good thing."

"But it's cancer. Cancer. It may be okay now, but for how long?"

"Did they talk about a plan? Are they going to do radiation? Chemotherapy? What exactly will the treatment be?"

"They're operating next week. It's a tumour and they said they'll try to remove the tumour without damaging the eye."

"I should come out there."

"Yes, you should come out. Leon and Isaiah from the reservation are organizing a peyote ceremony for Hugh. Susan and Will are coming out and I know he wants you and Jack and Oliver to be there."

Susan and Will are Hugh's kids from his previous marriage, and from the faint acceleration in her voice, I can sense her anxiety. Hugh lived an entire life before he came into our family. In truth, he's only been in our family for twelve years, but his impact has been monumental.

"Of course I'll come. Is Oliver still living at the house?" If this is sadness I'm feeling, it must be utter devastation for Ollie.

"No, he got an apartment in Santa Fe."

"His own apartment?"

"Yes. He's doing well on this new medication Hugh has him on."

"Well, that's good news at least," I offer weakly.

"Oh, what am I going to do?"

"Listen, when's the ceremony? I'll book a ticket now."

"It's this weekend."

"This weekend? As in, three days from now?"

"Don't yell at me, Murph. I didn't plan it."

"Sorry. Okay, I'm going to book a ticket this afternoon. I'll call you tonight."

When I get back to the loft, Kai, Jude, and Ingrid are sitting on the torn green couch like children outside the principal's office, staring up at me in expectation.

"It's my mom's husband. He has cancer." It feels strange to say that word about someone in my own life—about Hugh. Cancer feels like a secret club you know exists, one of the biggest clubs in the world, but rather than hoping to be admitted, you want to avoid it at all costs.

# twenty-four

I'M GREETED AT THE Albuquerque airport by Jack, Oliver, and Oliver's new girlfriend, Rosa. Despite the solemn air that surrounds our greeting as we walk to the parking lot and load my bags into the trunk, I can't help but notice that Oliver's car is clean. Like, vacuumed clean. As we drive the two hours from Albuquerque, New Mexico, to Fort Defiance, Arizona, Oliver and Jack joke and talk easily, and Oliver asks me what I've been up to lately, how "the rock star boyfriend" is, and a variety of other more specific questions. He's steering the conversation. Mom's right: he's doing well.

None of us know what a peyote ceremony is. Hugh has explained it to Oliver and Oliver has done sweat lodges, but none of us *really* know. I'm a little nervous about taking hallucinogens.

"But you've done mushrooms before, right?" Jack asks, as we pull into the dirt lot where the tipi is being set up.

"No, never."

"You've never done mushrooms?" Oliver and Jack say in incredulous unison.

"Get over yourselves. I've done plenty of drugs—I'm quite sure I have you both beat in that department, just not the hippie drugs."

"I've never done mushrooms either," Rosa confides, as we walk together from the car to the tipi. Mom and Hugh are talking to Leon, Hugh's best friend. We each hug Hugh and he thanks us for coming, but it's clear we've interrupted a conversation, so we step away and form our own circle.

After a bit, Leon comes over and says, "Ya'a'teeh," introducing himself to Rosa. We know *ya'a'teeh* from Hugh. It's a Navajo greeting that translates into something like "It is good." Leon is a small man with long silver hair, glasses that tint dark with the sun, and skin that resembles the dried clay of Arizona. He wears a gentle smile, as if he's a visitor here on earth, perpetually amused by how little we humans know of the real way of things. I'm pretty sure Hugh has asked Leon to talk to us. After he says hello, he stands for a moment and then brings his hands together in front of his chest, lowering his head to touch his fingertips to his chin. He stares down at the red earth in the circle formed by our bodies. He won't rush. He has the floor and we all know it; we know not to speak, that he's formulating his thoughts and to give him space for that.

Finally, Leon says, "We Navajo call our religion *the Way.* There is no separation between how we live and our ceremony. Spirit is everywhere in everything, in the ground and

clinic. I'm not sure what exactly he does at the clinic, but in his spare time, he's an artist. Hugh has a small painting of Isaiah's hanging over his desk. Isaiah is taking ash from the fire and sweeping it along the floor—with a small hand broom that he uses like a paintbrush—into long tendrils moving away from the flames. Throughout the night, Isaiah will trace lines in the pale sand, lines not meant to last but to speak of the moment, the sacredness of the moment. The lines will remain as the peyote is passed and the moments are blessed, and then they will be swept away to make room for a new design.

Hugh is seated next to the Roadman and Mom is next to Hugh. I am between Leon and Jack. "Usually, we do the peyote ceremony in a hogan, but it wasn't available, so we pulled this together at the last minute," Leon whispers to me, and chuckles. "It's better anyway, we're nineteen people, not counting Mo and Isaiah: too many for the hogan." Throughout the ceremony, Leon continues to whisper things into my ear and chuckle to himself. I keep nodding lightly to acknowledge that he's spoken but can't think of much to say back—except for later in the night when the peyote's been passed around maybe half a dozen times. Leon touches the peyote fan that Mom has formally presented to me as part of the ceremony. She is crying and says, "This is for my daughter." The Roadman blesses the fan and speaks of the bond between a mother and daughter. He calls the fan a healing gesture and a gift, in the true meaning of the word. When the Roadman finishes speaking, and the chanting and passing of peyote resumes, Leon reaches over and runs his fingers along the rust-coloured feathers of the fan and says, staring straight into the fire but clearly talking to me, "The red-tailed hawk is your father." My head is heavy with peyote and his voice is running water flowing through abalone, the shells clicking to hold and release liquid sound.

*Is he talking to me?*

He turns and looks straight into my eyes. "You think you have to do it all without a father, but you have the mightiest one of all guiding you. Your mother gave you this fan. Your mother gave you your father. It is as it should be."

I look at my mother, her face stained with tears. She has spent so much of her life in one battle or another. With Hugh, she has found some peace. They are holding hands and he leans over to kiss her on the cheek. I think of the time Hugh sat with me on the mountain; I think of how much he has given to our family; I think of how many ways there are to tell the same story.

When the sun rises and we emerge from the tipi into the new morning, made gentle by a light drizzle, we all share mutton stew.

Jack drives the whole way back to Truchas. It's a four-hour drive and we're all dead tired, but his fire experience has accustomed him to staying up for days in a row, so he's the designated driver. Sleep takes me almost instantly, but I half-wake as we bounce over the cattle guard set into the road in Chimayo. Oliver and Rosa are leaning into each other, fast asleep in the back seat. Jack drives slowly.

"Look at that one," he says, pointing to a wildly ornate

descanso, about two feet tall, at the top of a barren hill. The hill sits in front of the mountains, like a child in front of her grandparents. Those little crosses pierce my heart; every time I see one it momentarily takes my breath. Spread across the hills of the southwest, these crosses don't mark just any death, they mark car accidents, shootings, stabbings—the kind of violent, unexpected death that lingers and creates more trauma; the kind that leaves ghosts. These memorials are intensely private and personal in nature, but at the same time are left in warning, a reminder to all of the brutality of this land where the border between the living world and the other side is as thin as an inhale. Mountains and desert and sky ready to ferry us back to our true impermanence. I understand graveyards as places to keep death, to show reverence, to hold the depth of our unknowing. But from another angle, there is no small amount of hubris in thinking we can neatly place death in a manicured setting with a high iron fence, and there it will stay. Death is everywhere, all the time, irreverently. It's there even when no one has died. Jack reaches over and touches my hair. I fall asleep again.

After the peyote ceremony, Hugh gets better for almost five years. He's able to see me and Kai get married, to see Oliver release his first CD (which he dedicates to Hugh), to see Jack move up in the forest service from hotshot to smokejumper. He and Mom live up on the mountain, going about their routines as if everything is normal. For a while, it seems he is completely better, until one day he gets completely worse. It happens all at once, and within a month he is gone.

It is sweat lodges and peyote ceremonies that Hugh credits with keeping him alive for the extra five years. When he is in the hospital dying, he asks to be brought back up to Truchas. He wants to die there. Leon and Isaiah come from the reservation. It takes three days, and for that entire time, Leon and Isaiah remain outside the house chanting and drumming, blessing the Four Directions and preparing the way for his journey.

We each take a turn at his bedside saying goodbye until, on Thursday evening, he stops speaking and slips into a coma. While Leon and Isaiah continue to circle the house, we take turns at Hugh's bedside. Keeping vigil. Four-hour shifts. Jack and I are on shift when he stops breathing. Such a small thing. One last inhale, as if he forgot to close the door on his way out.

Before he goes back to the reservation, Leon brings me, Oliver, and Jack out to the front of the house and gives us each a prayer bag. Mine has two turquoise beads and a feather from the red-tailed hawk. He doesn't say anything about the small leather bags, about how to use them, he only gestures toward the sky. "Hugh is on the spirit way now." He and Isaiah wave goodbye as they pull out past Tafoya's general store, past the church, and on down the mountain. There is a descanso at the turn in the road where they disappear from view.

# twenty-five

MOM CRAWLS INTO the temporary hospital bed, curls up alongside Hugh, and cries into his chest. The hospice workers pull me aside and give me a small bottle of Valium.

"Nina needs to sleep."

They help me to gently untangle her from Hugh and bring her into the bedroom. She will stay there for the better part of two days. Hugh's daughter, Sue, is a hospital administrator—a professional at bringing order to crises—and she is given charge of the funeral preparations. I am designated her assistant. Hugh has requested a simple-wooden-box-type coffin and a bagpipe player and has asked to be buried by the Gambel oak grove on the north side of the house, facing the mountains.

Kai and I stay in Truchas for two extra days after the funeral and leave on a Friday morning. It is three a.m. when Kai peels me out of bed and stuffs me into the rental car to head down the mountain and south into Albuquerque. I've felt nauseous for two days and he's rigged a plastic bag inside a paper bag, which he puts on the floor in front of me. Kai has a huge concert this weekend and we can't change our flight.

He buys Gravol at the airport gift shop and assures me it will all be fine once I get some sleep. It's no surprise I'm sick, he says, given the all-night vigil followed by the funeral preparations, followed by the service itself. It's been an emotional ten days. But it isn't the catering from the funeral, and it isn't the ten sleepless nights. I know what's wrong with me. I knew it with the last words Hugh said to me, as I sat by his bedside, holding his hand. We'd each taken a turn saying goodbye. With what little voice he had left he said to me, "Have babies." He meant this as a kind of respect; a high imperative—birth and death were *where it's at* for him, everything was contained in those moments, and he wanted me to have that. It wasn't some sexist "go have babies and be barefoot in the kitchen," he meant it ... well, he meant it in the best way. The Hugh way.

A thin blue line across a white stick marks more than one passage.


"You have to tell your mother. I know you want to give her more time, but the truth is it's exactly the kind of news she needs. It'll do her good." Kai is flipping through real estate listings on his laptop and talking into his screen. I've heard that women have a nesting instinct when they're pregnant, but in our case, it's Kai who's become obsessed with buying a house. The phone rings.

"Hello? Oh, hi, Nina ... How are you? ... Yes, of course, she's right here."

It's only been two weeks since the funeral and I know everyone handles death differently and there are stages of grieving, but listening to her, one would think nothing had happened. Like there had never even been a Hugh. She's moving down off the mountain, she's decided. She's going into Sotheby's today and is going to list the property, is looking for places closer to Santa Fe, says there's a small town half an hour outside the city, called Jacona. She'll get a piece of property and build a house, like she did in Truchas. She can't live on a mountain in the middle of nowhere. She has to work.

It's impossible to get a word in edgewise when she's like this. But I'm having a baby and she's my mother. I have to tell her sometime. I burst out with it.

"Oh, Murphy! Well, isn't that wonderful. Congratulations."

"Yeah, we're pretty excited, we ..."

"Oh, hang on a sec ... Murph, I'm sorry. I've got to run. I'll call you later, but that is terrific news. Tell Kai congratulations for me."

"Okay ... well, bye ..."

I hang up the phone, not sure what to do with the answers I had prepared for all the questions she was sure to ask.

It's April and I invite her to come for a visit, telling her it'll do her good to take a break, change of scenery and all that. "Don't be absurd. I can't leave now, I'm in the middle of a project." In the fall, I invite her to come see the new house. "I'm sure you'll have design ideas." "Send me photos, I'll let you know what I think." At Christmas, I invite Mom, Oliver, and Jack to come for the holidays. Oliver and Jack accept, but Mom, apologetic, declines. "I'm sorry. I promised a friend I'd spend Christmas with him."

Kai's parents had also been planning to join us, but his father slipped on the ice and sprained his ankle. Kai and I will visit them in the new year. So, it'll be me, Oliver, Jack, and Kai.

Shortly before my brothers are due to arrive Jack calls, says he's packing for his trip and wants to know how I feel about him staying a little longer than the week of Christmas.

"Of course. We'd love it."

"Actually ... I was thinking of staying quite a bit longer, like for a few months, so I can help with the baby."

I laugh. "Seriously? *You* want to help with the baby?" The silence at the other end of the line tells me not to joke. "Yes, definitely. That would be great."

"I was thinking maybe instead of staying with Mom in the winter, I could be put to use up there in Montreal. Fire season doesn't start until late March."

Jack is on active fire duty from March through November, when the off-season begins, and he doesn't work. Up until now, he's always spent this time in Truchas. He's asking to come and spend the winter with us. Something is off. I'm not sure what, but I know enough not to ask. I surmise it has something to do with Mom's new "friend."

. . .

Oliver, who moved back to Massachusetts after Hugh died, arrives two days before Jack. He drives the five hours from Amherst in an old Volvo with no heater—in a leather jacket with no gloves. He has a small, battery-powered space heater he uses to keep the windshield from freezing over. He drives the whole way with one hand on the steering wheel and the other constantly adjusting the heater, so he has a clear patch of windshield to see through.

It takes Kai a while to *get* Oliver. It doesn't surprise me in the slightest to hear about Oliver's car. It's just how he rolls, literally. If the thing has wheels and an engine, everything beyond that is decadence.

"But why doesn't he get it fixed?" Kai asks me when we're alone.

"I don't know. Lack of money, probably."

"But you said he has, like, five cars."

"He does but none of them quite work. They sit out in the yard."

"So why doesn't he sell one of them and get his heater fixed?"

"Listen, Kai, we can sit here all night and you can ask me why Oliver does what he does, and I can come up with a variety of answers, but they won't add up to making sense for you. Can't you just let him be the enigma who is my brother? He's my brother. That's all you need to know, okay?"

"I'm sorry. I don't mean to upset you."

"I'm not upset ... but you don't have to get him, and you don't have to fix him. Just let him be."

"I can't. It doesn't feel right to let somebody drive in the winter in a car with no heat."

"Okay, fine. Take his car into the shop. I'm sure he'll be thrilled."

"Okay, fine, I will."

"Okay, fine."

"Fine."

Jack arrives in the late afternoon on Christmas Eve.

When we thought Kai's parents were going to be joining us, we had planned to make green curry, one of the many Thai dishes his mother has taught me to make. But since they aren't going to be with us, we've decided on something from my side of the family. Our traditional Christmas Eve fare had always been latkes. Kai and I peel and grate potatoes for almost an hour in preparation for Christmas Eve dinner. It was Frank who had introduced this tradition and I don't know what his secret was for frying them without filling the kitchen with smoke, but Kai and I manage to set off every smoke detector in the house—it's so smoky we can't see from the kitchen to the living room. The yield of latkes is not nearly enough to justify the two hours of peeling, grating, frying, sweating, and smoking up of the house. It is not a tradition I'll be continuing. Finally, we all sit down to eat. The only side dishes I manage: a bowl of applesauce and another of sour cream.

At the end of the three minutes it takes to eat all the latkes, I venture forth and ask Jack about Mom's friend.

"Yeah, he's a boyfriend." Jack fixes his gaze on his empty plate.

"That was fast," Oliver says, with an edge to his voice. "Not sure why I'm surprised. It's kind of her MO, right?"

Oliver has never had any filter when it comes to expressing his anger at Mom, but for Jack, respect and honour are everything. He contains his anger. It's not quite accurate to say he swallows it, it's more like he breathes it in through his pores and channels that into physical action. He lifts weights and runs up mountains and competes in Iron Man triathlons and fights fire and jumps out of airplanes: he takes it in and melts it down into fuel.

He's clearly containing a lot and has been for some time.

"Well, what's he like? This friend. Have you gotten to know him at all?"

He looks straight at me then, and everything he's been holding in seems to rise to the surface and press against the back of his eyes. It pushes its way out of his mouth.

"I don't need to get to know him, he's my friend. I'm the one who brought him to the house."

The trees outside the window are black scratches on the sky. There is no snow. We all stare at Jack. A thick heat circles my neck, constricting. My breathing turns shallow.

"How old is he?"

"Twenty-three."

"And when did this friend first come to the house?"

"About six months before Hugh died."

The heat rises from my neck up the sides of my head and squeezes. I feel the tears come. *How dare she. Why can't she just be normal? Just be a fucking mother. Be a wife, for Christ's sake.*

"Fucking bitch," Oliver says and shoves his chair out from under him, grabbing his jacket and storming out the door.

Kai looks at me. He wants to help in some way but has no idea how.

"She sure does make it hard ..."

It's obvious there's more at play than our mother having had an affair on her dying husband—whom we loved deeply—of her having an affair with her son's friend. *How many people can she insult with one blow?* I try to call up my rational self. I suddenly have a flash of Hugh sitting at the table with us, laughing, reminding us to laugh: "It has nothing to do with this young lad—or with me, for that matter. She's afraid of aging, of her mortality—she's enacting the metaphor and literally clinging to youth." *I don't care, Hugh. I don't care why she's doing it. How dare she. How can you be so forgiving?*

Kai puts his hand on mine. He's like any other guy who wants to fix things that are broken.

"Should I go after your brother?"

"He'll be back. It's forty below and he's wearing a leather jacket."

Oliver is back inside of five minutes.

He sits back at the table and finishes his entire beer in one swig. Jack is next to storm out. But he has a North Face jacket and a proper hat and gloves, so who knows when he'll be back?

Kai sticks to his mission to connect with Oliver.

"Something to drink, Oliver?"

"Sure."

"Anything in particular?"

"Red wine?"

"You got it."

Kai goes into the kitchen and Oliver goes over to the couch and picks up his guitar. I flip the napkin on my lap over and back again. I rub my huge, round belly and eye Kai's half-full wine glass. I haven't had anything to drink in eight months. I flip the napkin over again. I pick up the glass and toss it back in three swallows. I look over at Oliver, who's watching me. He doesn't say anything, just keeps playing his guitar. I wouldn't say Oliver never judges anyone, he judges anything he perceives as bourgeois, hates that with a passion, but the only weakness he judges is his own ... and perhaps his mother's.

When Kai comes back into the room, Oliver is playing "We Three Kings" quietly. Kai puts the glass of red wine on the coffee table in front of him and remains standing, bottle in hand, watching Oliver play. After a verse, Kai starts humming along and then—as if to explode the sombre energy—bursts into the chorus of "We Three Kings" down an octave, in an exaggerated baritone. Oliver takes the cue and plays louder, more boisterously. When they reach the end, they finish with a flourish, and both start laughing. Oliver lifts his glass and

Kai holds up the wine bottle and they tap them together in cheers and Kai drinks straight from the bottle.

"Do 'Silent Night,'" I call out.

We are in the first chorus of "Silent Night" when the door bursts open and Jack comes in, slamming the door behind him.

"Fuck, it's cold up here." He lasted ten minutes.

2013-2017

# twenty-six

MY MOTHER BUILT her house on wetlands. The groundwater specialist, the structural engineer, and the surveyor all told her the same thing: "It's a beautiful piece of property, gorgeous—a natural spring? Quite a rarity in New Mexico. And that view of the Jemez Mountains, spectacular! Unfortunately, you won't be able to build on it. Maybe you could put in a horse pasture—or a yurt. Those are popular these days." The men— two Pueblo and one Chicano—gave the Anglo woman—my mother—the silent *you-people-are-into-that-sort-of-thing-right?* look. They stood under the Russian olive tree at the top of what would become the driveway and looked out over the land. She didn't know how she was going to do it, but do it she would. She smiled politely and told the men that no, she wasn't going to put up a yurt, she was going to build a house. She would be in touch.

They had successfully lit a fire under her.

I was there for the whole summer that year. Kai was on tour all of July and August and with Isabel barely six months old and not yet sleeping through the night, I happily accepted Mom's offer to stay with her for two months.

Each day after breakfast, she would walk the land, and when she was in the house she paced. Until one evening, we were having dinner with Roberta at the Santa Fe Bar and Grill and the answer came to her all at once. "Like being hit on the head," she said.

We were in a booth by the window, and Roberta leaned forward conspiratorially, pressing both forearms into the edge of the table. "There was a terrible fire in Los Alamos this morning. The entire building was levelled. Apparently, three people were killed and sixteen hospitalized for smoke inhalation." Her eyes widened as she detailed the devastation. "All that's left of the building is a pile of rubble. They think it may have been caused ..."

*Rubble.* Mom told me later it was that one word. That one glorious, enchanted word. She drifted into her thoughts as Roberta continued with her story. For weeks, Mom had been trying to think of how she could work with the water, could redirect it rather than trying to get rid of it. Her mind had swirled around ideas of pipes and small streams and how she might construct something that was at once structurally sound, aesthetically pleasing, and economically viable. She wanted to work with the land. She had circled and circled, day in and day out, remaining single-minded, as was her nature. She hadn't given up; the right idea hadn't presented itself yet, but it would.

It would. The word *rubble* entered her brain and tapped lightly on her posterior cortex, and everything that had been swirling fell into place.

She popped an overloaded tortilla chip into her mouth and, holding her napkin up to her mouth with both hands, tilted her face up into the air as if to say thank you. She smiled and then laughed and replaced her napkin on her lap. She sipped her wine and looked across at us—staring back, aghast. Roberta had just told us how one of the people had been crushed so thoroughly, their body was found in several different pieces. In a split second, Mom managed to flip the corners of her mouth downward to produce the appropriate frown. "How awful. It's unthinkable."

The next day she began to draw. Throughout the days that followed, she alternated between walking the perimeter and studying the terrain maps of the spring: the various elevations and water levels. It had to be perfect. It had to work both below ground and above. She crumpled pages and threw them aside. She started again. After several days, she had a plan that satisfied her. She took the final drawings to be blueprinted. She called the city of Los Alamos and asked after the rubble, said she wanted it for a "large-scale art installation." They laughed and told her, "Be our guest." She rented a massive truck and contacted Diego, Eduardo, Philemon, and Javier, the team on her previous two houses.

Diego was a stocky man with a wide-brimmed cowboy hat shading his umber skin, and a mischievous smile that he flashed often—in spite of the fact that he was always chewing something: a straw, a piece of hay, gum, it didn't really matter what, he just seemed to need his mouth working at all times. He arrived two days before the others. He looked at the plans, and while chewing a mangled plastic straw, told her what she already knew. "These are wetlands. That's a natural spring there." He pointed behind them. She told him she was the one who had drawn the plans; she was well aware what the elevations meant.

"But you can't ..." he began.

"Trust me," she interrupted.

Diego readjusted his cowboy hat, flipped the straw to the other side of his mouth, and climbed into his backhoe, shaking his head. He reluctantly did as he was told and dug into the wetlands. He followed the blueprint and created what would be the hole into which they would lay the foundation of the house. It was filled with water. Philemon, Eduardo, and Javier arrived with the first truckload of rubble. They transported and dumped truckload after truckload into the deep pit in the middle of the property. The sun beat down and Mom was particular and demanding, and lengths of pipe and rebar, a few long I-beams, and large hunks of stone and concrete were laid in just so, according to her specifications. At first, it seemed an exercise in madness, but the men were accustomed to the heat and were getting paid, so they smiled and went along with her. They'd built houses for her before and those had worked beautifully, so there was faith mixed with the disbelief. The still inchoate design was not yet revealing the brilliance of its conception.

What they couldn't see was that they were not only creating support for a house, they were also making pathways for the water to travel along. The water wouldn't sink back into the ground but rather would flow under the house and out the other side. She had designed serpentine tributaries that led from the natural spring at the east of the house, through the rubble laid in the foundation, and out the western side into the new pit Diego was busy digging, which he gradually came to realize was to be a pond. They didn't know yet what she was doing, but they recognized that look in her eye and knew intuitively that they were going to be part of something big. They were all genuinely fond of her and knew from experience that her craziest ideas were usually crazy like a fox and soon enough they would see.

Once the three large truckloads of rubble were laid in, we stood back. It was late afternoon on a Friday, and we all stood up on the little hill, next to the Russian olive, and watched in awed appreciation as the waterways snaked through the rubble, on top of it, between it; the water did not sink back into the earth but rather flowed into her pond. We marvelled at her genius: she had created both a workable foundation and a structure that contributed to the ecology of the land. Plant species would flourish, frogs and snakes and all variety of ground animal would come to call this land home. She had created her own Fallingwater, an oasis in the middle of the desert. And those four men would be the ones to build her house. They would listen to her outlandish ideas with the knowledge that her mind worked in a way they didn't understand, wouldn't understand until they saw her vision realized in the landscape before them. Isabel and I left before the house was finished, but I followed the progress thanks to daily updates from Mom.

From that day forward and for the rest of the project, when Diego, Philemon, Eduardo, and Javier laughed at her off-the-wall ideas, they were laughing with her. They were a team, imagining what people would think if they saw what this group of lunatic builders was attempting, and they were proud to be part of it. She wanted to use two twenty-five-foot I-beams to support the roof; they told her it would take a crane and about twenty men to lift them into place. To which she said, "Well, we better get twenty men." She wanted the beams visible and jutting from inside straight out over the porch to the edge of the pond. She wanted the visual connection between inner and outer space. The porch would have no railing and be like an overhang in nature, without manufactured intervention. She insisted on two-foot-thick rammed earth walls, even though most builders had long since eschewed that traditional style of building, replacing it with faux adobe over wood frame. She wouldn't hear of it.

And one day, driving back from visiting Leon and Isaiah on the reservation, she passed some workmen taking down an old barn. As she drove by them, she slowed down and pulled off the road. She looked in her rear-view mirror and then turned to look back over her shoulder. She told me it was a full fifteen minutes that she sat there, thinking.

The basic structure of the house was built, and she'd moved on to thinking about the details. When she turned her truck around and pulled over by the halfway-deconstructed barn to ask the workmen if she might buy the vigas and latillas that had once made up the roof, the men looked confused.

"You want to buy that wood?" They looked back and forth between themselves, and then the one who seemed to be the leader said a price, a nominal amount. Mom countered with a slightly lower number and the boss said, "Done. They're yours. But we don't deliver."

She called Diego, Eduardo, Philemon, and Javier, and together the five of them loaded the wood, half onto the bed of Eduardo's truck and half onto Philemon's. And with those beams, at the southern end of her house, she built a small log cabin. You walked through the open-style rammed earth house, across the earthen floor under the jutting beams, until you reached the southern end where light poured into a glass passageway that led from the house into her log cabin bedroom. The sound of a gently flowing stream ushered you from the large open space across a gently curved footbridge, over the plants and flowers banking the water's edge, and into her bedroom. The water flowed through an opening at the base of the eastern wall and out the western side, forming a tiny waterfall that let into the pond. One year after they had begun, the house was finished. And it was spectacular.

· · ·

Ten years have passed when Jack and I meet the realtor at the top of the driveway, where the Russian olive shrieks skyward. As the realtor attaches a Sold marker over the For Sale sign, the two of us stand by the ancient tree and look down at the house. How had this happened? Had we not paid close enough attention to the shift that came when Hugh died? Had we turned our backs on her? Left her all alone out here in the desert? Or had we been normal kids living our own lives? In the years that passed, this house has been the backdrop to scenes of festivity, dinner parties, friends visiting from Boston and California, and local friends stopping by just because. But none of it could fill the hole that was being alone. I wade through the messy algae of memory in search of clues, something solid we can point to and say, "This is when it happened, this is what started it." But the truth is, it started long before she built this house, before she moved west, before we were even born.

From the outside she was everything you'd expect her to be, a mother who visited her children and grandchildren, a woman with a beautiful home who loved to entertain, was social, and gardened. But maybe, the darker and more unstable things became in her mind, the greater the illusion of perfection needed to be, dinner parties and travelling and spending more money than she had. A skeleton of unhappiness cloaked in layers of abundance. She had a boyfriend from the Pueblo named Rod, who stayed with her roughly half the time. As an active member of his tribe, he often had dances or ceremonies or council meetings, and in these cases, she was left alone. And being alone had become intolerable.

When she visited us, she would refuse to stay in our guest room, calling it "gloomy," and Kai would be relegated to the couch so she could sleep in bed with me. When I had to work, she would insist on coming with me, promising to sit quietly in the back while I rehearsed. If I made plans to go out and visit Jack in California or Oliver in Massachusetts and she got wind of these plans, she would accuse us of trying to leave her out. We would tell her that was nonsense, that we'd love to have her, and she would book a ticket. I think we intentionally overlooked the weirdness of it, because it was clear there was no bottom to her loneliness. Her need to be with us was greater than our need for freedom.

The realtor hands Jack the contracts, and the two of us stare down at the empty house. I remember coming to visit when Isabel was four. On the airplane, I'd told her all about the pond and how there were so many frogs. And the morning after our arrival, while I was having coffee with Mom, Isabel's strange, upside-down voice calling from the porch made me leap from my chair. I raced outside and crouched next to her where she was draped over the cantilevered edge, gazing into the green water at a frog who sat at the edge of the water with another frog sticking from its mouth—white belly and skinny legs tipped skyward, hanging from the overstuffed gullet of the dominant amphibian. It took me a minute to figure out what I was looking at, like an Ouroboros image. It left me unsettled for the rest of the trip.

As we, her children, grew and got married and had children of our own, had we left her behind? Is this the nature of life? Is feeling left out an unavoidable by-product of aging? Or was there nothing organic about it? Had it all been chemically induced? Every biological organism reaches a point where growth stops and shrinking begins. Maybe that was it. Our mother had no intention of going gentle into that good night. Raging was more her style.

I squint until the landscape blurs like one of her horizon paintings, blending the lines between land and sky, light and dark. Looking into one of her paintings felt like falling, like being submerged in pure depth; one felt the smallness of being human. She painted a loneliness beyond the boundaries of the word. I look out past the house to the Jemez Mountains in the distance, immortal and mighty. How small we are, constructing our mazes: roads and streets and houses that the mountains will watch crumble with time, abraded back into the land, blown away as dust. The land that so inspired my mother had come to claim her.

# twenty-seven

I STEP OUT OF the theatre so I can hear her. The applause is loud, and I hold the phone tight to my ear, covering my other ear with my hand. "Mom, I'm at Isabel's award ceremony. What is so important?"

"Well ... I'm sorry to bother you. But I thought you would want to know. I'm moving."

The anger that propelled me to the lobby begins to meld with confusion. It has been three months since Jack and I stood at the top of her driveway with the realtor and posted the Sold sign on her house in Jacona. Three months since she moved into a small house in Santa Fe. We've been having roughly the same conversation on repeat since well before that: she's unhappy in the Santa Fe area and wants to move—she'd moved to the southwest with Hugh, and now, more than a decade after his death, the reasons for staying have long since dried up. And though I have avoided looking at it, something inside my mother has become brittle too. All that had once been expansive in her thinking has begun to contract.

None of what she is telling me is new information. What is new is the verb tense. She didn't say "I have to move," or "I want to move." She said, "I'm moving." If she's truly moving, then this is news.

"Wow, Mom. Do you not like the new house?"

"I can't live in a retirement community."

"So … where are you moving?"

"To Montreal."

There's a long pause while I try to locate my breathing. The lobby is filled with parents and teachers chatting and laughing. Isabel's math teacher is walking by and touches my arm. She whispers, "Vous êtes fière, non?" I find myself unable to produce words, let alone French ones. I manage to make a thumbs-up sign.

"Hello? Are you there?" She's starting to get agitated.

"I thought you hated the winters. You call it the polar ice cap up here. Weren't you thinking California might be more your speed?"

After Hugh died, she began visiting us kids regularly. In the beginning, this was fine—great, in fact. She came to all my shows, my friends love her, and of course, the girls love her. But it was on these visits that I started to notice the shift. She became less interested in things like museums or long walks or playing with the girls. For the last few years, her primary and, in fact, sole interest has been in sitting around and talking, drinking wine and talking about her life. It isn't a conversation, per se—we aren't discussing a book she's reading or politics or art. It's a one-sided diatribe in which she complains and I listen. She sends food back at restaurants and contests prices everywhere we go. Back in New Mexico, she's been involved in not one but two lawsuits with previous clients.

She continues. "Yes, but it's almost summer. And you're always saying how nice Montreal is in the summer. I thought I'd give it a go."

I walk out of the building into the sunlight. I need air. I need to move. She sounds happy, and I don't want to spoil that, but at the same time she absolutely cannot move to Montreal.

I'm not one who subscribes to the whole positive thinking trend which seems—to me, anyway—to be the source of so much anguish. I lived with Hugh long enough to get a basic grasp on the concept of the shadow. Everyone has one and pretending we don't only makes it bigger. But with my mother, I am perpetually, desperately, trying to bring in some positive thinking. Shadows fill every corner of any room she's in. Even when the conversation is light and there is laughter, the threat of thunder is ever-present. It's hard to say if it's been a few months or a year or three years or ten, but she has an edge now: a sharp, dark edge I try to avoid.

"So you're thinking of coming out soon, then?"

"Cassie, I'm in Oklahoma. Roberta's with me. We're halfway across the country."

"You're what?" I yell, causing a few heads to turn.

Kai has stepped out of the building and is walking toward me.

"Oh. Well, you don't sound very happy about it," she says, her voice dropping down into hurt-angry.

"It's a little ... sudden. What will you ...? Where are you going to stay?"

"Well, I'll stay with you until I find a place." Silence. "It'll just be until I find a place ... God, Cassie, I thought you'd be happy to see me."

I tell her that Isabel's award is about to be presented and that I'll call her back after the ceremony.

Later that night, at dinner, Kai and I steer clear of the subject.

"But Mama, I didn't know adults could go to school," Lucy says.

"Well, they can. It's called a master's degree and it's what some people choose to do after they finish college."

"Why would anybody choose to do more school?"

"Well, I'm choosing to do it because I have an opportunity to teach, but I need to have a master's degree. But also, I will learn writing, how to use words. Do you remember when you were little, how you would get so upset that you had a hard time expressing what you were mad about, you could only slam the door and cry? And I would tell you to use your words so that I could understand why you were so upset? Well, it's the same with adults. We need to use our words too."

"But you already know how to use words. You're a grown-up."

"Some grown-ups can be just like children." I take a large gulp of wine, putting the glass down with too much force, and a wave of red wine sloshes over the rim onto the tablecloth. Lucy frowns and tilts her head. I blot at the wine with my napkin, unable to find my words.

"Are you going to have homework and stuff like that?"

"Probably."

"Are you going to have a backpack?"

"I'm sure I am. Will you help me choose one?"

"Yes!" This satisfies her and she gets up from the table. Kai says, "Listen, it's summertime in Montreal. Even your mother can't be unhappy in Montreal in the summer. It's a contradiction of physics."

"My mother doesn't follow the laws of physics."

But for a moment, I allow myself to imagine ... *Maybe it will be great, maybe this is the change she needs—I can look at it as an opportunity. How can she not be happy in Montreal in the summer?* I resolve to set aside everything I know about my mother and put a positive spin on the situation.

# twenty-eight

I FIND HER A LOFT space the very next day: one thousand square feet with a decent bathroom, a nice kitchen, and a large window at the front. It's hard to imagine her moving from her sprawling adobe home, looking out over the Jemez Mountains, to this artist's loft in an industrial building, looking out over the garment district. But she's already done the hardest part and transitioned to a smaller house, and my role in this relationship is to do what I'm told. And that's what I've done. Mom arrives one day later with Roberta—who shows signs of having spent three days in a car with Mom and announces that she'll only be staying for two days rather than the seven she had planned. So, Roberta leaves and Mom stays here. In Montreal. Where she now lives.

Every night she comes for dinner at our house, and every night we discuss her problems: where to live, how to find a new partner, what to do with her life. She is lonely and I want to help her. Kai and I spend hours, sometimes listening, other times suggesting places to live, offering to make phone calls, to set up an appointment with a realtor.

I try to get her to a yoga class, to the Y for swimming, I take her to the museum, get her on a bike, help her stretch a canvas—but not only do these attempts not help, they push her further away. Nobody wants to be "fixed" but at the same time, something is undeniably broken and just listening night after night is bottomless.

Finally, I have the wild thought that I'll take her to the Notre-Dame Basilica. We didn't grow up with religion, I don't even know that it's a conscious thought that propels me, but maybe, just maybe, there is some part of me that knows we need *help*.

I take her for dim sum and then we walk the last stretch from Chinatown to Old Montreal. "Where are we going?" she asks as we trudge up the steep hill that leads to the Basilica. I tell her I want to show her something. We arrive in the little square facing the cathedral and I stop to gesture at the magnificent structure, smiling.

"A church? You're taking me to a church? Are things that bad?" She jokes.

*Yes, things are that bad.*

"Come on. Let's go in."

"Fine."

We sit inside under the great vaulted ceiling, spires reaching heavenward, and I feel the predictable humbling that comes with being in such a space. I feel like a fleck in the ever-forward-and-up motion of life; life is a river, and we will be lifted and will fall, will go under and rise. We only exist as a part of something greater, we are pieces, we are—

"I need a coffee," she says and walks out.

That night at dinner, I tell the girls about the Basilica and suggest we go as a family sometime. And Mom tells them about the humble churches of New Mexico and the church in Truchas she helped to renovate. Then she is explaining how the Spaniards used religion to colonize and destroy the Indigenous people. She is working up to a rant as she segues into her connection to the Navajo and the fact that she was gifted a chief's blanket that's gone missing, and she knows someone is stealing from her and she's going to find out who. It is one of her projectile monologues that I usually try to deflect, but as I look at her hand on the wine glass, I stop listening; the whole room goes quiet. She lifts the glass to her mouth and my eyes open to what is right in front of me, has been right in front of me all along. She tilts her head back and closes her eyes. This delicate gesture I've seen all my life but never fully took in, as familiar as how she uses her hands to give shape to her words, painting everything she says. I think back to the last time she visited, how she had had a flu so serious I'd taken her to a clinic to see a doctor and when we got home, I tucked her into bed and gave her medicine and as I turned to go put the kettle on, she stopped me: "Murphy, can you grab me a glass of wine?" I had laughed, thinking she was joking. She wasn't. And there was no talking her out of it. There, propped up in bed with a fever of 102 degrees, she drank her wine.

I remember finding out my good friend Betty was an alcoholic. I had been completely surprised to discover she'd been sober for five years. "I had no idea you even had a problem." Betty told me the alcoholic is remarkably adept at hiding their drinking. "We're women. Hiding what's really going on inside of us is second nature." We shared a laugh before she turned serious again. "Alcohol completely distorts one's perception; the loneliness is a chasm. And one drinks until there's nothing left but the shame and terror of being alone. It's truly dreadful." Betty's high British accent seemed incompatible with the kind of misery she was detailing. She told me her meeting group was almost exclusively women. "Strong, intelligent, hilarious women."

The dinners are dreary, and I am worn out—we're all worn out. For three solid months we have forged on, thinking some change was right around the corner. It isn't until she silences the girls for three consecutive nights that I put my foot down. It's a hot night at the end of August, and while Lucy and Isabel go out front to play hopscotch and Kai goes upstairs, she and I have a talk in which I do the talking. I tell her the girls need some time with their parents, that I also need some space. I suggest she come to dinner four nights a week instead of seven. Maybe sometimes the two of us could have dinner at her loft. She doesn't say anything to contradict me, or in fact, to reply in any way. I watch her eyes go dark.

the rest of the forest. Any average person, if they saw those furry little creatures, up in flames and running for their lives, would pity them. But firefighters curse them: acres and acres of land, scorched to a crisp because of a bunny.

I remember her coming to visit me at Carnegie-Mellon, to see me as Bernarda in *The House of Bernarda Alba*. She had come with us, the whole cast, to Bar One in Squirrel Hill afterward. The next day, my friends kept coming up to me, pulling me aside in class. "You have the coolest mom ever. You're so lucky." And I had felt lucky. She was young and beautiful and able to talk about all the stuff we were talking about. She was charming and artistic and could win people over like magic. But even thinking about it—I feel the anger creeping in to steal away that version of the memory and replace it with its own: she dominated the conversation, she was drinking and never once suggested we go home, knowing I had class at 8:30 a.m., a full day and another show that night. No, rather, she was the one who kept ordering another and another, this is what my friends thought was so cool, she could out-party us. I remember dinner parties when I was little—I always thought she was the life of the party because she did all the talking. Ten guests gathered at the table and Mom holding court. But maybe she had done all the talking because nobody could get a word in edgewise. She's the *give-her-an-inch-and-she'll-take-a-mile* type, the *always-an-hour-late* type, the *tell-you-she'll-do-something-and-then-doesn't* type. I feel the fire entering the untouched part of the forest, descending into a deep wood. Just when the flames are almost contained, the little beast has jumped the line and my pristine memories begin burning before my eyes. I know it will take down anything in its vicinity. I vow to contain the damage.

*I can't give you any more of my oxygen.*

I go over to the couch, take up my bag, and, pulling out my keys, say, "I think you know that's an absurd and unfair thing to say. If you want to leave, that's your decision. I hope you'll at least come and say goodbye to the girls before you go."

She doesn't say anything else to me. Not another word. She calls Roberta, who reluctantly agrees to come up and help her make the drive back. There is nothing that can be done to convince her to stay, and to be honest, I don't try very hard. They come to the house the last day after packing everything up. We're all standing on the sidewalk alongside the overstuffed pickup truck, Kai is chatting with Roberta, and the girls are bouncing a ball back and forth. Mom and I stand there, awkwardly, not saying anything, until she announces she's going to use the bathroom one last time. I have the thought to follow her, so we can have a moment alone. This is my opportunity to tell her I love her, that we'll figure things out, not to worry. I am just inside the entry when I see her in the kitchen. She's trying to reach a bottle of red wine from the top shelf. It's high and the bottle is all the way at the back. She pulls a bar stool around from the end of the counter and climbs up onto her knees. She stretches out her arm, lifts her face, and manages to get hold of the bottom of the bottle to slide it off. She looks like a child grabbing for something she can't quite reach, that she knows she isn't supposed to have, but that she'll do anything to get. She fills her travel mug, takes a few gulps, refills it, and replaces the bottle on the shelf. As she screws the lid on her cup, I slip out the door.

She comes back out onto the sidewalk with the mug close to her chest and goes to the car to set it in the cup holder. She hugs the kids and Kai, but when I hug her, her body goes slack and her eyes glaze over. I ignore this and, not letting go, I pull her closer and say, "I love you, Mom" into the back of her hair. I realize she's waiting for me to let go. I realize I'm crying. I have an overpowering sense that I won't see her again. I say it again, "I love you."

We wave and say goodbye as they pull out. Roberta waves out the window while Mom looks straight ahead, hands rigid at ten and two. The kids play with their ball and Kai puts his arm around me. After a while Kai and the girls go inside, but I am an animal frozen in a bright light, standing in the middle of the empty street long after she's gone.

# thirty

JACK AND I SIT on a piece of driftwood, back where the sand meets the long, blowing beach grass and watch Iona and Kai at the water's edge. Iona is wrapped in a fisherman's sweater with a BabyBjörn strapped to her chest. She holds one hand on the back of Chloe's red-capped head, while with the other she points something out to Kai, further down the shore. We arrived in California yesterday and despite the cool weather, Jack and Iona have brought us down to the beach in Pescadero. Lucy and Isabel, barefoot with their pants rolled up to their knees, are running in and out of the water. The waves are high, but the turbulence is thrilling to the girls, who race to dip their toes in the swirling eddies left behind as each wave slides back into the angry ocean.

I hug my arms around my waist and look down at my bare feet. I push the cold sand around with my toes. It is two weeks since Mom left Montreal and drove back to Santa Fe.

"I suppose she'll probably start coming out here next," Jack says.

"Probably."

Wind rolls in off the water and Jack tucks his head, the brim of his baseball hat blocking the gust. Foam skitters across the tide pool beside us.

Last night, after the girls had finished dinner and gone into the living room to watch TV, Kai and I told Jack and Iona about Mom's time in Montreal.

"Jesus!" Iona was shaking her head. She looked at Jack and let out a small laugh, "How did you two turn out so normal?"

We'd had a lot of wine. We laughed. It was a simple, unambiguous moment. Iona was trying to lighten the air, teasing us. But as the conversation continued, my mind circled the word *normal*, wandering this way and that through its implications. Did she mean Jack and I as opposed to Oliver? Or did she mean all three of us? Has Iona even met Oliver? By *normal*, did she mean unscathed? Without injury? Free from harm?

"What do you suppose Iona meant when she said that Jack and I are normal?" I asked Kai later that night as we lay in bed listening to the rain, which came in waves, alternating between heavy and downright deafening.

"What do you mean?"

"I don't know. I don't know what I mean."

He rolled over to face me.

"Never mind. I think I've just had too much to drink."

"I don't think she meant anything, really. Your Mom is … well, something's not right. But you know that. That's what the whole conversation was about. It's hard to explain your mother to someone who doesn't know her that well. I think Iona is still trying to get a sense of the big picture. How many times has she met Nina?"

"Probably like two or three."

"Yeah. Wait until she puts in some real time—like me." He smiled boastfully. Kai and I have been together for two decades, he's earned the right to boast. "Your mom reminds me of that book Isabel had when she was little with the holographic pages, where you tilt the page one way and it's a lion standing still and you tilt it the other way and the lion roars. Most angles of your mother are incredible. She really is amazing, and some people only see those sides, but if you tilt her the wrong way, things can get very dark very fast. These days, it's kind of like she's stuck on that angle. I think Iona just meant that you and Jack aren't like that—you guys don't really have dark sides."

The silence between Jack and me is Mom. She's as present as if she were sitting on the driftwood between us.

Sometimes the formation over and around an injury is not a scab but a carapace. An outer layer that's an exact replica of the original, that protects the original, hiding inside. This kind of shell takes time to cultivate properly. It takes years. The shape of mine is *independent, competent*. Jack's is *charming, happy-go-lucky*. And Oliver has his guitar; Ollie's is *music*.

But sometimes it's hard to breathe. The calcification is unyielding.

Jack says, "I do all my phone-calling in the car. It takes me an hour each way to get to the station, so I usually call Mom when I'm on the road. Once, when I called her—this was almost a year ago now—I was on my way home from shift and she was going on and on about how she needs a new boyfriend, how she needs to move from New Mexico, and all of her friends are awful and—you know the drill, we're supposed to sit quietly and listen."

Here, he pauses and picks up a stone about the size of his palm and brushes the sand off. He flips the stone over and back again as he talks.

"Well, I must have fallen asleep, because I woke up to a massive truck honking and bearing down on me. My car had drifted into the breakdown lane at seventy-five miles an hour and was headed for an embankment."

"What?"

"It's okay. I woke up instantly—like being stabbed with an EpiPen, I woke up. I whipped back onto the highway and—once my adrenalin levels settled—I realized she was still talking. Her voice was piping from my phone into the car speaker. She was complaining about how there's nowhere for her to exercise. Her voice had hypnotized me. I know you'll think I was tired from work, but it wasn't that. I promise you it wasn't that. We'd had a slow night. It was her voice, the same thing over and over and not being able to respond because you can't contradict her, you just can't ..."

"I know."

"It felt like how, with certain animals you squeeze them and they go unconscious. It was like I *had to* leave the scene but there was no way out—I was trapped. My body had decided falling asleep was the only way."

Back in Montreal, I call and email her regularly in the weeks and months that follow—all through the fall and into the winter and spring—but she doesn't answer the phone or return my emails. Not one email. Not one phone call. It will be a year before she speaks to me again, and when she does, it will be a different person I hear at the other end of the line.

# thirty-one

THE DAY TRUMP was elected, my mother drove her car into a ditch. This was our first real sign that we had lost control of the situation. We could no longer sit back and wait, let things follow their natural course. We had to do something.

Snow had come early to Santa Fe, and in addition to the roads being all white, her claim was that this particular road, the one she was driving on, had just ended. That's what she said: "It just ended." She was adamant about this: there had simply ceased to be a road in front of her, there were no signs and, "It's very dangerous, that whole section of road is under construction, you know." It wasn't.

This kind of confabulation, as the doctors explain it, is supposedly one of the symptoms that marks Wernicke-Korsakoff syndrome. But for my brothers and me, it's hard to see it as a new symptom; fabrication is something she specializes in—the difference now is that she's no longer very good at it. It would be easier to let these small disasters go, help her find a way to chuckle at them, if she didn't get so fired up when anyone questioned her version of the truth. "They should be sued for not having it properly marked. In fact, I might call the police." For some reason, she's become fond of saying she might call the police.

Growing up, we knew not to question her stories. We were accustomed to being told exactly what we were to say to this or that person when we were asked why we were late or why she hadn't come to a parent-teacher meeting or why we'd been absent from school. At first glance, you might wonder why she bothered with these lies, as the truth would do just as well. But it was as if she saw these occasions of having to explain herself as opportunities to stick it to someone. As in, "Screw them for wanting to know our private business." For instance, once I missed a day of school and the simple, real reason was that I'd missed the bus and Frank had taken the car into the city to pick up leather supplies, so she didn't have a vehicle to drive me the five miles to school. But rather than say "I'm sorry" or "It won't happen again," she had said, indignantly, that I'd gone to work with my father, because parents are the real educators of children, and perhaps the school should consider adding a bring-your-child-to-work day to the school calendar, since children certainly learn much more from their own parents. Perhaps that was part of her genius. She could turn a question around 180 degrees and refashion it into an accusation—repositioning the finger of blame. Before they knew it, *they* were apologizing to *her*.

...

The engine hums louder at the back of the plane. I rest my hand around the empty plastic cup with its one lone cube jostling against the turbulence and look out into the night. I had an old drama teacher who used to say that when an irresistible force comes up against an immovable object, you have dramatic tension. A rivulet of water crawls down the window, determined. The doctor—when I was finally able to reach him—had explained that we couldn't force her into rehab, she had to go voluntarily, and even if we got her as far as the door, she could leave at any time. Kai has become like a broken record on the subject of not thinking about it, of not letting it take over my life. "Try to think of something else." I pull the SkyMall catalogue from the seat pocket in front of me.

Jack is holding Chloe in his arms, standing off to the right at the end of the long glass hallway in the Albuquerque airport. On the drive to Santa Fe, Chloe sleeps while Jack and I circle the Mom situation. We have four days to get a handle on things. We speculate and hypothesize uselessly about things we can't control. Maybe Alzheimer's came first and she's drinking to self-medicate. Maybe it's the drinking that's causing the memory loss. Maybe the move from her big house into a small house in a retirement community has made her overly disoriented. Maybe we could get her into rehab. Maybe Roberta can help us. Is Mom still dating Rod? As we get closer to Santa Fe, the conversation slides into silence. At the intersection of St. Francis and Cerillos, I watch two gophers—the exact colour of the ground—scurry along the railway tracks and disappear down a hole.

She stands before me as if she's about to turn and go into the kitchen, that sort of midway stance she does. She lifts her hands and gestures before the words come. "But ... I'm sorry, I don't want to sound ... whose baby is that?"

"It's Chloe, Mom. Jack's daughter."

"Jack? You mean my son, Jack?"

"That's right."

"Jack, the firefighter? Who has all the girlfriends?" I'll have to remember to tell him that one—if he ever decides to come back in the house. I could use a little help fielding these waves of distance. We've been here all of an hour and already she's terrifying me. She seems worse than even a few months ago. She lifts her hands before she speaks, like someone who's trying to get directions straight. As in, "... so after I take the left ... I'm going to make a right ... or do I stay straight?"

I bounce Chloe on my hip to cover the shaking that's coming over my body.

"I don't mean to sound—I don't know what you'd call it, but I think it's a little rude of him to not tell me he had a baby."

"But he did, Mom." I'm not sure how to lead her back onto solid ground with sensitivity. "Remember, we went out to California a month ago?"

"I was in California?"

"Yes, you and I visited Jack and Iona."

"And Jack lives with Iona?"

"Mm-hmm." *What the fuck? What's he doing out there? He said he'd be five minutes.*

She keeps on. "And is he coming here to visit too?"

"He is here, Mom, that's how Chloe got here. We all arrived today. He's right outside, talking on the phone, he'll be in in a second."

I can feel her coming back onto the path. I can see it in her face. "Oh, I see." She comes over and does a scrunchy face at Chloe, taking her tiny pink fingers in her own thinning bird hand. "Hi, little sweetie, little ..."

"Chloe."

"Sweet little Chloe."

Finally, the screen door closes and Jack comes back in, tucking his cell phone into his back pocket. "Hey." He looks at his mother with his daughter and smiles at the pretty picture they make.

"I was just explaining to Mom who Chloe is," I say, ruthlessly.

He looks at me. "What?"

Mom stops making baby faces at Chloe and looks up again, confused. "Well, I don't know why you would have a baby and not tell me about it," she starts up again and I watch his face fall. I don't know why I did it. I guess I'm scared and I want him to be scared too. I want this to be a fugue state, an anomaly—I want to wake up in the morning and find her returned to her old self. I tell Jack that I'm going to change Chloe's diaper and I walk out of the room, leaving him with Mom.

There's a two-hour time difference between Montreal and Santa Fe, and being an early riser, my normal six a.m. wake-up becomes four a.m. I tiptoe into the kitchen and survey the scene. There's an unpacked box on the counter in the far corner, a kettle on the stove, and a Bodum next to that. I fill the kettle and put it on. I check the cabinets for cleaning products. Nothing. I go into the bathroom and try not to look at the vanity area—which belongs in a New York City subway station—or the toilet, which is worse. I can't see in the mirror for all the splatter. I look at the clippings of Mom's hair in the sink, and realize she's probably cut her bangs in anticipation of our arrival. She often trimmed her bangs when someone special was coming to visit. I feel a pang of longing at this glimmer of the old her reflecting back from the scunge-lined sink.

The kettle whistles. Over coffee, I make a new list. I have a second cup of coffee and double-check the list. I look at my watch. It's not even five a.m. yet. I decide to take Mom's dog to the dog run on Alameda. "Come on, Bowie. Come on, sweet boy. Let's get you some exercise."

Jack and I start with the interventions that very morning and continue with them every day we're there, realizing almost instantly how futile they are. She listens, seemingly happy for the attention, and then says something like, "You kids are so dear. I'm fine. My memory is fine. What do you

mean my friends have been calling you? Like who? Oh, well ...
Roberta. That figures. Do you know Roberta used to complain
about the light I had over my garage? She had some problems
herself. I wouldn't listen to anything Roberta—I'm listening ...
Of course, I love you ... No, I'm not trying to torture you. But
I don't have any problems with my brain. I promise I'm going
to cut back. I've actually been meaning to cut back ... Oh no,
I don't want to go into a hospital. What would I do, sit there?
Would I have to stay overnight? No, I don't think I want to do
that ... Well, I've had a lot of depression in my life, you know."

The intervention sessions are all virtually identical and
are always followed by her going to the kitchen and pouring
some "orange juice." She's always very pleased with herself,
thinking she's tricked us.

After one such failed intervention we take her to the bank
and get ourselves put on her account—the bank manager
is relieved to see us. We sign all the papers. Then we visit
her financial adviser, Doug. Doug is a tidy, gentle man,
sitting perfectly straight behind his clean, empty desk. We
explain much the same thing to Doug as we explained at
the bank. We choose our words carefully: "She's under a lot
of pressure lately and is having trouble remembering all
the details of finances and things like that." We give him
the *you-know-what-we're-here-for-right?* look and he gives
us the *yes-I-most-certainly-do* look. He confirms with Mom
that he will send her monthly statements to us and keep us
updated on her finances in general, and she signs some papers
to that effect.

After our appointment with Doug, we head home to eat something and attempt some sort of cleaning. Once Chloe falls asleep for her nap, Jack announces, with some desperation, that he's going for a run. He takes Bowie and heads out. Mom and I are left in the living room. As she nibbles her cracker, monologuing on the subject of how inconsiderate her neighbour is, I watch the crumbs fall into the cracks of the ninety-three-inch pale-wheat down-cushioned sofa, remembering when she ordered it from the Crate and Barrel catalogue. The sofa has moved from house to house with her, each a little smaller than the one before, her accommodations shrinking alongside her mental capacity. The enormous sofa is necessary, however, to maintain the illusion that nothing has changed.

Finding it impossible to sit still and listen as she complains about the woman who has attempted to help her plant some flowers, I suggest that maybe, in this beautifully landscaped retirement community, a house with a blue tarp nailed to the side, draped over an enormous stack of mouldy furniture, atop a lawn with long yellowing grass might be considered an eyesore to some. Here comes the tone. I pretend to look something up on my phone.

"No. Now first of all, Cassie, it's the house that's too small. It's not my fault. Where am I supposed to put all my things? I'm not going to pay for a storage unit when I have a house. It's my lawn, I can do what I want."

She claims she hung the tarp out of consideration for her neighbours. To keep everything contained and protected from the rain. And how's she supposed to know which plants are weeds and which might be considered wildflowers? I resist reminding her that she was once a landscape designer. She says she likes the look of the wild growth and wants her lawn to be like that, and her neighbours "can damned well deal with it."

I try to explain that she doesn't own the house, she's renting it. She's part of a community now and has to sort of go with the flow. This is such an outrageous suggestion, she actually laughs. She gets up and heads to the kitchen. She needs more wine. There's a part of me that's taking perverse pleasure in provoking her. I call out to her in the kitchen, "Why don't we give the furniture to Habitat for Humanity." I realize I've been doing that a lot lately: intentionally suggesting something I know will set her off.

She comes back into the living room—still monologuing angrily—and sits on the couch. I walk out of the room. "I can hear you—I'm just grabbing a sheet from the closet."

"What?"

I am moving at a speed she can't keep up with. She's talking about freeloaders now, and how she's worked her whole life and she's not giving a single thing to Habitat for Humanity. I go to the couch she's not sitting on, and holding a folded sheet in one hand, lift a couch cushion, only to recoil, dropping the cushion and stifling a small cry. She hasn't noticed. All around the inner edge of the sofa is a solid ring of black mouse droppings and old crumbs. I ask where the vacuum cleaner is. She chuckles. "Oh, Murph. You don't need to vacuum. The house is fine."

The sound of the vacuum drowns out her voice. I keep vacuuming long after the mouse droppings are gone. I am vibrating as though I've had ten cups of coffee. I shut off the vacuum as she finishes the last swallow from her glass. She heads to the kitchen for a refill, calling out, "I'm just getting some orange juice. Would you like a glass of juice?"

"No thanks, Mom."

I remember when her house was magnificent, when it was featured in *House Beautiful* magazine, when friends would stop by just to see what she's done with the place.

The next morning, she's in the kitchen trying to make coffee—one of the few things she still does in the kitchen—but her Bodum doesn't work anymore. Grains pass the filter easily and make the coffee sandy, but she refuses to get a new one. I plunge the coffee for her and then hold the little strainer over her cup to catch the grinds.

"We're going to Walmart today," I announce. I've started a new list. The lists have become a kind of security blanket, giving the necessary illusion that I have some sort of control. Today's list: silverware tray, dish rack, mop, shampoo, and conditioner. She tells me it isn't necessary, that she has everything she needs. But having just discovered she hasn't showered in four months, I insist. She reluctantly accommodates me, and we go. We are standing in the kitchenware aisle perusing silverware trays. I pick up a nice bamboo tray for $14.95. "What about this one?"

She takes it from my hands, turns it over and back again, and then, catching sight of the price tag, twists her face as

# *thirty-two*

THE NEXT DAY, Jack drives us to Mom's assessment appointment with the neurologist. It's a ten o'clock appointment and both Jack and I notice she's foregone her usual morning "juice." She's in top form and seems almost like herself. We'll come to learn it isn't an accident she's managed to go this long, living her life as if nothing's wrong: she knows when to pull out her performance face, and It. Is. Good.

We sit in the waiting area of the hospital while she goes for her brain scan and her assessment with Dr. Nguyen. He's much friendlier with her than he is with us; it's clear he thinks we've wasted his time. After the appointment, she and Dr. Nguyen walk out of the room together talking and laughing like old friends. Dr. Nguyen tells us he'll have the results quickly, but he doesn't think we have anything to worry about. He says he'll have the test and the scan sent over to Dr. Valdez, her physician.

Later in the day, when we go to Dr. Valdez's office to hear the results, Mom listens quietly as Dr. Valdez tells her that her scan is in an acceptable range: "There is some shrinkage of grey matter, but there are a number of incidents in your history that could account for this." He also tells us she performed well in the assessment and that all looks good. He says this with a smile. This is good news. Jack and I exchange a look. We watch our mother, grinning happily. "Well, I'm happy to hear that I'm normal. And who, exactly, proclaimed this?" She has had many glasses of "juice" between her morning appointment with the neurologist and this four o'clock appointment with Dr. Valdez.

"Dr. Nguyen, who you saw this morning, said you did very well on your tests."

"I saw a doctor this morning?"

His face falls. "Yes ... Do you remember seeing Dr. Nguyen this morning?"

"No. I'm here now, at the clinic, but I didn't see anyone this morning."

He leads her along with some clues as to what the appointment was, and she seems to get that she's supposed to remember having had a doctor's appointment.

I want to scream, "Leading the witness!" But it's too late.

"Oh yes, of course, I remember. Dr. Nguyen, wasn't it?" Dr. Valdez has said his name at least ten times in as many minutes.

The doctor smiles. It's clear he wants all to be well and for us to be out of his office. But he isn't going to get his wish.

The story Mom concocts to describe her appointment has Dr. Nguyen's office as a kind of space station, she says she had to answer strange, inappropriate questions, and that the doctor hovered over her menacingly the whole time, occasionally even making threatening statements.

When we're leaving the office, Dr. Valdez concedes that though she tested well, she's clearly suffering some memory loss. He recommends that she see a psychotherapist at his clinic, to get a better sense of exactly how bad things are.

We have wanted to trust doctors throughout this process— to put our mother into the hands of professionals and say, "Please help us." Dr. Valdez seems, on the surface, to be a nice man, likeable. But that's all—he doesn't want to do anything that will result in Mom not liking him. Doesn't want to make more work for himself. Whatever she has asked of him, he has said yes. This is my first impression. I want to be wrong. I want to discover that there is more to this man. But later that night, Jack and I find Mom's toiletry bag. It contains roughly ten prescription bottles, all with the name Dr. Valdez written on the label. That's when Jack explains to me what benzodiazepines are. Jesus Christ. He reads off the bottles: lorazepam, diazepam, Zoloft … *hammer, eraser, black ice, broken bottle, snake eating rat, battle cry to an empty field, river with no dam, sentence with no period.* Finally, he stops.

# thirty-three

"SO, LET ME GET this straight." Kai is standing with his hands on his hips, his brow deeply furrowed. "You're going to ask Oliver to go out and take care of your mother?"

"I know it's not the perfect plan ..."

"Not the perfect plan? That's a bit of an understatement."

"What would you suggest we do?"

"Get her into rehab, take the car away, put her into assisted living."

He's starting to annoy me.

"Do you really think my mother is going to sit idly by while we take her car away and stick her in a home? Maybe you're not aware, but there are actually laws that give a person rights over their own existence."

He sighs heavily.

"God! Can't you just trust that I've thought this through," I yell, hoping a display of outrage will distract from the fact that I *haven't* thought it through. Or rather, I have but without arriving at any satisfactory solutions. It's been a month since I went out with Jack, and there are things we have to address, and this is the only option we have at the moment. Of course, I know she works Oliver's last nerve, that this is way too big of an ask for him—for anyone. She likes to go on roughly ten errands a day, keeping busy is what gives her life shape, and Oliver is not going to want to cart her all around town. These are things I know. But we have to get her off the road and he's willing to help and that's something. Besides, he'll have a roof over his head and a small salary, so they'll each be getting something out of the deal.

Ollie sends me a text a few days after he arrives.

OLIVER:
Driving Miss Crazy

He begins with diluting her wine. He puts his foot down about the number of errands he's willing to run. My phone rings constantly: Mom calls to complain that Oliver is acting like her boss. She wants me to come out and tell him to stop it right now. He gets her shut off at her two local haunts. He gets her to an AA meeting. (She leaves after the first five minutes, and he finds her at a bar across the street—but at least he got her there.) He says that he's talking to her about alcohol and about quitting and that she seems to be listening.

Jack and I are surprised and thrilled. So much so that we book tickets to go out. We will make a solid try at getting her into rehab—the three of us, together. A formal intervention. There's a rehab centre in Santa Fe that has a six-week program with recovery activities like horseback riding and painting. We are hopeful, cautiously optimistic.

Oliver picks us up at the airport and tells us about Mom's new boyfriend. For the briefest of moments, when he says the word *boyfriend*, I have a flash of hope. Might it be someone who can help us?

"What's he like?"

"Have you ever seen *Leaving Las Vegas*?"

"Oh shit."

"Yeah, he's like that, only not good-looking."

"How long has he been on the scene?"

"About a week."

To get to the kitchen in this new, even smaller house she's moved into, after being evicted from the last small house, I have first to pass by her bedroom door and then through the living room. It's 4:27 a.m. and I slip out of my room without making a sound. She won't fully wake up until eleven thirty, but she often gives a false start at five a.m. I tiptoe past the closed door, listening for movement within. I'm so preoccupied with being unseen and unheard, I nearly miss the man sitting in the living room, a spectre in silhouette lit by the faint flickering of the television on mute.

I start at the sight of him there on my mother's couch, with his feet on the coffee table. He's tall—even sitting down, this is apparent; red face, shock of yellow hair, belly sagging into dirty, blue-jean lap, legs ending in worn-out cowboy boots, some sort of power drink clutched in the hand resting on the arm of the couch, the other hand scratching the back of his head.

This is my mother's new boyfriend, Kenny—or Kenneth, as she grandly calls him. I've already met him—just last night—but my mind must have weeded him from my consciousness, because he has taken me completely by surprise. I pass in front of him and move toward the kitchen. I walk the way I used to walk in New York when I finished a late shift, my every surface an impenetrable shield of iron. The sun is not yet up, I'm not awake enough to think clearly, but my animal instincts have shifted into high alert; and what they're signalling is that this man, sitting in my mother's living room, defiling her couch, is a man staking a claim, a man who will not be easily blocked out or pushed aside.

"Can't sleep either?" he says to my back as I enter the kitchen.

"Jet lag." I give as little as humanly possible.

"Been up since two," he continues. His mouth is worn down by chewing tobacco and years of drinking hard liquor, and his words come out somewhere between speech and slur. "Just watching a movie. Y'ever seen this one? Got Tom Cruise in it and that coloured guy, what's his name again?"

There's no actual door to the kitchen, so I can hear him easily, but I figure the threshold between rooms gives me a pass on answering. My empty stomach is beginning to turn. I put the kettle on.

I want to say he's an anachronism there in my mother's living room, on the Crate and Barrel couch, framed by linen curtains, feet resting on the brushed-stone coffee table. But the couch is dilapidated, the curtains are dirty and torn, and there's a crack across the centre of the table. The illusion she has managed to maintain these past few years has lost its sheen. Nevertheless, Kenny is one step too far, a glitch in the system, that new symptom after all the lesser symptoms that lets you know what you thought might have been the flu is in fact leukemia, or possibly a brain tumour. He's that patch of light on the scan that lets you know the cancer has metastasized. He's the anti-Hugh. I need to concentrate.

Why is he awake? He was so drunk last night he fell face down on the floor carrying a plate from the kitchen to the dining room. In the course of the half an hour we were at the dinner table, he managed to call my mother's octogenarian neighbour "a bitch," "a cunt," and "a rich she-devil." Mom had chuckled as if he were a naughty child. "Kenneth! Watch your language."

Shouldn't he be sleeping that off? Does he do cocaine? Crack, maybe? I intuit that he's up because he knows that we, the kids, are going to be his biggest obstacle in getting his hooks into Mom. I intuit that he's too stupid to have any sort of plan, that he's going to feel it out as he goes, that the most important thing—in his mind—is to be present, to not miss anything.

The kettle whistles, and I realize I'm looking over my shoulder—that for all my bluster I'm afraid of him. I recognize underbelly when I see it.

I walk back through the living room with my coffee. I don't say a word to him or even look at him. I close the door to my room. There's no lock, so I push my suitcase against it and climb back into bed to begin today's list. I have barely picked up my pen when there's a knock at the door. I freeze. Before I can think what to do, the suitcase begins sliding into the room.

"Murphy? Are you up?" Mom pokes her head around to see what's blocking the door. Her tired, red eyes widen at the sight of the suitcase. "You aren't going anywhere, are you?"

I exhale. "No, Mom. You can go back to bed. I'm still on Montreal time, that's all."

She rubs her eyes. "You'll still be here when I wake up?"

"Of course."

"Okay." She pulls the door closed behind her.

I click on my browser. I open Twitter, then the *New York Times*, then click on my email.

I have four junk emails and one non-junk. From my father. One line.

*I'm standing under the neon exit sign.*

My father has lung cancer. When I found this out, I thought about calling him, thought about the various things I could say, ways I could say I'm sorry. But it didn't feel right, so I emailed him a poem. I didn't know if he still checked his email or if he would write back, but he wrote back the very same day. A full page of commentary. So a few days later, I sent him an another poem. He wrote back. And in this way, for the last few months, we've had more regular communication than we had my entire growing up. I prop my pillows against the headboard and google Bashō.

Several hours later, I'm sitting in the kitchen on a stool by the back screened door, laptop on the counter beside me and Bowie on the floor at my feet, when Mom enters. She doesn't see me. She moves as if pulled by forces greater than herself, drawn straight to the fridge. I can almost see the demons sitting on her shoulder, helping her lift the bottle of wine, petting her long strands of thinning hair while she fills a glass to the rim with her nectar of withering. She is sipping herself into the underworld.

"Oh! Morning, sweetie," she says, noticing me there by the screen door, breathing the only fresh air in the house. I offer to make her some toast. She puts the cap on the wine bottle and closes the fridge. She takes a sip from her glass, and then sets it on the counter to push up her sleeve and contemplate her forearm. It's as thin as a twig. The veins are visible through her papery skin. She doesn't like it. It's not attractive. "My arms have seemed so thin lately. What do you suppose it could be?" I pause; I know that saying it out loud doesn't help, but what's the alternative? Leave the elephant in the room to trample us all? I know it will make her angry and sad. It makes *me* angry and sad. "Do you think it might have to do with how much alcohol you drink?"

"Oh, fucking hell." She slides her sleeve back down and takes up her glass. "Here we go again. You kids have no idea about my life." I'm still looking at her, she knows she's not off the hook. "I have this much wine with dinner." With the hand that isn't holding the glass of wine, she uses her thumb and forefinger to indicate an inch. She has put so much effort into hiding her drinking from us, she's unwittingly hidden it from herself in the process. She has maintained the architecture of her daily routine, buying no more than two or three bottles at a time—because buying ten bottles would be a bold admission that she has a problem. When she pours her daytime wine, she tops it up with orange juice, and when she insists that it's just juice, it gradually becomes clear that in some submerged, deluded way, she believes herself. She must, because when we get in the car and I tell her she has to dump it out, she says, "It's just juice. Taste it if you don't believe me."

It's possible, I reason, that she pours the wine and then—like with everything else—she forgets. And it's hard to yell at her as she is now: ninety pounds at most, the unwashed hair, the little black spots under her fingernails and toenails, the daily nosebleeds. This is what those in the know call end-stage alcoholism. She has lost any possibility of choice. I can feel the fine line between anger and grief, though I know she perceives only the anger. I am alienating her more and more each day. Since I arrived, she has been affectionate with me, touching me gently and showing me this and that around the house, and all I have been able to do is shrug her off. It's not only my mother who has become a small child.

She is now standing in the doorway. I sigh. I know how

# thirty-four

"COME ON IN." Leslie's office is in the back of her home on a side street off Canyon Road. It's very northern California, decorated with teak retro furniture and a palm tree in the corner. Leslie, senior care advocate, is equally West Coast, with short, tousled grey hair, freckles, and eyes at once serene and alert. She wears a loose black top over beige pants.

After bringing me an iced tea, she gets straight to it. "So, why don't you tell me about your mother."

"Um, well, she's an alcoholic and she's suffering memory loss."

"Has she always been a drinker or is this a recent development?"

"Fairly recent. Well ... I mean, she's always had wine with dinner."

"Nightly?"

"Yeah, pretty much."

"How much wine?"

"I guess like two, sometimes three glasses."

"Then the alcoholism is not new?"

"Um ..." I'm not sure if Leslie is asking a question or making a statement. "Well, it's nothing compared to what she drinks now."

Leslie continues, "It's quite common for someone with a two-to-three-drinks-a-night habit to slide into heavy drinking later in life when, for example, a spouse dies, or retirement age comes, or with any of these kinds of changes that come after midlife. You find a *lot* of elders in AA."

I find it difficult to think of my mother as part of a demographic. I want to tell Leslie that my mother is one of a kind but can't think of how to express this without sounding ridiculous.

"My mother is not your average alcoholic," I say, realizing as the words are out of my mouth just how ridiculous they sound. I look at Leslie to see if she's laughing. She's not. She's listening. "What I mean is it's challenging to get people to help us because they meet her and she's beautiful and charming— she *really* knows how to pull out the charm, it's amazing—and then people end up annoyed with us for wasting their time. We're completely at a loss, we don't know what to do."

"You said she has memory loss. Could you describe that? When did it start?"

I think of Mom's summer in Montreal. "I'd say maybe a year ago. She's always suffered from anxiety, and while the drinking part of it has accelerated, I'd say there's been a deeper change that began well before the heavy drinking started. Like she's been getting darker or something."

"Could you give me a bit of a timeline of the last few years, when the drinking and the memory loss accelerated, as you say?"

"First, we noticed that when we talked to her on the phone, she would repeat herself. She's a talker, you know, like phone calls with my mother are usually an hour long, at least. And in the past couple years it's become a thing that she'll repeat a story—like a full ten-minute story, two or three times in the same conversation. And then she'll call me again, later in the day, forgetting that we've already spoken. And shortly after that we started getting calls from friends and neighbours, and I suppose that's when we noticed she was drinking pretty much all day every day. So my brother and I came out here to try to ... I don't know, do something about it, I guess. And now, looking back on that trip, it seems so ridiculous. Like putting a Band-Aid on a severed limb or something. We took over her bank account and cleaned her house and tried to do interventions and tried to get her licence taken away and tried to get her a caregiver—she absolutely will not hear of moving into a facility. But pretty much everything we tried failed because she was countering us at every turn. She saw us as trying to control her, which obviously we were, but what else are we supposed to do? Oh, and now there's a boyfriend on the scene who's an even worse alcoholic than she is."

I realize I'm scratching the side of my neck. Stress activates my eczema, and my neck and forearms are covered in welts.

I stuff my hands into my lap and squeeze them between my legs to keep from itching.

Leslie asks, "And what about you and your brothers? How are you taking care of yourselves?"

"What do you mean?"

"How are you dealing with this trauma?"

The word throws me off momentarily. "We're trying to get her some help. That's why I'm here."

"What you are doing to help your mother is very noble and I think I'll be able to help you with that, but what about you? How are *you* dealing with this trauma?" she asks, ignoring my reticence. I know where she's headed, I know that the words *narcissism*, *boundaries*, and *self-care* are about to come up. *Mental health people are so predictable. Where's Hugh when you need him.* I want to leave. I want this meeting to be over. I know Leslie is trying to help, but my skin is itching like mad and I'm getting that vibration in my chest that makes it difficult to concentrate. I force myself to focus on Leslie, who is saying, "You might be finding that a single word from your mother sets you off, because this current behaviour, while at a whole new level, is not fundamentally new, it sounds like it's an amplification of familiar dynamics. And this awakens anger and guilt and shame, which can be difficult to cope with on top of trying to care for your mother. I would suggest that when you're out here you give yourself space whenever you can. Find moments when you can be away from her. Walk out of the room if she's pushing your buttons. You need to take care of yourself."

. . .

The next morning, I accompany my mother and Kenny to his old house to pick up his things. I drive with my mother sitting beside me and Kenny barking directions from the back seat. He fits back there about as well as an ogre in Cinderella's carriage. We pull up in front of a small adobe house in a suburban neighbourhood on the south side of Santa Fe. There's a tall man in a baseball cap adjusting a sprinkler on the front lawn. Kenny speaks to him for a few minutes, they shake hands, and Kenny walks into the house through the open garage door.

"What do you think of Kenny?" Mom asks.

"I think it's too soon for him to be moving in and that he's taking advantage of you," I say, knowing I should couch my concerns in gentler terms, that she's going to get defensive. But since Kenny is, at this very moment, getting his things to move into her house, it's clear a harder line is going to be necessary.

"You don't even know him."

"*You* don't even know him, Mom. He has a problem with alcohol, and I don't exactly think that's the best thing for you to be around right now."

"What's that supposed to mean?"

"I think you know you have a problem with drinking. It's not the first time we've talked about it."

"You kids completely exaggerate how much I drink. I have a glass of wine with dinner and that's all."

"Okay, Mom." I roll my eyes.

"What?"

"I must be concerned for nothing."

"You are concerned for nothing." Pause. "So, what do you think of Kenny?"

I want to cry. Her memory is gone. Completely gone.

"I think he's great," I say.

"He is pretty great, isn't he?" She smiles as we watch him through the windshield, emerging from the garage with a brown paper bag clutched in one hand and a beer in the other.

He gets into the back seat and leans forward to set his beer on the console between me and Mom. He puts the bag on the back seat. I turn around fully to look him in the eye. I speak slowly and clearly, my words freighted with the declaration of war they contain. "Sorry, Kenny, but we're not going anywhere with that beer in the car."

"Cassie. Don't be rude," Mom says, trying to catch my attention, but I keep my eyes on Kenny.

There is a long silence. He meets my gaze in reptilian stillness.

"*I'll* drive if you have a problem with it." Mom tries again to break the tension.

After what feels like an eternity but is perhaps only a matter of seconds, Kenny abruptly changes his demeanour, dropping confrontational for happy-go-lucky.

"Of course. What was I thinking, I'll dump it out."

This toxic specimen of human flesh is a top-notch actor. I watch him throw the can of beer in the black trash can just inside the garage. The nature of evil is like that of smoke or shapeshifters or illness: it adapts to its host. Just as the cancer cell mimics the healthy one, so evil infiltrates the vulnerable, attaching itself inseparably. As I turn the key in the ignition, I realize my brothers and I are in for a fight, and the battle-ground is going to be our mother. Kenny climbs back into the car, sliding his bag over beside him. And with that brown paper bag of belongings, he moves into my mother's house and into her life.

# thirty-five

*I'M WALKING UNDER a waterfall. A cave and a precipice. The sound of falling water is loud, light streams through sound and the falling water transforms into ribbons of warblers and starlings* and I land in a sun-drenched tangle of legs and sheet and hair. The singing of birds is deafening. The last of the water slides back through the loose seams of sleep. I'm in a room with a door in the corner. I'm in a bed next to a table with a lamp. There is also a pad of paper and pencil if I remembered to leave them. I scribble fast and light, holding the pad to my face. *Asleep under waterfall, Dad called on phone I answered but he wouldn't speak. I kept saying, "Dad? Are you there?"* I stop struggling to hold the pad and pencil up to my face. They fall to my stomach, and I turn toward the strong desert light. Through the screen by my bed, a small rabbit is eating grass. The grass is long and dry, and the rabbit is looking at me sideways the way rabbits do. The dream of my father lies open in my hand.

. . .

My father married a woman named Darlene, an ultra-religious, climate-denying, Trump-supporting southern conservative. They've been together for seven years now. Two months ago, near the end of March, Darlene called to tell me and Oliver that our father was dying of lung cancer. Six months was optimistic.

I went to visit.

Getting off the plane in Knoxville, Tennessee, was like stepping in under the big top. Darlene met me at the airport and drove me to the house, crying and talking the whole way, and we pulled up in front of the small ranch-style home sooner than I was prepared for.

Inside the door, gravity increased. Time stood still as I took in my father there at the other side of the room, near to drowning in the velour recliner that held what was left of his tiny body. His overlarge teeth seemed to have come loose inside his skull, his eyes were huge blue marbles looking up at me in childlike innocence.

"Cassie!" He lifted his thin arms.

Was he making a gesture to hug me? I fought against the earth's pull, set down my bag and went to him. I crouched in front of him, and we managed a hug. He was wearing a pressed dark blue shirt that I surmised he had put on especially for my arrival.

Having not seen my father in three years, I was hoping Darlene would leave us alone that week, but instead, she came right up beside him, sat on the arm of the recliner, and leaned against him, fluffing his white hair. My dad and I let go of each other. "Isn't it cute?" Darlene asked, indicating his hair. "Grew back all curly after the chemo." I wasn't sure what to say—my father and I didn't have the kind of relationship where I would call him cute. I noticed that Darlene was studying me. Somehow, seven years of living with my dad had led her to the conclusion that Oliver and I were people he needed to be protected from, that our estrangement from him was somehow the result of *us* leaving *him*. That we were the reason he was here, dying in this recliner. She explained how the radiation had created a hole in his remaining lung, and that they couldn't do any more surgery because he was too fragile. "Body doesn't like air in it. Tiny hole's all it took."

I looked at the tubes coming from my father's nose and at the oxygen tank beside his chair and asked Darlene where the bathroom was. "Oh now, where are my manners? Let me show you to your room. You'll sleep in Brandon's room if that's all right." Brandon is Darlene's nine-year-old nephew, who lived with them.

"As long as it's all right with Brandon," I replied.

"Oh, he'll do what he's told," Darlene said, earnestly. *Earnest* was her default mode.

Later that night, I helped Brandon with his spelling homework: Jesus is my best f-r-i-e-n-d. He also had math and Bible reading to do.

"What is Heb?" he asked, pronouncing it like *web*. "I have to memorize Heb. 11."

I told him I thought it stood for Hebrews. We looked for the passage. He said he thought it had something to do with "having faith in things we cannot see." We looked through the table of contents and found the passage he was looking for. *Now faith is the assurance of things hoped for, the conviction of things not seen. For by it the people of old received their commendation. By faith we understand that the universe was created by the word of God, so that what is seen was not made out of things that are visible.*

He studied it until he could almost recite it back to me without looking. Partway through, though, he got distracted and picked up his toy dinosaur. He held it in the air, making loud roars, while he marched it through an imaginary landscape. Darlene came out of the kitchen, waving a dishtowel at him. "Brandon, no playing with your toys until you finish that homework. You hear me?" He complained that he was tired and had already done a lot. She explained consequences to him. It was much the same as when I explained consequences to Lucy and Isabel, except that in Brandon's case if he was naughty, rather than being sent to his room, he'd be smote by God.

When my father woke up from his nap he said, decisively, that he'd like to talk to me. Darlene set down the dish she was drying, told Brandon it was time for bed, and took him out of the room. I was pretty sure my father was going to tell me about how with the radiation came the "light," that God had saved him, and that Jesus was King. I was in the ballpark. He said he wanted to explain his relationship to God. I was thankful when he acknowledged that "it must seem a little strange," and he said it had all been pretty surprising to him too. I was having a hard time reconciling my Ivy League–educated, long-time Democrat musician father with any of this.

My dad grew up in the rolling hills of Pennsylvania. He was at home in the natural world. When he and Darlene had split up for a few years, just before he was diagnosed with cancer, he'd gone to live in the woods by himself, à la Henry David Thoreau. He said that when he got back together with Darlene, part of the deal was that he'd go to church with her, that he'd stop swearing and give up being sarcastic. She'd said she wouldn't expect any level of participation in church, beyond listening. He told me that at first, he'd gone to appease Darlene, so that after the weekend he'd get to live out his side of the arrangement: two nights a week in the cabin by himself. He'd go to church on Sunday and then from Monday to Wednesday he'd be at the top of the mountain. As it happened, going to church started to be less and less of a chore; he started reading scripture on the mountain and seeing God everywhere he looked. It turned out that a cabin on the mountain and a pew in church seemed to put one in touch with the same thing. He said he didn't find God, it was more like he opened himself to the possibility and said, "Okay God, I need to see you. Show yourself to me." And according to him, God did. Not only in nature but also in his body. He said that after a year of treatment, the cancer disappeared—right at the time he'd asked God to show Himself. Also, his relationship with Darlene had flourished, the more he'd welcomed God into his life. "God saved Darlene," he explained. "She would probably be dead if it weren't for the church. There are levels of poverty down here you just wouldn't believe."

He was having a hard time talking. It took a lot of air to make sound, and everything he'd said had come out in little five- and six-word packages, as he struggled for oxygen. Finally, needing a break, he said, "But tell me about your life. How are the girls? How's Kai?"

Trying to think of something to say to my father was like fishing for a shadow. I didn't want to talk about my kids, I wanted to tell him about my own childhood, about everything he'd missed. I wanted to tell him about lilacs in the spring and sledding and wet mittens and baby goats, I wanted to tell him about my birthday dress against the cracked banister. For my fourth birthday, he'd made me a photo album, a beautiful book I still have, with black-and-white photographs printed on fibre paper and glued to card stock, with narration he'd written by hand in silver Sharpie. Even as a teenager, I'd kept it in my room, on my bedside table. Once, when I was about sixteen, Mom came in to drop a stack of laundry, and on her way out she'd casually picked up the book, flipped through it, and chuckled, "You know the funniest thing about this book?" I didn't answer. "The year he gave it to you, you were turning five, not four." She'd dropped the book on the bedside table. "He never could do anything right," she'd said, and walked out of the room.

But I didn't say any of that to my father. I gave him the information he asked for, told him about Isabel and Lucy and Kai. I tried to stay off the subject of Mom, but inevitably, magnetically, all at once, there we were.

"Ah, Mary," he said, upon hearing the update. Nobody called my mother Mary anymore, not since she was a child. She had started calling herself Nina as a teenager, and that had gradually become her name. She even had it on legal documents. I don't know how she managed that one, but I don't know how she manages most things, so I'd never given it any thought. By calling her Mary, he was refusing to accept her definition of herself.

"Here I am, hanging on to life by my fingernails, willing to do anything for a little more time, and it would seem she's trying to speed up her departure." Then, after a pause, he added, "She ruined my life."

He said this so matter-of-factly that I didn't feel any impulse to call him on it.

There was a long silence, and then, "Have you ever been in a motorboat with a leaky engine?"

I'd guessed this was a rhetorical question, so I didn't respond.

"You're going along the river, looking at the beautiful scenery, the fish in the water, the sun shining, the wind blowing through the trees, not realizing your leaking engine is leaving a wake of oil ... killing everything, slowly, beneath the surface ... Your mother is like a motorboat leaking oil. What a wake of disaster she's left behind." He paused, apparently to contemplate how much of a disaster that might be. "But we don't need to talk about Mary. Let's talk about you and me."

He closed his eyes, then, as if to say, *the words will come when they come, these are things that can't be rushed.* I felt a deep ache for this man dying in front of me, who I had wanted in my life but never had. How much easier it would be to write him off if he were a tyrant or a drunk or unfeeling, but this man was sensitive and gentle. To meet him was to like him, to want to have him in your life. Even Frank had said, "Your father was one of the kindest, most intelligent people I've ever met. He loved you kids." And then he'd added, "Your mother emasculated him in ways you can't imagine."

I can imagine.

# thirty-six

I CLOSE MY journal and text Oliver and Jack, who sleep in the next room. We decided yesterday, today is the day and we're getting an early start.

CASSIE:
Are you guys up?

OLIVER:
Yup. Meet outside in ten?

CASSIE:
Sounds good

The three of us slip around the side of the house and into the car. Oliver puts the key in the ignition and turns. We hear the dull sputter of a half push by the engine and then nothing. He reaches for the radio. "Shit. I got this stupid radio off a friend. I have to pop it out every time I shut off the car or it drains the battery."

Oliver currently has five cars and each one has its own issues. There was the Volvo with the broken heater he drove from Massachusetts to Montreal that Christmas. Or his old Volkswagen Rabbit, where the driver's side door was held closed with some duct tape and a length of rope; the passenger door was the only way in and out.

"Hang on." He gets out of the car and starts to push it backward. It's moving slowly, and Jack and I open our doors to step out into the pace of backward pushing. We hit a tiny incline and the car starts to roll on its own. At this, Oliver jumps in and puts the car in gear. We jump in too, and when he turns the ignition, the car starts and off we go.

"What crazy magic was that?" I ask.

"I just had to pop the clutch," he says.

This crafty manoeuvre, as he explains it, essentially boils down to tricking the car into thinking it's in gear. He smiles. These little moments please him. I think he hates that his life is held together with duct tape and rope, so magic counts for a lot.

The road is shiny from the sun. Piñon and sage line the streets. I'm glad I took Leslie's advice and got out of the house for something that has nothing to do with Mom. Oliver's arm hangs out the window and the Rolling Stones pipe from the battery-draining sound system. "Can you see why I want to stay here?" He's smiling. "Every day is like this ... every day."

I smile at him and at the sun and the road and the pale sage poking through pink clay. I can see why. On the narrow concrete island, a haggard woman is selling newspapers. Oliver gestures toward her. "I remember once walking somewhere with Hugh and we stopped to get a paper from one of those people, and as we walked away, Hugh said, 'Schizophrenic, but managing nicely.'"

We all laugh. Hugh always said things like that. Once at dinner, someone said something innocuous like "How was your day?" and he slammed his fist down on the table and said, "Why do Anglo-Saxons have to be so goddamned happy all the time?" He let it land for just long enough and then began laughing. Or once we were out to dinner and he told us the couple across the restaurant was separating and this dinner was a last-ditch effort to get back together, but that the woman would soon get up and leave. And sure enough, a few minutes later, the woman left. Or another one that sticks with me: "Be careful with kids born by Caesarean near an open window. They may have the impulse to jump."

When Mom and Hugh moved out to the Navajo Nation in Fort Defiance, Hugh became completely immersed in Navajo culture and cosmology. He was always walking around with a book or papers held up to his face. "Listen to this," he'd say to nobody in particular. *"Be'yoteidi, One-who-grabs-breasts, is a creature of versatile and conflicting characteristics. He is described as the son of Sun, who had intercourse with everything*

*in the world. This is the reason so many monsters were born.*
Brilliant. Absolutely brilliant." He would spout these random
sentences that made no sense to the rest of us but seemed,
to him, not only to make sense but to force everything he
knew, or thought he knew, to either fall into place or fall by
the wayside. With Oliver's guitar as constant refrain, Hugh's
words became like song lyrics; even if we didn't understand
their meaning, we felt their weight.

The *Santa Fe New Mexican,* lying next to me on the back
seat of the car, lists local bands playing in the plaza: poets
and drummers who will be in town and art exhibits not to
miss. On October 14, Gary Snyder will be speaking at the
opening of the New Mexico History Museum's exhibit *Voices
of Counterculture in the Southwest.* Oliver says Snyder lives
somewhere between Cordova and Truchas.

Before Oliver moved west to live with Mom and Hugh,
when he was still living in Massachusetts, Hugh had arranged
for him to begin seeing a Jungian psychotherapist who'd been
recommended by his own psychiatrist. The three of them
were part of those Robert Bly men's groups, that whole *Iron
John* period, and when Oliver moved west, Hugh took him
to those meetings too. The doctor put Oliver on medication, and Oliver went to his sessions every week, diligently.
During this time, I hardly recognized my brother. He was
communicative and friendly and—dare I say—organized. He
lived in an apartment—and it was clean. But then the doctor
wrote a best-selling book and ditched all his patients to write
a second book and a third and Oliver was, once again, left

to fend for himself. *A minimum of 131 songs is required for the war ceremony.*

Just after the turn-off for the Santuario de Chimayo, there is a cattle guard set into the road and Oliver slows down as the car bounces over it. After another mile or so, we come to the intersection where the road through Chimayo ends and the road to Truchas heads off to the right. There's an odd jumble of signs giving every variety of direction. One in particular jumps out: John 3:16. *For God so loved the world that he gave up his one and only Son, that whoever believes in him shall not perish, but have eternal life.* I wonder if Gary Snyder has ever done a men's group meeting. I wonder what men do at men's group meetings.

Roberta Hart's gallery has an Open sign on it, so we pull in and park. On the small gallery door, underneath the Open sign, is a note that says *Tap on the back door of the house and holler nicely,* so we do. Roberta hollers back from the bedroom for us to come in, so we do. From where we stand in the small entry, we can see her sitting on the edge of her bed. She gets up slowly. It's a strange sensation to be standing in this house that was once ours, so many years ago, when things were good ... when things were the best they would be.

I call out, "Hi, Roberta, it's Cassie, Jack, and Oliver Wolfe, Nina Wolfe's kids."

"Cassie Wolfe? How interesting. Cassie, Jack, and Oliver Wolfe. How interesting." She hobbles out of the bedroom. A little overweight, two hip replacements. From the neck up she's vibrant and funny and has this way of asking a question and then watching you with a little smile; you can almost hear her reconstructing a version of your story that she'll recount later in gossip to Margaret or Francisco. We tell her about Mom's drinking and the new boyfriend and what a disaster he is, how she's ruining her friendships by accusing people of taking things from her. Roberta gives a long sigh, and says, "Ah, Nina. She's always worked from a place of scarcity."

Mostly it's the way she says "Ah, Nina," sinking on the *Nina* and invisibly shaking her head. It's not the first time we've heard this kind of sigh, the kind of intonation that lets you know she's notorious. All the neighbours know, her recycling bin is always chock full of bottles, other dog owners at the park give her a wide berth, at the Whole Foods where she shops it's obvious the checkout people know, and people who used to be her friends don't call anymore. When her old friends talk to us, it's with sympathy. Roberta is expressing exactly that. "Margaret was up here just last week, and we talked about Nina for half an hour at least and about you kids and how you're managing ..." Roberta's good at leading phrases like that, sentences that hover somewhere between a question and a statement. She isn't asking anything, but you're definitely meant to respond. I say, "Well we're open to suggestions if you have any." *Back at ya, Roberta.* "Well, I suppose there's nothing really you can do." It's the pleasure of sharing the exchange, a badinage that's in stark contrast to Mom's monologues that invade your territory with no sense of boundaries or fair play.

Roberta can tell we need a break from the subject, so when we ask her what she's been up to, she takes the opportunity to tell us about the memoir she's writing about her years in Truchas. "You wouldn't believe the characters you meet up here." And when she gets going, the segues from one anecdote to the next are barely perceptible, such that when we try to recall later how a particular story fits in, we aren't able. She begins by telling us about Jesus the bartender who needs a wife. Roberta suggested to him that he consider her, since she, in turn, was looking for a husband. He asked her if she could cook and she said, "Yeah, I can cook." "What kind of food?" Jesus asked. "You know, American. Like meatloaf and mashed potatoes," she said. And then she told us that since she'd done the whole Julia Child thing, she added that she could cook French too. "French," Jesus had exploded back at her. "No way—they eat horses, I need beans. This will never work out." She then made a mystery segue to Clarence the rapist who wouldn't rape you if you looked him in the eye, and how Margaret was visiting and saw Clarence on the street and—knowing the rumour—locked eyes with him so fiercely he was forced to turn away. When Roberta asked what on earth she was doing, Margaret explained and Roberta laughed and said, "Oh that's not Clarence, that's Calvin ..." She begins another story and I look to the window at the end of the table where Oliver is sitting. Hugh's temporary hospital bed had been set up just there. That exact spot.

We say goodbye to Roberta and start walking down toward the back field, hoping our memory will kick in and we'll find our way. Jack taps me on the shoulder and points to a barely visible path off to the right. We step onto the path and start walking. Once our feet are moving, we begin to recognize things. The lone black tree in the long, yellow grass off to our left. Blackfoot daisy hangs over the arroyo beneath a sign marked Coyote Crossing.

The altitude turns my breathing shallow, my eyelids become heavy. My foot lands on soft pressed clay and the heat rises as we enter further into our collective past. *When the Holy Ones, after great difficulty, had prevailed upon Dark Thunder to agree to the restoration of Rainbow and the two war parties had carefully prepared themselves, all of the gods who were invited came except be'yoteidi.*

I take a photo of the Coyote Crossing sign. Water trickles through massive corrugated metal pipes. Up ahead I see the gate. There is some orange rope now tied around the wooden pillars. *Buddhist?* The house comes into view. Oliver is a few paces behind, as is his way. A long-haired grey cat runs out of the acacia and trots along with us. It's her house now, she'll show us the way. We cross the arroyo and walk toward the house, the first house our mother built in New Mexico.

"Here it is," Jack says.

Oliver and I turn to see that Jack has stopped walking. He's about three yards off the path, standing by the Gambel oak grove. We turn away from the house and traipse through the dried grass to stand beside Jack, who takes his cap off and wipes his forehead with the back of his arm. Oliver crouches down and pets the cat. There's a simple bar on two supports that marks the spot. Not like something that would typically mark a grave, like a cross or a stone. Just this wooden arch. I turn around and face the way Hugh would be facing. The mountains have a dark anvil-shaped cloud hanging between them.

When cumulus clouds grow vertically, they're becoming thunderclouds. This is due to the heat from the ground that pushes the cloud upward. Mountains are your best bet for seeing this in action. The heat nestles in the valleys and its only escape is up. When a cloud gets that anvil shape and starts to tilt from the weight of the rain, darkening on the bottom, it's about to come crashing down. This is why lightning and thunder happen late in the day; it takes a while for this heat to gather and push up into the sky. *When the gods assembled to consider the war between Dark Thunder and Winter Thunder, Changing Woman was the first to enter. As soon as the subject was broached, she said decisively, "I did not bear these children to go to war, but to rid the world of monsters."*

"Cumulonimbus," Jack says, reading my mind.

It'll rain before nightfall.

# *thirty-seven*

"YOU'RE WASTING YOUR TIME," Oliver says.

"But we have to try. We can't just stop trying," I counter.

"Suit yourself. But don't say I didn't warn you."

Oliver has called to tell me he can't take it anymore. He's moving back to Massachusetts. I beg him to wait until Jack and I get there. I tell him we'll be out in two weeks, and we'll try one more intervention, one more attempt to get her into detox, and it'll be best if it's all three of us. He relents; he'll wait until we get there. Two weeks later, the three of us are together again, two months since our last detox effort. And we try, we really do try, but Oliver is right: it's a waste of time. With Kenny around, nothing positive is going to happen.

The four days we've been here feel like four hundred, and at last the hour of our departure has arrived. We're in the living room and Mom is standing in front of the door. Her eyes narrow and it's clear she's making a determined effort to walk in a straight line. She's angry that we're leaving and is going to make it as difficult as possible for us to go. "I can't go anywhere until I find my phone and call Kenny." She stands against the door and crosses her arms. "I'm sure he'll be here soon." It's hard to be authoritative when your memory only extends to the end of the sentence.

Jack continues to use his slow, calm voice. "Mom, Kenny told you this morning he's busy and we should go to Albuquerque without him. Oliver will drive us, so you don't even need to come. Just hang out, Kenny will be back in an hour."

This is unfathomable, so she decides he simply hasn't said it. She's been doing this a lot lately; if something happens that makes her even mildly upset, reality becomes malleable. "I need to find my purse and then we can pick up Kenny and leave."

She wanders into the kitchen. Jack groans.

"We have to get out of here. Should we call an Uber?" I look at him in desperation, knowing there's nothing either of us can do to make this situation better.

"What will that cost, like a hundred bucks?" he asks.

"Probably more."

"I suppose we could. But we're not really in a hurry, we don't need to be there at any particular time."

"It's not the checking-into-the-hotel part that's time sensitive. It's the getting-the-fuck-out-of-here that can't happen fast enough."

264

Oliver strolls into the living room with the guitar strapped to his chest. "What's going on?" he asks, noodling up and down the strings.

"Mom lost the car keys, and we need to go."

"Oh. Well, I hate to break it to you, but you're not getting out of here any time soon," he says, not grasping the situation.

"We have to get out of here. Now," I say, and watch his face until I see the realization click. He's been living out here with Mom for six months. He knows well the sensation of not being able to take another minute. He's gotten good at hiding behind his guitar, in his guitar, strings making sound, creating music that lifts him up and out of Hades. Musical oblivion in the face of alcoholic oblivion is a studied state he has mastered, a door only he can open.

He sets down the guitar. "But wait, don't *you* have the keys?"

"Yes, I *did* have them," Jack answers, "but she snuck up behind me, grabbed them out of my hand, and ran away—literally ran away, laughing. She stopped halfway out of the room to turn around and laugh in my face, so I could see ... I don't know what ... that she had won? I suppose I could have wrestled them from her, but I'm trying to stay above the crazy."

"Right. Good luck with that."

None of us say anything for a moment. And then Oliver says, "Okay, well we should look in the kitchen and her bedroom first. The keys are usually in one of those two ... places ..." His voice drifts off as he walks over to the window, suddenly distracted.

"Shit. Kenny."

Jack and I join him at the window.

"Fuck. He wasn't supposed to be here for another hour at least."

"I'm sorry to tell you guys this, but she's not going anywhere without Kenny."

"Oliver, will you please drive us?"

"I will, sure. But we still need the keys."

"Why do we even listen to her? What's the matter with us?" I ask uselessly. Why are we still acting like she's our mother? Jack's right, the woman we knew is gone. She's been replaced with a drunken, petulant child who revels in being naughty.

In a conversation with Doug earlier in the week, when Jack and I went in to sign some final documents regarding Mom's finances, Doug had suggested we check out Al-Anon. Jack and I had exchanged a look when he said it. "Thanks Doug, yeah. We'll check it out," Jack had said, both of us knowing that was never going to happen. We've spent our lives shaping our actions and choices around our mother, joining a group because she's an alcoholic had no appeal whatsoever. The only twelve steps I wanted to take were out the fucking door. I appreciated the thought but was in no way, no how, not a chance, going to go to an Al-Anon meeting.

I did, however, later that night, in the privacy of my own room, check it out online. In the online support chat room, the most common thread was something along the lines of, "In the end stage of alcoholism, it's not the alcoholic who's acting insane, it's the people around the alcoholic, those who tolerate the behaviour, who continue to listen, continue to try and talk and persuade the alcoholic. It's those people who are acting insane." Well, I had to concede, they were right. I felt insane.

Mom is crossing the dead yellow lawn like a shot. Kenny's taking a case of beer from the back of his truck. Of course it's beer. It couldn't be soil for planting flowers or tools for fixing the back screen door or groceries for dinner or equipment he needed for the work he did, because he worked instead of collecting unemployment. No, of course not. It's beer. He hands the case to Mom while he fishes around the cab for something. The six-foot-two man hands the case of beer to the ninety-pound woman.

"What a fucking piece of work," Jack mutters under his breath, as we watch the scene unfold from the living room window.

"You're coming with me when I take the kids to Albuquerque, right?" Mom manages to ask Kenny from under the beer.

"I guess I could," he says, emerging from the cab and stuffing something into his front shirt pocket. I don't even want to imagine what. "Want to go out on the town after we drop them?" he asks, leaning in as if he's going to kiss her. We're about to turn away when a small red Toyota pulls up behind Kenny's truck. Connie, the property manager. Shit. We race for the door, piecing together in less than a second that she could only be bringing bad news and if Mom is the one to speak to her first, everything will be that much worse.

"Hi, Connie," I call, halfway across the front lawn. Jack intercepts Mom, taking the case of beer and leading her and Kenny into the house.

"I'm sorry I'm not here with better news," Connie says, handing me an envelope. "Your mother's being evicted."

I look down at the envelope blankly. "Oh, okay." I try to think of something to say to counter Connie, but really, I knew this was coming and we have no defence. "How long do we have?"

"Thirty days."

"Thirty days? Is there any way you could give us more time, like maybe sixty days? We're working on getting her into assisted living, but these things take time."

"I'm sorry, Cassie, I really am, but the owners won't budge. The other residents are complaining. Last week, someone found her passed out in the car with her head against the steering wheel, a bottle of wine in her lap and a six-pack on the console," Connie says, her tone trying for something like compassion, but not managing to get past *this is the last straw*.

"Oh."

"They took photos."

"Okay. Right."

As Connie gets into her car and drives away, Oliver and Jack come out of the house.

"What was that all about?"

"Mom's being evicted," I say, leaving out the rest.

"Shit," says Oliver.

The three of us stand at the edge of the lawn.

"What are we going to do?"

"I don't know."

"Nobody is going to rent to her now that she has not one, but two, evictions on her record." Oliver states the obvious.

"She really needs to be in a facility." Jack states the other obvious.

"We'll figure it out. But we're not going to solve anything right now. We need to get out of here," I say flatly. "Let's find the key." I want to run screaming from everything this small plot of land contains—but we can't go anywhere until we find the fucking key.

As we look, Oliver keeps apologizing that his own car is in the shop. He keeps on with this all through the search, the one-hour-and-fifteen-minute search. "If it wasn't in the shop, I would just take you in my car." As I look on windowsills, in drawers, in the fridge, under couch cushions, in baskets, under books, Oliver's constant apology sends my mind wandering to a joke my economist father-in-law used to tell about a mathematician, a physicist, and an economist who are stuck in a lifeboat with a can of food but no can opener. The mathematician suggests all sorts of formulas having to do with the density of seawater versus metal, the physicist suggests ways to transform the molecular structure of the metal, and the economist says, "Suppose we had a can opener." And that was the punch line. I never really got it, which I would apologetically tell my father-in-law, which he loved, because it opened the door for him to explain economics to me, which is all about imagining things you don't have.

*Imagine you have a key*, I think, as I rummage through my mother's dresser drawers, swearing under my breath. Oliver finds it in the garage, on top of the mouldy couch we tried to have carted away by a junk collector, but Mom had fought us tooth and nail, saying she was going to sell it on Craigslist and get a hundred dollars for it. We assured her she wasn't going to get a dime for it and tried to make her see that keeping this rotting furniture in her carport, when she's been told time and again to clean it out, was going to get her evicted. She not only refused to listen but made a dramatic show of standing in front of the couch, blocking it with her full body as if we were enemy invaders trying to take her child.

With the key in hand at last, Jack and I announce that we're ready to go and stand by the car, waiting. It takes what feels like an eternity for the whole rigamarole: fighting with Mom about the fact that she isn't allowed to drive, forcing her to empty the travel mug of wine, waiting for her while she goes in and searches for her purse, uses the bathroom ... All the while Kenny sitting in the back seat, fumes rising from him like a distillery.

# thirty-eight

JACK PULLS INTO THE PARKING lot of Whole Foods so we can get some food for our night in the hotel. No sooner has he found a parking space and shut off the car than Mom is out of the car and trotting into the store ahead of us. Jack and I exchange a look and follow her, leaving Kenny in the car.

"Fifty bucks says she's getting wine."

"Not even worth betting," Jack replies, as the glass doors to the market slide open, and we walk past a display of wild-flowers, little bundles wrapped in twine and held in Mason jars that spoke of a life impossibly far away.

"I'm thinking of contacting that realtor who sold Mom's Jacona house."

"You're thinking we should buy something?" Jack turns to me, surprised.

"I don't know what I'm thinking, other than that we need

to get a roof over her head, and it's pretty clear nobody's going to rent to her."

"What about Meadowbrook? Doug said he's heard good things."

"How many times have we talked to her about assisted living? And what are we going to do, drag her there? Yes, she should be there. I just can't figure out how we're supposed to go about it. Oh—and speaking of Doug, he called yesterday to say Mom had come in asking about her finances."

"When?"

"Must have been when we were at Leslie's office."

"Okay ..."

"Kenny was with her."

"Please tell me Doug didn't talk about money in front of Kenny?" Jack asks.

"Not only was he obliged to talk about her money, but apparently Mom said, 'Kenneth is my husband, whatever you have to say to me, you can say to him.'"

"What? Oh, fuck."

"Obviously, they're not married, but what would be the implications if they were?"

"Oh my God."

We walk down the aisle in dazed silence.

Once we have our drinks and takeout boxes from the buffet, we get in the express line, where Mom walks up behind us with a sandwich, a cranberry juice, and a bag of chips.

"Well, fancy meeting you here," she chirps.

I stare at my mother's food, confused. Had we misjudged?

. . .

Jack pulls onto the highway and Mom reaches through to the front seat with her open bag of chips. "Want some chips, Murph?" she asks.

"No thanks, Mom. I'm okay."

My mind is cycling through our options for housing. All of my edges are buzzing, like I'm stuck between two cement walls unable to move.

Mom reaches through with her sandwich, "Want a bite?"

"No thank you."

"Let's have some music. Here, put this in." She reaches through a third time with a CD; she's chipper, bordering on manic. *What's going on?* Jack is sitting straight as an arrow, his twitching fingers on the steering wheel the only evidence of the stress he's containing. Something is up.

*Just let it be.*

Mom starts to hum, happily.

*Just look out the window and breathe. You're almost there. You'll be away from all this soon, don't turn, don't ...*

The wine in the bottle is a deep yellow, not the light colour of a Sauvignon Blanc or a Pinot Grigio, more like a cheap, overly oaky Chardonnay. It is tumbling from the bottle into an empty Starbucks cup tucked between her legs. I see the yellow liquid fall in slow motion, a gentle back-and-forth wave. And all the energy I have put into holding things together for months on end lets go, becomes one with the yellow liquid.

Something inside of me spreads out. My breathing slows down.

*A wave that ebbs and then flows* ... My mother's tiny hands are on the bottle; there are three more bottles poking out from under the driver's seat in front of her. She had sprinted into the store to get the wine, hidden it in the car, and then made another trip in with the express purpose of tricking us.

She's not looking at me, but she's aware I'm looking at her. "I'm just so thirsty, I need a little something to drink."

Kenny shifts uncomfortably in the seat beside her.

"Give it to me," I say in a voice just above a whisper, vaguely aware that my body is shifting as the wave gathers and reaches its height. The molecules in my body begin to contract.

She stops pouring. "No," she says, and looks right at me. "I'm not giving it to you."

*I will break you in half like a twig.* The wave curls and I realize—feel it down to my core, that the gathering is not preparation for a fight but rather, restraint. It will take every ounce of my strength to *not* hurt her, to not destroy her and, with her, all that she has wrought. The urge in my body is overpowering. I want to rip roots from the ground, blow down houses.

"Give me the bottle." I thrust my hand between the seats.

She's holding it to her chest like a baby. She turns and presses against the car door, crushing the cup and soaking her legs. "It's mine! You can't have it."

"Give me the fucking bottle *now*!" I reach past her shoulder and rip the bottle from her hands, nearly clocking her on the chin as I yank it back.

"Give me the lid."

Instead of reaching for the lid, she reaches for the bag of chips and throws it at my head, potato chips flying all over the car. Then comes the cup. She grabs her sandwich and is about to throw that too, but I catch her tiny wrist and rip the sandwich from her hand, crushing it into a ball, all of my impotent anger pressing into two thin slices of white bread, bits of lettuce and tomato exploding through plastic wrap.

As I feel my anger from the past two years—from my life—crashing against the inside of my head, I watch her eyes cloud over, see her brain dilate. She's leaving the scene. It's her new superpower. Just like that, she's gone.

"Why are you so mad?" She looks at her wrist in my hand. She's scared and confused.

"Give me the lid to the bottle," I say quietly and slowly, keeping my voice as even as I'm able.

She reaches down on the floor, and when she hands me the lid, I pull her close and lower my voice further. With each syllable the sky inside of me is darkening. Any last drops of pity or compassion have been sucked into the typhoon that has taken me over. I want nothing but to pull her down with us, to drown her in the darkness she has blanketed across our world. "Do you ever think about us, Mom? Jack and Oliver and me? Do we ever factor into your thoughts? Let me help your liquor-soaked brain piece it together: Jack is a paramedic. A paramedic! That means that if we were pulled over with alcohol in the car, if he was caught behind the wheel of your little booze-mobile, his career would be over." Her face is blank. I flick her wrist away. Guilt and pain and rage have fused into an ore of molten fury and I'm at the bottom. Nothing human exists here. In the bleak, empty face of everything that has happened in the past year, it hits me: this is reality—stripped of all illusions. I'm trying to fight what life has dished up for me. It's a simple law of nature: you can't fight life. She's proof of that.

The situation is clear. This woman is the child and we're the parents and it's as simple as heads or tails: care for her or abandon her. That's all. Choose.

Jack looks over at me and then down at the phone, face up in his hand. He looks at me and then at it, as if guiding me to look too. It's open to the GPS and says, *sixteen minutes until destination.* Sixteen minutes. I can handle sixteen minutes in the same space as her. I am trembling. My fists are clenched and finding my breath again is climbing a rocky pass between two mountains. Jack keeps the phone where I can see it. Fifteen minutes. The ground is levelling out. The shaking has rendered my edges unclear. I hold my gaze on that phone. A person needs to know there are edges. Everything eventually transforms into something else, you just need to make it to that edge. Twelve minutes.

Mom sits in the back seat, seeming, in every possible way, like a distressed four-year-old. She has already forgotten everything.

"Murphy? Are you mad at me?"

# DECEMBER 2017 AND JANUARY 2018

# thirty-nine

KAI'S LAPTOP ILLUMINATES a perfect billboard of light atop the rolling hills of the down comforter. His fingers click-tap across the keys. I stuff my face into his hip where it's perched upright against the pillows.

"Shoot, sorry. Did I wake you?"

I'm a light sleeper, and normally he goes downstairs when he wakes early, but for the past few days, I've been falling asleep in brightly lit rooms with the TV running or the kids fighting, falling asleep with my face on the counter at any time of day. Easily. Deeply.

"It's okay. I need to get up anyway."

"I'll put the coffee on."

I roll back over and close my eyes. I didn't cry upon receiving the news of my father's death, just felt overwhelmingly tired. Kai has managed to hold back the phone calls and emails by diverting them to Jack, but by this, the fourth day,

I accept that I have to get back to it. Oliver has returned to Massachusetts and she's all alone. With Kenny.

"Hello?" Jack sounds like he's in his car.

"We're moving her to Meadowbrook," I say.

"Oh, um ... okay."

"Doug's going to help."

"But she isn't going to want to ..." he begins half-heartedly.

"We're done asking her what she wants," I reply. "Doug is going to bring her to his place for a few days; he lives an hour north of the city in the middle of nowhere. When she asks to go home, he's going to say his car won't start and from there he'll improvise and do whatever it takes to keep her there overnight." With over a decade of sobriety under his belt, Doug has turned out to be one of our best allies in this fight, never questioning the lengths we are going to, driving across town to bring her money or disconnecting her car battery in the dead of night, explaining things to her with the patience of a monk.

"Okay ..."

"That will give us two days to book her a spot at Meadow-brook, hire movers, and move her in. We'll need to put a lot of her furniture in storage. I've made an inventory."

"What about Kenny?"

"We block his number on her phone. I think that's about all we can do."

"What about the restraining order?"

"The adult protection services officer I spoke to said that restraining orders are hard to get, even when the at-risk person wants the order, but since Mom doesn't want Kenny gone, it'll be next to impossible."

"Okay. I guess it just feels kind of sudden."

"Does it, Jack? Really?"

Silence.

"Do you think it'll work?"

"I have no idea. I hope so. It doesn't matter, though; we have no choice."

"It makes me nervous."

"Yeah, I know. Me too."

The movers arrive at seven the next morning, right on schedule—only they refuse to do the job without haz-mat levels of protection due to the condition of the house. Additionally, they want to be paid double for the risk. I tell them to do what they need to do; the move has to happen. I get a phone call halfway through the day. "Hi, Ms. Wolfe, it's Kit from Kit's Moving. I just wanted to let you know, we have a woman who packs all the clothing, and she says your mother has no undergarments."

"Are you sure?"

"Yes. We're all finished. There was nothing."

"Okay. Thank you for telling me."

"Ms. Wolfe? I hope I'm not overstepping. I just wanted to say ... my father died of alcoholism. My heart goes out to you."

. . .

Doug brings Mom to Meadowbrook the next day. Leslie is waiting to greet her at the front. She stays with Mom all through the first day and introduces her to Rosie, the caregiver I've hired to be with her each day from five p.m. to nine-thirty p.m. Mom is confused and disoriented through it all. Tina, the administrator from Meadowbrook who signed us up, helps with hiring a dog walker and booking laundry service and arranging hourly check-ins. I accept everything that is proposed, and all goes as planned—all except for Kenny, that is, who finds her within a matter of days.

"Are you ready for this yet?" Kai asks, appearing at the top of the stairs with a cup of coffee.

"Could you set it on the bedside table?"

I roll over, trying to hold back the ever-creeping to-do list for a few more minutes, but it needles its way through the frontal haze of my waking brain: *call Meadowbrook about dog walker; toiletry bag for Isabel; email Lucy's teacher about class photos; defer thesis; order basics for Mom at Walmart; call Jack …*

Kai opens the curtains on a heavy grey sky. When I was little, my mother would tease me about my lists. "They're so cute, the first item is always wake up." According to Mom, I started making lists at about age five. These days, it's that first item that's the hardest.

Once the kids have gone to school, I set up at the kitchen counter.

"What about Jack? Can't he go out instead?" Kai thinks I baby my little brother.

"He's starting his new job."

"Your father dying doesn't trump his new job?"

I don't look up from my screen and he doesn't say anything further, anything that might indicate regret. The kettle whistles and he pours water into a second Bodum of coffee. He takes a spoon and begins stirring. The spoon clacks against the glass carafe. Over and over. He stirs it for a long time. I stare at the pot and will him to stop.

"You need to take a break is what you need to do. Can you not see the insanity of this?" He tosses his whole shoulder into plunging the coffee like he's wrestling someone to the ground. I watch him without responding. He brings the coffee over and refills my lukewarm remains. He's on the opposite side of the counter, inside the kitchen. My mother designed this kitchen for us. When the renovations were finished, Kai had stood in the kitchen with his hands on the wrap-around bar counter and smiled. "Our own personal command central. I love it."

I don't tell Kai that Jack's already offered to go out, offered to handle everything for the next two weeks. Instead, I say, "I've already booked my ticket. It has to be me. It wouldn't help me if Jack went, I'm the one who's been dealing with Meadowbrook and the DMV and the psychiatrist. I need to see this through. By next weekend everything will be taken care of."

"And I don't understand why you don't defer *everything* … Why just the thesis?"

I don't respond.

"Well, it's clear you're not exactly open to advice at the moment." He takes his coffee and leaves command central. He pauses halfway through the dining room and then changes his direction to come back and sit next to me. I can feel the willpower it is taking him to not walk away. He sees me as acting stubborn. He's trying hard not to be mad at me. I don't have the fight in me to tell him I'm doing tasks because it's the tasks that are keeping me afloat. He thinks it's too much, that I should lie down or something. Let my feelings out or something. Thinks I'll have a complete breakdown if I don't. I know this because he says, "You need to rest, let your feelings out, that's what you need to do. Otherwise, you're going to have a complete breakdown." I don't tell him that if I let it all out, the million shredded pieces of me will blow away in the wind, that the tasks are the glue. Without the tasks, I'd be finished. I suddenly feel tired. I take my coffee and laptop and head upstairs to work from the bed. I lie under the covers and close my eyes against the too-close ceiling.

As part of the same home renovation as the kitchen, Mom had designed this bedroom. A small second-floor accès au toit is what the guidelines allowed for. The room is tiny, but the roof terrace is large: our piece of outdoor space in the city. On the day the workmen were finishing the ceiling, they'd explained that there was a five-degree grade to the roof, and did I want to keep that grade for the ceiling inside? Or did I want them to level it out? I'd asked Mom and she had instructed me to absolutely level it out—an angle that small would drive me crazy, particularly when I was lying in bed. But then, on the day I was to pass that direction on to the workers, I'd had a fight with her. It was a bad fight and she'd slammed the phone down on me in mid-sentence. And so, out of pure spite, I'd told them, "Keep the angle." I'd practically shouted. I'd show her.

Now every morning, I wake up facing that ceiling and feel like I'm falling backward. I hate the angled ceiling and the vertigo it gives me. I should have listened to my mother.

"Are you listening to me?" Kai has followed me up the stairs and is sitting on the edge of the bed.

"Yes, I'm listening," I say, though I have no idea what he's talking about since I wasn't listening. I wish he would leave me alone.

"You keep telling me you need to see this thing through. I'm just asking you, Cassie, what do you think *seeing it through* means?"

"What?"

"You said you need to *see this through*. What do you think *through* means?"

"You mean the fact that my mother is slowly killing herself? Yeah, strange as it seems, I do feel compelled to do something about it." I get out of the bed and start down the stairs, not sure where I'm going and wishing he would stop following me. Halfway down the stairs I stop and turn around. "I know you're trying to help, but you're not."

# forty

I WAKE TO the cold humming of the airplane window against my head. "We are descending into Albuquerque. Please return your seatbacks and tray tables to their fully upright and locked position ..." I hand my empty plastic cup and crumpled napkin to the flight attendant and close my eyes. I go over what needs to be done: *get sandbag, fill sandbag, put items on top shelf, try not to think about house being washed away, move animals to shelter, stack sandbags, watch water rise, keep hope up, keep water down, pump water, take out rowboat, fill sandbags, watch water rise.*

The water is up to my eyeballs, and I seem to have gotten hypothermia on the inside. There is only a thin layer along my surface that has a sense memory of how a mother behaves, or a wife, a friend, a colleague, and I've slipped into that outer skin and walked and talked and lived these past weeks on a faulty autopilot.

. . .

"Cassie?" Tina, the administrator who signed us up for Meadowbrook several weeks prior must have seen me pull into the lot because she has come out to greet me. "Boy, are we glad to see you."

"Oh. Hi, Tina." I drop the car keys into my purse.

Tina guides me down a little hallway behind the reception desk and into a small office. Her tone is gossipy, as if we're the popular kids and Mom's the school loser. "You weren't kidding when you said she was an alcoholic. Boy oh boy. She never goes anywhere without that glass in her hand. Where should I start?" She seems to know exactly where to start because she doesn't even take a breath before continuing. "Well, the kitchen staff are at their wits' end trying to keep her in the dining room: she follows the waiters away from the table when they tell her she's reached her two-drink limit, tries to break into the kitchen to get to the fridge. Oh, and I've called the steam cleaning place for you about that couch ... she won't allow the cleaning staff in to get laundry and she won't allow Rosie to help her with showering—Rosie is the caregiver you hired, by the way, not sure if you've had a chance to meet her yet. There are no cleaning supplies in the apartment, so I had Rosie pick up a bunch of stuff over at Walmart, I have the receipt here. We've taken the car keys, but she managed to call over to Honda and have a new set made, so you may have to call over there and tell them the situation. As far as the dog, I found someone who's going to take Bowie and I can get that ball rolling—"

"Hang on a second." My voice has emerged from my mouth without me having sent a message for it to do so. I try to catch up. I need to remember that this woman is here to help. Had I been hoping for the modulated caregiving tone I've come to know and depend on? Yes. Had I been imagining someone more like Leslie? Yes. But—I remind myself—Tina is an administrator, not a caregiver. She is the saleswoman who signed us up. I remind myself to do the opposite of what I feel; I will be polite.

"I'm sorry, I'm just a little confused as to why you would be concerning yourself with her dog. You told me they allowed dogs here and Jack signed us up for dog-walking services, didn't he?"

"Oh yes, I must have forgotten to tell you—Jim, our dog walker, tried to stop by on her first day to pick up Bowie, but she turned him away, said she didn't need that service. There hasn't been a dog walker."

"What?" Calm voice gone. "Did you just forget to tell me?" *Too loud. Calm down.* Yes, she forgot to tell me. "So how often is the dog being walked?"

"Well, clearly not very often because the carpet is a mess, let me tell you. We are going to need to replace that."

I lower my voice. I speak slowly. "My mother has dementia. I'm confused as to why you are waiting for her permission. I thought the reason you called me multiple times a day is that my brothers and I are the ones making the decisions. No?"

"Okay, I understand your confusion now. The issue is that she's here in independent living rather than assisted living, so technically *she's* the boss."

"Why is this 'she's the boss' rule only coming into play about the dog? About the missing dog walker *you* forgot to tell us about?" *Too snarky. Need to modulate.* Tina doesn't respond. "Okay, Tina. How about we switch her to assisted living."

"Well ..."

"When we signed up, you offered that as a possibility. If I'm not mistaken, you said it could even be in the same apartment, that it was just a level of care."

"Well, yes, we could do that. That might be a step in the right direction."

"Great. Let's do that then."

"Well, that can't happen overnight. We'll need to get her assessed by our wellness director."

"Is your wellness director on-site?"

"Yes."

"Then let's set up an appointment." *Why is she dragging this out?*

"I'm not sure you fully understand the situation, Cassie. I'm trying to put this gently ... your mother is unmanageable. We may not be able to handle her anywhere in the facility."

Through the window beyond Tina, a care worker in a green nursing smock is guiding an old man hunched over a walker. They move at a glacial pace.

"Thank you, Tina. You've given me a lot to think about. I'll stop by in the morning, and we can discuss it some more."

"You're welcome," she says. "Your mother is in unit 243. You get off the elevators, take a left, follow the hallway to the end, take another left, and then keep going until you see 243."

I want to ask about the long, nondescript hallways in a place for people with dementia—*What's the idea? Inside joke?* But I smile my winningest smile instead. "Thank you," I say, taking hold of my suitcase with one hand and shaking Tina's hand with the other.

And then it happens: she is with me, in me. It's been happening with increasing frequency, not like an intentional channelling thing or an *I'm-going-to-try-to-do-what-she-would-do* thing. Rather, in certain necessary moments, Nina helps me out. She's an easy woman to criticize, to be frustrated with. It's easy to wish her otherwise because she is—or was—demanding and inconsiderate and doesn't listen. All of this is true—but like any coin, if you flip it, there's also the other side. She doesn't take shit from anyone because she knows people will shovel you shit if you let them. "If you apologize to people, they'll walk all over you," she once told me. She took control of situations, whether they needed to be taken in hand or not. She gripped them tightly.

I turn to Tina and say, "We have someone who will be taking Bowie, a family friend. That's in two weeks. Until then, he stays with my mother. I will arrange a dog walker immediately. I do not want to hear that anything has happened to the dog. The dog is all she has left and will remain by her side until I say otherwise." And then I use Mom's technique—the one she would employ if I had committed some highly punishable offence for which she would have every right to punish me but instead would stab me with, "It's okay. I just thought you were smarter than that. Oh well."

I add, "I'm sure even you, who don't actually do *any* of the hands-on work with the elders, have enough compassion to understand that she needs her dog."

I wander down a river of burgundy and beige, getting lost no fewer than three times before making it to my mother's unit.

She opens the door not with a greeting but with the announcement that her bank account is low—which I already know, since I'm the one who emptied it. She turns back into the apartment. I decide that it's kind of interesting to not partake of the whole "So good to see you, I've missed you" thing. I decide to appreciate this new aspect of our relationship as emphasizing that we're on a continuum. I look at the dry-erase calendar I put on the wall the last time I was here, more for Kenny than for Mom. I'd filled the days: December 1 to 5: Jack visiting, December 7 to 12: Oliver here. It wasn't accurate but rather designed to let Kenny know we were going to be around. One look at the dry-erase board tells me that it, like most of my great fix-it ideas, has failed. Kenny has wiped it clean and scrawled in red Sharpie, "U and me babe 4-eva!"

*You could wield a hammer and a Skilsaw, knock out a wall, or milk a goat, or shoe a horse or build a fence or plow a field—for someone who doesn't need men, why do you need them so badly?*

I buy cleaning products and meet with caregivers and lawyers, I call the Motor Vehicle Division, I buy Mom underwear and healthy food. I scrub her carpet and her couch and wash her sheets. I try to explain to her that she can't climb over the kitchen counter when she reaches her two-drink limit at dinner, that she can't hit her caregiver. I get her into the shower. I take her for a walk. I buy her shoes. She asks where Kenny is every hour, every half-hour, every fifteen minutes. "Where is he? Is he mad at me? Is he coming back?" She wants to know who is stealing her wine. She wants me to fire Rosie.

## forty-one

I LAND IN MONTREAL at five p.m. In the taxi on the way home from the airport, my phone rings. She's crying. Bowie is missing. She can't find him anywhere. She's worried that maybe she forgot him at the dog run, she can't remember. She's worried something might be happening to her memory. "You know when you're waking up from a dream and you can't remember where you are? I feel like that all the time."

"Hold on a second, Mom." I pay the taxi driver and pull my suitcase up the front walk to the porch stairs and sit. "Mom, it's okay. It's going to be okay. I think I know where Bowie is. I have to call someone, but I'll call you right back. Don't go anywhere, I'll call you back, okay?"

The lilac bush beside me is bare. Beneath it, the leaves we didn't rake have become mulch. I am floating above the scene. I can see myself gesticulating wildly, pacing up and down the front walkway. I must have started yelling fairly soon into the call because Kai has opened the front door. The conversation is jagged shards of glass. I can't piece them together enough to get a clear sense of the scene.

"... well aware she's an alcoholic ... No—I want to know. Tell me. In the daily phone calls and emails has there been a single request on your part that has gone unanswered by me? ... It's not her you've offended—it's me. I realize my mother is little more than fodder for gossip in the back office but she's a *person*." I see myself holding the phone away from my face and yelling into it, treating it as the useless object it is. Supposed to be a device for communicating but it's clearly not working because none of my communication seems to land. Anywhere. "This is my family at our most distraught and you've just pulled the rug from under us. No, I do *not* want to speak to someone from head office, what I want is the fucking dog back before the end of the—Yes, she drinks. Yes!—ten points for you—Bravo!"

"Cassie, I think you should hang up." Kai puts a hand on my shoulder, I swat it away.

"You've played your winning card, she's 'unmanageable' and what can I possibly say to that? How about a little compassion, isn't that the field you're supposed to be in? That dog was all she had left, and you took him away. How dare you."

I kick my suitcase into the mulch.

"Cassie, I think you should—"

"... 'what's best for the dog'? How about what is best for the fucking human? You were supposed to do what was best for

the dog when I asked you two weeks ago for a dog walker—
that is on *you* ... No, I cannot control my ... I sat in your office
just last week, I sat across from you and told you that in two
weeks, two fucking weeks, our friend was taking the dog ...
How dare you."

"Cassie, hang up the phone."

I hang up and wheel around on Kai. "There. Are you
happy? They took Bowie. Now she has nothing—nothing!"

I storm off down the street. I have no idea of where I'm
going, walking on the edge of running. Off the pavement and
onto the mountain, on paths, off paths, through trees and open
spaces, I start running up and further up until I'm at the top of
the mountain. The dog, the blessed dog, the last kind being on
the planet. Everyone says, "I'm not judging." But it's a bald-
faced lie. *I judged you, Mom—what a shit thing you've done,
making us clean up this massive mess that is you.*

*And what a shit thing I've done to let you fall so far.*

I stop walking and hunch over my knees, wanting to
vomit every last bit of it. I turn to the hundred-foot cross,
lit up against the darkening sky. "Jesus Christ. Yes, you," I
yell, somewhere between angry and sad and desperate and
conceding, there at the top of the mountain, that I know
absolutely nothing at all.

My phone rings. I answer it.

"Murphy? Did you figure it out?"

## forty-two

"MAMA?" LUCY IS SHAKING me on the leg. "Daddy made popcorn."

Kai comes in with a dishtowel over his arm, both hands cradling a massive bowl of popcorn, and sits on the edge of the couch in front of my prostrate body. The cushion dips with his weight and I roll against him. He rests the popcorn on his lap and wipes butter from his hands before reaching out to take Lucy's outstretched palm. She and her sister are curled tightly at my feet, a tangled clump of arms and legs and synchronized responses. Their blue-lit faces drop in unison as a tiny boat tips over the edge of an endless waterfall. There is screaming. I take some popcorn and pull myself in the direction of sitting but stop halfway and decide instead to reach for a pillow that has fallen to the floor. I wedge it under my head and lie back down.

Kai has been overwhelmed with picking up the slack at home. I've been away a week out of every month going on almost a year now, and after trying to figure out how to deal with the crying jags and interpersonal dynamics of a ten- and a fifteen-year-old girl and worn thin by hours and hours of *My Little Pony* and *The Gilmore Girls*, he's decided to brand his personal parenting style as unabashedly masculine and stakes his flag on the hill of screen time: December will officially be *Lord of the Rings* month—and the movies will be viewed on a ten-foot projection screen. The part of me that might argue has gone dormant. I have become winter. This is for the best, I think vaguely. The absent parent doesn't have a right to tell the present parent how to do their job.

My cell phone buzzes. I pull myself up out of the couch.

"Hello?"

"Hello Cassie. It's Dr. Katz."

I drag myself off the couch and out of the living room, "Hello, Dr. Katz."

The doctor tells me that my mother didn't make it to the appointment; when Leslie went to pick her up at Meadowbrook, she was nowhere to be found. Dr. Katz says it doesn't matter, in fact my mother wandering only strengthens the diagnosis she's formulated. She tells me my mother has dementia, but that she can't properly diagnose the level until we get the alcohol out of her system. "You have to detox her."

I chuckle.

Dr. Katz continues, "It's getting quite close to the holidays. I'm not sure I'll be able to arrange the follow-up doctor for December, but if we plan this for early January, she could go into geriatric psychiatry at UNM after she's detoxed.

Dr. Matthews over there is excellent. I'll keep you posted, but either way, let's get things rolling."

"Okay," I say, having no idea what *get things rolling* means. I take a sticky note from the kitchen counter and write, "Get things rolling, detox early January." I know the words must mean something. I will look at the note in the morning and know what to do.

I ask Dr. Katz how much I owe her.

"You don't owe me anything. I'm very sorry you're going through this. I will help you in any way I can, let's just get her into the hospital."

I feel—and not for the first time—that the kindness of strangers will be the feather that knocks me over.

"Thank you."

"Call me once you've settled on a hospital."

"Okay, talk to you soon."

I climb back into the pile on the couch and pull the blanket up to my face.

"Can we start the next one, Daddy?" Lucy asks.

"Already on it."

We're on hour three of our fantasy saga and I have no idea what Kai's rules are going to be for bedtime, so I don't see any problem with sleeping right here on the couch. An army of the dead is summoned, and the two girls cling to each other more tightly. Lucy is scared. Again, vaguely, I think perhaps I should do something. This isn't age appropriate. But I don't say anything. *She'll be fine.* The young travellers are climbing a jagged cliff face. Lucy is shaking my leg. "Mommy, what does it mean, 'the ring always wants to get back to its master'?" I open one eye and look toward the screen glowing bluish gold. Kai is coming in from the kitchen with a second round of popcorn and rescues me. "Well, it's a magic ring. And it's like that big eye is its home and it's always wanting to get home, like a magnet that's always pulling." I feel myself drifting off again, trees are being cut down, lands laid to waste, fires burning, and a ring is being pulled homeward. Our nature is defined by gravity; we exist on land, tangled with each other and elemental, we use the word *free* but there is no state of being that isn't held, tethered to other humans. Always pulled, always feet on the earth—unless you're an elf. I roll over, and Lucy and Isabel adjust accordingly. *I'm wearing a white dress and Viggo Mortensen is by my side. I'm trying to move gently and exude a sense of calm and peace, but I know it's a lie and this knowledge is making me more agitated by the minute. All this pretending. There is no doubt I'll get found out and my elfly ability to walk on air will be revoked when they realize it was given to me in error. "You are not free of mind and spirit, how can you call yourself an elf?" Wand wave and down go my feet. Cursed to touch the earth for all eternity. "I sentence you to a life in gravity." They know that it's always pulling, it wants to bring me back to her, forever entangled, it knows that I want it, that I feel its pull, but I must throw the ring back into the fires of Mount Doom and to do that I have to go all the way to her, right up to the edge of her mind and peer inside. "And you must love her," says the elf king, standing ten feet taller than*

I give over to movie watching and pulling the kids to school on the sled, activities I'm able to do while being half-present and half-lost in the Arctic tundra of my brain, the region where my thoughts are supposed to coalesce with some logic but is instead a place of glacial movement where cohesion is impossible.

# forty-three

THE LAST THREE WEEKS of my mother's "freedom" are the most harrowing of all. She's like a kitten on a freeway. The snow falls in Montreal, and I set up a mini office at command central in the kitchen. For nearly all the hours that the girls are in school, I'm on the phone. In long conversations with Turquoise Lodge and Life Healing Center, two of the main detox centres in Albuquerque, I'm told, yet again, that I can't bring her in against her will. No matter that she's in bad shape. I search on Google, go down endless rabbit holes, look further afield. I'm told time and again, "The addict must take control of their life if they want to beat the disease." I ask, "So, which is it, a disease? Or something one can control? And what if the addict is no longer able to string a sentence together and is incontinent and falling apart at the seams?" I'm told that it's sad, "tragic really, but thankfully we've left the dark days of the institution, when women were locked up against their will. The overcorrection, if you want to call it that, is that modern laws make it very difficult to abrogate a person's right to free will." I ask again why they bother calling it a disease if they aren't going to treat it like other diseases. If a person is incoherent from diabetic shock, the hospital doesn't say, "Sorry, but we need to hear the patient's voice out loud saying they want to be here." Clearly, they've heard my arguments before because they have an answer for everything and all the answers, as long and seemingly compassionate as they are, all add up to the same thing: no.

It's a broken record of misery. I call every day and she sounds like she's on heavy narcotics, unable to follow any thoughts, to have anything resembling a conversation; her voice is faint and distant, like she's at the end of a tunnel. I start to suspect Kenny is drugging her. Her caregiver, Rosie, reports that she's found the dozen pairs of underwear I sent stuffed into a cardboard box in the corner of her bedroom, covered in feces. When Rosie tries to get her into a bath or a shower, Mom hits her. First with her hands and then with things like hairbrushes and keys. She has bloody noses daily and can hardly walk for the pain in her knees. Every day I follow her further down this dark road.

I skim over Christmas with my family—my days and nights occupied with calling doctors and hospitals. I am persistent; in spite of the fatigue, I stubbornly refuse to accept that there's no one who can help us. Leslie pulls strings to speed up our doctors' appointments and finds us doctors who will accept extra money for an immediate diagnosis. Embattled

# forty-four

LAST NIGHT, JACK CRIED. We were in the parking lot at the airport hotel, remembering the good years. And he cried. It was a long day, but at the end of it she had looked at us. She understood. We were talking to *her*.

Maybe things will be better when she gets out of the hospital. I don't expect things will be better all at once, but there are therapies, there is hope. I've decided to tell my daughters what is happening. To tell them the truth. Last night in bed, I searched the internet for information on alcoholism, something medical-ish. It turns out that alcohol is responsible for more hospital admissions than heart attacks. According to the Centers for Disease Control, an estimated 140,000 people die from alcohol abuse in the United States every year ... then I found something saying that alcohol affects the alcoholic's brain differently than it does other people's. I'm not sure how verifiable it is; I found it in a medical journal and it seems legit enough, so I decide to go with it.

I sit on the edge of the bed and double-check the notes I've written. I call my daughters upstairs. I sit them on the bed across from me and tell them about alcoholism, that anybody can get it. I tell them that even Grandpa Frank had it, but that he stopped drinking, so he got better. "Grammy is in the hospital right now getting the alcohol out of her body. That will take a few days and then—we're hoping—she'll start to get better." I tell them the alcohol has affected her short-term memory but there are therapies that will help her get some of that back.

Lucy turns her head to face the window while I talk. I can tell she is crying by the way she tilts her head and touches her eye. Isabel is sitting on the edge of the bed, staring at the comforter cover, folding it over and back with her fingers. I resist the urge to hug them or tell them everything will be all right. Finally, I acknowledge that they must be curious. I tell them they can ask me anything they want. Their questions are similar to the ones my adult friends ask: Couldn't you make her stop? Will she get better? Why did she do that to herself? And then they ask a question my adult friends haven't asked. "Does she remember us?"

"Yes, sweetie. She does." I'm *pretty* sure she remembers her grandchildren, or she will, though it's been at least a year since she's asked about either of them.

. . .

It takes a few days of being home to return to my body. I sleep a lot. I wake before the sun and reach for my pad of paper and pencil, holding them to my face in the dark, writing as fast as I can before the dream recedes.

*I make a sculpture of Mom, a large hollow figure made of broken glass and held together with clay. Through cracks in the glass and crumbling bits of clay, a tiny doll is visible, broken with patches of hair missing, her dress is torn, and she has no shoes. You can see the blue of her dress and the light straw colour of her hair.*

I call my mother at the hospital several times a day, and she's sleeping every time. When the doctor returns my call, he tells me he's stopped the Ativan. "She's more somnolent than I would like, so we haven't had her on anything for twelve hours now. When she wakes, she's calm but confused, which is to be expected. There haven't been any seizures and her heart rate is good. All in all, it's going well."

The next day when I call to speak to her, they tell me she's been released. My heart begins to race. "She's been what?"

"She's been released into Dr. Matthews's care at UNM Geriatric Psychiatry. They moved her this morning."

I call the number I'm given.

"Hello, Geriatric Psychiatry."

"Hello, I'm calling to speak to my mother, she's a new patient there, Nina Wolfe."

"Connecting you to the common room."

I am connected to a line that rings and rings and rings. After about twenty rings, someone answers.

"Hello?" comes an angry voice, scratchy at the edges, possibly a patient.

"Yes, I'm calling to speak to Nina Wolfe."

There is a bang as the phone is set on a table, and then "Who is Nina Wolfe? Is there a Nina Wolfe here?" is called out into the ward. A minute. Two minutes. A shuffling sound.

"Hello?" Her voice is half an octave higher and full of air.

"Hi, Mom, it's Murphy."

"Oh hi, sweetie. I'm so glad to talk to you."

"Me too."

"Now, there are usually a few people in this area, but it seems everyone is out. I think they're preparing a big turkey dinner."

"Oh wow. Well, that's nice." I imagine the patients setting a huge table with a turkey on it. It seems odd, but I think *maybe they cut everything up in advance so there are no knives.*

She has things to say. "You know Rod Cordero?"

"Yeah," I respond, wondering why she is talking about her old boyfriend.

"From the Pueblo?"

"I know Rod."

"Well, he was arrested. We were in school, and they just came and took him right from his desk. They took him from school and brought him to the religious place."

"The religious place?"

"Well, you know I got notice too. I was going to be

incarcerated. And this place is very religious, you can't open a door—or you have to be careful where you put your hands—or the manager will say, 'That's the men's room' or 'That's the women's room.' They're very strict, there's a lot of religion. I was there for five hours. And I don't have my purse. The manager took it and I do need that back."

I ask why the manager took her purse.

"Well now, Doug, you know, from First Financial—well, he has the purse and I need to set up a meeting because I need to get it back. I mean, I almost couldn't get on the plane to come here because I didn't have my ID. And what if my friend and I want to get a glass of Chardonnay and I don't have a passport. I can't go anywhere."

"You need your purse."

The full realization that she is making no sense whatsoever sinks in; the terrible, undeniable fact that something has happened to her, something that has made her even worse than before, is turning into a terror that I funnel into fury about her purse being taken away. I feel months of emotion and rage that have been directed at her, now shifting to those who have hurt her. I want her words to make sense—I want there to be some reality in which she did take a flight, did speak to a financial adviser, a reality in which she was at school with her old boyfriend—but I can't make it fit. I want to believe it's some medication that's causing this, but a part of me knows this level of dementia is not caused by any medication. This is the new her. I don't feel the tears as they appear in my eyes or when they roll down my chin and fall onto my chest. Only when the phone slips in my hand do I realize it's over.

"Well, Murphy's on the TV. Now look, look at that, can you see that? I told my friend that I would need money to go out because Murphy's coming, and I'll need money to go to dinner. Oh, and did I tell you, I think I saw Bowie downstairs? I mean, it could have been my imagination, but he looked just like Bowie. I have to ask the manager about that."

"Mom?"

"Yes, sweetie?"

"Jack is coming, okay?" I try to keep my voice even. "He'll be there in the morning when you wake up. He can help you with everything. Don't worry about anything, Mom. We're here. We're going to help you."

"You're here? Where are you? Are you going to sleep over? If you bring your jammies, we can have a sleepover."

"I'll bring my jammies when I come, I promise. I'm not there right now, but I'll be there very soon."

After I hang up, I call the doctor.

"Excuse me." I am percolating. "Why did you take my mother's purse away?"

"Well, it's a psychiatric unit and the patients can't have anything pointy or with long straps."

"You *have* to give her back her purse. She *has* to have that. Taking things in and out of her purse is what she *does*. It's her *thing*. You're supposed to be taking care of her. Why does she sound like she's on heavy medication? She's supposed to be clean. What's going on?"

"You mean she doesn't always sound like that?" Dr. Matthews asks.

"No, she doesn't sound like that. She has memory loss and she talks in a loop around the same four subjects, but when she talks she can put sentences together that have a beginning, a middle, and an end—she doesn't talk about going to the religious place or being in grade school with her old boyfriend, when I know full well she's been in a psych ward all day."

He tells me that she was given gabapentin in the morning and that yesterday she was given olanzapine because she was severely agitated and anxious, but that both medications have a short half-life and would be out of her system by now—and that in any case, they don't cause dementia like that. Dr. Matthews tells me that if what I'm saying is true—that she wasn't like this before detox—then his guess is that her brain "suffered an insult" from the withdrawal, and this is her new normal.

## forty-five

IT'S FORTY DEGREES below zero, the temperature at which Fahrenheit and Celsius meet. Smoke from the chimneys slows as it hits the icy sky. Once the girls are bundled into every possible layer of winter gear and Kai takes them to school, I call Leslie. Leslie says her top recommendation for elders with dementia is a facility called Acequia Madre, right in Santa Fe. I hang up and call the facility. I speak to a woman named Sonia, who tells me that a spot has opened up and they'll be ready to receive Mom in two days. I call Jack, who has just landed in Albuquerque, and give him the name and address of the facility. He calls me later that afternoon and his voice has an energy I haven't heard in a long time. "They have a peacock and rabbits and goats, and everyone seems so kind. It's a small adobe building with a large, open common area. The whole thing wraps around a bright, sunny courtyard and Sonia says they spend a lot of time outdoors. Their philosophy is that they are a family and the facility is their house."

"It sounds like we should sign Mom up right now."

"Yes. I think so."

"How does she get from UNM to the facility?"

"Sonia will go and pick her up—she seems very gentle, Sonia. She's going down to Albuquerque tomorrow morning to do an assessment. As long as UNM is prepared to release Mom, Sonia will take her right then and there. If not, she'll go down the following morning."

Jack will stay until she is fully settled. And when he leaves, I fly out.

Kai, Lucy, and I wave goodbye to Isabel through the glass wall as she winds her way through the security lineup. It's twenty-six degrees in Spain, and she's packed summer clothes and gifts for the family she'll be staying with. We double-checked her packing, weighed her bags, and bought snacks for the plane. She'll be away on the exchange for three months, the first time she's been away from home all on her own. I feel a churning in the pit of my stomach as I watch her pass through security, take her bags off the conveyor belt, and disappear down the hallway of lights. I strain my eyes against the thick glass, desperate for one last glimpse, but everything blurs and becomes liquid. I want to keep my daughter tucked under my wing, to keep her safe. We are walking back to the car when I am overcome with an acute pang of longing for my own mother. All at once, I am fifteen again and I want my mom. I want to tell her what's been going on. *Oh Mom, you wouldn't believe it.* And she would say, *No! You're kidding, Murph. She drinks how much? That's absurd.* Oh yes, she would have a thing or two to say about this. We'd have toast and coffee and gossip into the morning.

"Don't cry, Mama." Lucy throws her arms around me and squeezes.

It's six p.m. when we pull out of the airport. At four the next morning, I will turn around and come back.

# forty-six

"WE ARE BEGINNING our descent into the Albuquerque area."

The sky is a lambswool dawn, wing tip through clouds. The plane lands and there is the sound of seatbelts snapping open. I have slept the entire flight. I follow the herd off the plane.

*Nobody is there to meet you*, I say to myself one more time, just to be sure I've heard. Nevertheless, there she is at the end of the hall: her spectral presence legion.

*Standing off to the right, shimmering and glamorous. It's Christmas and she's prepared a feast and cut down a tree—my brothers will be there, we'll make margaritas, and sit by the fire. She takes my bag and says goodbye to the woman she's been chatting with.*

*She's at the front of the crowd: Mother of all mothers, reaching to take Isabel from my arms. "Look how big you've gotten, you sweet girl." She bounces her granddaughter on her hip, then* turns to me and says, *"You must be exhausted. Let's go have some dinner and a glass of wine ..."*

Time cradles my relentless thinking machine and loosens the screws.

*She's all the way at the back: transparent and lonely. Her house in Jacona, beautiful but empty, her blond hair unwashed. She is hanging onto youth despite her seventy-three years. Her clothes a little dirty, a little loose, in her hands a pad of paper on which she has written names and numbers she's beginning to forget.*

I pass through the crowded greeting area and turn back for one more look.

*I am holding her up. It's January 15: Detox Day, D-Day. The airport: a decoy. She is wandering.*

I close my eyes to comfort the image. *All is grace.* I walk with my suitcase out into the brilliant desert sun.

In my mother's unit at Meadowbrook, I tear a piece of masking tape and stick it to the Crate and Barrel couch. With a Sharpie, I write *consignment*. I have one day to clean out the apartment or we'll be charged for another month. This "independent living" apartment consists of two bedrooms, a kitchen, a living room, a bathroom, and two closets. I have three hours to pack it all.

Paintings of land, horizons, fire, and pond: save. But how will we transport them? I write: *save (transport?)*. There is the chest of drawers from the farmhouse in Natick where she kept her art supplies. Its brass pulls now broken or missing, there's no top, and the drawers are filled with old screws and hardware: *junk*. We've hired a company that will come and pick up everything we don't keep or give to consignment. Back before Christmas, I thought maybe I could interest her in art again. *Start small*, I'd thought, *pencils and a pad of paper*. They sit untouched in her closet: *for Isabel and Lucy*. The slatted bedroom set: *consignment*. I find a stack of pictures of Hugh in the bottom of a small wooden box with a broken hinge, lacquer chipping at the edges. I sit on the bed and flip through the pictures. I place them back in the box: *save*.

There's the stone bust of our great-grandfather, the one she refused to put in storage, and instead carried with her from house to house, even in the smallest of her apartments. This stone head-and-shoulders of one of the forefathers who had borne her into a life of trauma—she has literally carried it with her everywhere, all her life. That bust is part of our mythology—even if I don't know its meaning, I feels its pull: *save*.

A juicer that she bought at the beginning of the end, when she felt the alcohol taking its toll, when she felt her appetite disappearing and knew she had to get vitamins somehow—"a juicer will be the thing": *consignment*. In the back of the bedroom closet, I find a red laptop with an American flag on the front: Kenny. I put on the yellow dish gloves and carry the laptop downstairs and out the back door of the facility. I stand a good ten feet from the dumpster, so I can throw it. So I can hear it crash.

In the bottom of the dresser, I find a stack of pictures of the house in Natick and think of Irene.

I take off the gloves to dial. When she answers, I don't know how to start. I haven't spoken to Irene in years. I launch clumsily, directly, into telling her about Mom, about the last two years, about the chaos; I tell her that Mom was detoxed, but now speaks in word salad. Between my sentences, Irene gasps, and when I finish, she wails into the phone. I wait patiently; Irene's not being dramatic, it is wail worthy. After about a minute, she switches to words. "Words—how she loved words. To take a simple newspaper headline and turn it inside out and we would be laughing so hard, both of us. Oh no. Oh *no*."

Irene asks me for the address of the facility and if it would be okay if she flew out and visited Mom. I say that it would.

Bottom drawer bottle of diazepam, empty wine bottles under the bedside table, boxes in the closet from her last move labelled *dining room* that haven't been opened. The Navajo rugs, her peyote fan and prayer bag: memories from Hugh's years on the reservation.

My phone buzzes with a text.

IRENE:
Can you imagine how much effort it
must have taken to keep up the illusion that everything was fine? O sweet
Nina! She loved you kids so much. It
may not feel like that now, but you were

everything to her. Just think of all that
she has given to this world!

I call Sonia at Acequia Madre to let her know I'll be visiting tomorrow morning. Their policy is: five days with no visitors so "the elder" can get settled. Sonia explained that this is Nina's new home and she needed to begin to experience it as hers before family visits.

"For her room ... should I bring some paintings? Rugs? A vase of flowers? And what about music? She loves music. I bought her a little CD player that I could bring over ..."

"I'll tell you, Cassie, maybe one or two small paintings that we can hang on the wall. We generally don't have much else in the elders' rooms because we don't lock anything; the whole facility is open, so the elders can go in any room they want. And when there are nice things around, they tend to pick them up and take them. They aren't 'taking' things, as we see it, they will just see something and think it looks nice and pick it up. So, if you want to bring the CD player, we can keep it for her in the office. And if you're visiting and want to listen to music, we'll bring it out for you."

"What about pillows?"

"We have pillows and blankets and all of that."

"I'm just worried that if she doesn't recognize anything from her home, she'll feel disoriented."

"We can look at the room together tomorrow. It's a new home for her, so there will be a period of adjustment, but she's doing really well so far."

"Okay. Thank you, Sonia."

"You're welcome. I'll see you in the morning. Oh, Cassie?—do you know who Murphy is?"

"That's me, why?"

"Oh, I see. That makes sense. Well, she's doing great during the day, but she's not sleeping as much as we'd like, she wanders into the other rooms in the middle of the night, saying she has to tuck Murphy in."

"Oh."

"I'll see you tomorrow."

"Yes. Okay, thank you."

Roberta comes by as I'm packing the last box. There are two of Mom's paintings we've decided to give to Roberta. She is using a cane now. She sits on the edge of the couch. Sticking out from under her leg is the end of the masking tape label. All that is visible is: *signment*. Boxes extend from Roberta's feet outward into the room. She sits with that defeated posture I've seen on my brothers, that I've worn myself many times over these past two years, that *how-did-we-get-here?* posture. There is a tear rolling down her cheek. I stop packing, butter dish in hand. As Roberta blows her nose, I look down at the piece of elongated stoneware. It's the butter dish we gave Mom for Mother's Day the year Jack went off to boarding school, the one shaped like a rabbit. The ear had cracked off almost immediately after we gave it to her, but she superglued it back on and it's lasted ever since. I run my finger along the crack.

Roberta says, "When we helped her move out of her house in Jacona, I found something under the bed." Roberta is looking at me as if she's not sure she should continue. "It was a long pole, like a broom handle, and duct-taped to the end was an enormous knife." Her face falls into her hands again and she presses the tissue to her eyes and lets it all go. Her shoulders shake. "She was sleeping with a spear—a *spear*. She must have been so afraid. I knew she was suffering but instead of helping her, I stopped calling, stopped taking her calls. What kind of friend am I to not have been there for her? I knew what was happening and I just didn't want to deal with it. Oh god. Oh my god."

I say, weakly, "It's not your fault."

Roberta looks up at me, searching. "How did this happen?"

I want to answer the desperation in her eyes, her heaving chest. I want to give her a proper answer. I want to feel like there *is* a proper answer.

*It was the doctors who let her down.*

*It was the benzos and the booze.*

*It was Hugh dying.*

*It was her overbearing father and her depressive mother.*

*It was her kids ... It was us, we left her ...*

"I don't know, Roberta."

After I help her bring the paintings down to her car and return to the room, I stand in the doorway and survey the scene. I imagine the long pole with the knife at the end in the hands of my mother. I imagine her as a great warrior leading an army of orphans and addicts and abandoned souls

# forty-seven

AT ACEQUIA MADRE there are two massive front doors and an intercom system with a buzzer. Your name must be on the approved list for you to be let in. Next to the door is a sign that reads, *The reality of the elder constitutes the only reality.* I smile. This has always been true, long before she was an "elder." The buzzer sounds. Through the doors is a sunny anteroom containing a sitting area and a desk, on which sits a large sign-in book. Past the desk, on the other side of the room, is a second set of locked doors leading from the anteroom into the facility.

I am not waiting long when I hear a buzzing sound. In comes a small, round woman with dark curly hair and wire-rimmed glasses, like a younger version of a fairy-tale grandmother. This must be Sonia. I am expecting to shake hands, but the woman pulls me into a hug instead. After we introduce ourselves and she explains the whole sign-in process, she buzzes us through the second set of doors. "She'll be so happy to see you. Wait here, I'll get her for you." And then, all run-of-the-mill, she adds, "They're just changing her."

"Oh. Okay," I say, flinch imperceptible.

"I'll be right back."

I wait. Two cockatoos in a cage study me silently. After a moment, Sonia returns by herself. "She's not there. Let's check her room."

The "house," as they call it, is small, as these places go. We look in her room. There's a single bed with a sea-green bedspread, a nondescript bedside table, and an equally plain chair. We leave the door open and pause again in the hallway.

"They always change her after lunch," Sonia says, thinking out loud.

"Right, okay." We stand by the cockatoos. We hear someone coming down the hall and I turn to see Mom, hanging, sad-seeming, on a nurse's arm. She sees me and her tiny body lurches, a single sob escapes. "Murphy!" She walk-falls to me and I take her in my arms. Her body curls against mine and she starts to cry. "I hope I don't disappoint you. I'm sorry. You're not going to leave, are you? Please don't leave."

"I won't. I'm here. Don't worry, I'm not going to leave." I lower her down into an armchair and kneel in front, holding her hands in her lap. Sonia pulls over a chair so I can sit and asks if we need anything. I tell her we'll be okay. But as Sonia turns to go, Mom pulls her hand out from mine and signals to Sonia. "Could I just have a small glass of wine when you have a minute?" She holds her fingers apart to indicate an inch.

Sonia gives me a knowing smile and then says to Mom, "Of course, dear. I'll get it now."

She walks off toward the kitchen and Mom starts speaking immediately, urgently.

"I never expected he would go, but he did, and he knocked on the window and that was where I waved to him. That's my husband, Hugh. You remember, right?"

"Yes, I remember."

She is holding onto me with one hand but has removed the other hand to gesture with. "Well now, when Hugh died, his wife was very sad, and I decided I wanted to make a painting to take to him, and so I took the glass and painted her face and I got everything carefully, especially the sadness, big sad marks here and here." She lets go of my hand and makes her own hands into little fists and runs her thumbs downward along her temples to just past her cheekbone. "On both sides. Sad on both sides—but I knew he would be at the window, so I went over there, and I thought I would just wave hello. I haven't seen him for a long time, but I knew he would check his window because it was me and I was always there on the eighteenth. That was what we decided. And he did walk up and wave and I waved to him, and he went to answer the door and I just sent him a kiss and said it was from his wife, and I touched his forehead like this, and he was very, you know ... saying prayers and everything ..." *You were our queen, we would follow you anywhere, through the day and into the dark night. We raged at you and wanted to be set free, we bathed in your light and proudly proclaimed you our mother. How many times we wished you other ... We wished you humble and modest and thoughtful instead of talented, free-spirited, and stubborn but we followed ... we will always follow you ... our warrior, our mother.* "And for the next eighteen years or very long period of time or so I always made a point to go over there. It's for celebrating that point in his life and his wife to say, 'Good morning,' and bless him and his wife." *I'm sorry, Mom. I'm sorry. I'm so sorry.* "Because they knew it was from me, and so for the last several mornings, several months of mornings, I haven't been able to get over there ..." *I love you.* "I haven't been able to find someone who will just sit here so I can go, I haven't felt sure ..."

We both look up as Sonia arrives, setting down a tray with cookies and "wine"—apple juice in a plastic wineglass. Mom smiles and drops her story entirely. There is a glass of apple juice Chardonnay for me, too. It has been two weeks since I went with my friend Betty to an Al-Anon meeting, since I became one of the beleaguered Anonymous, meeting in church basements and libraries, quietly fighting the rising tide of alcoholism that swallows so many great women in its deadly undertow.

Sonia asks if we need anything else.

"No. Thank you, Sonia. We'll be okay."

Mom closes her eyes as she sips. And then, holding her glass up to the light, asks, "Isn't this a nice wine?"

# Acknowledgements

A HEARTFELT THANK you to everyone at Anansi, especially my editor, Shivaun Hearne, who pulled these pages from the open submissions portal and helped me turn them into a book. I am grateful to my family: Dylan Reeves, Damon Reeves, Océane Usher, Coco Usher, David Usher, Ann Usher, George Reeves, and Lisa Paris. And to my mother's friends who were there when being there wasn't easy: Barbara Zook, Erin Coyle, David Krogdahl, Dick and Joanne Bartlett, Mark Rael, and Greg Woeffel. I am grateful to my early readers: Anne Day-Jones, Peter Behrens, Trevor Ferguson, Sina Queyras, Kate Sterns, and Sean Michaels. And to Lucy Simic, Stephen O'Connell, Tony Chong, and Carol Prieur: I am lucky to have such friends as you. Thank you to the Mile End Bookies book club: Bronwen Low, Sepideh Anvar, Sabina Walser, Alem Sklar, Andrea Neuhofer, Joanne Robertson, Laurie Gelfand, and Laura Shea. And thank you, Carla Palmer, for suggesting I submit my manuscript to Anansi in the first place.

© Tony Chong

SABRINA REEVES grew up in Boston and New York and currently lives in Montreal. Her artistic practice has primarily been in writing performance texts and plays. She founded the performance company Bluemouth Inc., with whom she's written and staged over a dozen original works and performed all over the world. In 2018, she completed an MFA in creative writing at Concordia University, where she was awarded the Dean of Arts and Sciences Award for Excellence in Creative Writing.